JUDAS BURNING

JUDAS BURNING

Carolyn Haines

RIVER CITY PUBLISHING
Montgomery, Alabama

Published in the United States by River City Publishing
1719 Mulberry St.
Montgomery, AL 36106.

Designed by Lissa Monroe.

First Edition—2005
Printed in United States of America
1 3 5 7 9 10 8 6 4 2

Library of Congress Cataloging-in-Publication Data

Haines, Carolyn.
Judas burning / Carolyn Haines.— 1st ed.
p. cm.
ISBN 1-57966-061-4
1. Women journalists—Fiction. 2. Murder victims' families—Fiction.
3. Missing children—Fiction. 4. Fathers—Death—Fiction. I. Title.
PS3558.A329J83 2005
813'.54—dc22
2005008755

Newspapering is not a job but a calling. Journalists are the watchdogs of the community, and this book is dedicated to three reporters who aren't afraid to bark—Pat Sellers, Ronni Patriquin Clark, and Alice Jackson. And to the late JoAnn Sellers, a teacher whose influence will be felt for generations.

Chapter One

His skin is golden against the tangled sheets, his chest moving softly in the rhythm of sleep. Dim air, tinted with gold, slips through a crack in heavy draperies that cover the window beside the door. The room is filled with the cold drone of an air conditioner. Outside, children run, laughing. Their footsteps echo hollowly on the cement front of the motel.

The man stirs. Beside him a faceless woman reclines on one elbow. She watches him. His left hand is on his chest, and she stares at the gold band that encircles his ring finger. She touches his chest, her long, dark hair sliding across his face as she kisses the hollow of his sternum. Her tears fall onto the sheet that covers his lower body.

She slides from the bed, her body pale, sunless, her hair a shield for her face as she steps into the bathroom. There is the sound of running water, the clean smell of shampoo. In a moment she returns and picks up her jeans from the floor.

He is awake now and stands, naked, and wraps his arms around her, murmuring into her ear. Her hair swirls around them, hiding them from view, and she wishes they could step beneath the dark strands and hide forever. She has to leave. The clock beside the bed shows a blinking red 11:45. She must go now, the pressure like a chill grip on her neck. She shivers.

His kisses move from soft to demanding. "Don't go. Stay here and play with me." He speaks without moving his lips. His kisses drop lower, to her breast.

She has to go, but she can't. Her body fills and becomes languid. She drops her jeans to the carpeted floor and kisses him back. The bedside clock reads 11:53.

Thunder echoes far away, above the sound of the air conditioner. Lightning flashes, and she looks toward the window where the shadows of flames leap against the draperies.

"Something's wrong," she whispers, pushing him away.

"Don't leave me." He carries her to the bed. "Don't leave. You're safe here."

A boom of thunder shakes the building.

Dixon Sinclair awoke from the dream sweating and gasping for breath, her thin nightgown stuck to her body. She staggered down the hall of the old house and into the bathroom. Leaning against the pedestal sink, she turned on the cold water, splashed some on her sweating face, and lifted her dark hair off her neck. She pulled her nightgown off and dropped it to the polished wood floor.

She closed her eyes and thought of a glass of ice cubes, the crackle of the bourbon hitting the ice, the sweet fire of the liquor going down her throat. She would give a lot for a drink.

There was no liquor in the house. She'd made sure of that. The town of Jexville was dry; so was Chickasaw County. She stared into the mirror. Could she make it without drinking? Not unless the dream stopped. She began to shake.

She went to the bedroom, pulled on a pair of jeans and a T-shirt, and picked up her truck keys. It was just after eleven. The closest liquor store was nineteen miles away. She could make it before the store closed at midnight.

She was about to walk out the door when the phone rang. She hesitated, then walked back down the hall to answer it. Like it or not, she was in the business of late-night calls. She picked up the receiver and recognized Tucker Barnes's worried voice.

"I've got a problem with the typesetting machine. The film is stuck."

"I'll be there in fifteen minutes."

CHAPTER TWO

The marble head of the Virgin Mary lay at the base of the statue's stone feet, in the glare of the sheriff's spotlight. Someone had decapitated the statue and splashed blood all over it. Blood soaked the statue, the ground, the zinnias in the flower beds, the church walk. It was a tide of blood.

Although the early-morning hour was sticky hot, Dixon shivered. The metallic odor clogged her throat, and for a moment she thought she was going to be sick. She hadn't made it to the liquor store. The typesetting machine had been fixed quickly, but an anonymous call to the paper had sent her to St. John the Baptist Church.

She focused on the broad back of the sheriff as he worked the crime scene. For a local yokel, J.D. Horton seemed to know what he was doing. So far, he hadn't noticed her. She'd been in Jexville for two weeks, and every attempt she'd made to meet the number one lawman in the county had been countered with a cool rebuff. Or if not an actual rebuff, then an excuse. Horton had no use for newspaper reporters, and he made his sentiments clear. At the moment he was absorbed in conversation with Beatrice Smart, the pastor of Jexville's Methodist church.

Father Patrick Leahy came out of the church. She saw the way he averted his eyes from the statue. It was a shocking act of vandalism, but the story was in why it had occurred.

"Father Leahy." She caught up with him as he moved quickly to his car. "Do you have a moment?"

His expression said he didn't. He sighed. "What can I do for you?"

"I need a quote."

"So you're the new publisher." He nodded. "I've heard about you. Big-city reporter come to a small town. Jexville might be a tight fit."

"I'm sure I'll fit in just fine," she said. She shifted the focus away from herself. "Who would do such a thing to the statue and your church?"

"I have no idea," he said. "The parishioners were delighted with the statue. It was an amazing gift, not only a work of art but a perfect example of God's miracles."

"Could you explain that?"

"Alan Arguillo, the Mexican artist who created the statue, was blinded in an accident. He thought his career as a sculptor was over. But he got this piece of stone, and he couldn't leave it alone. He worked on it by feel, his hands becoming his eyes. And when it was done, his vision was restored by a miracle of God."

"How did the statue come to be in Jexville?"

"Dr. Diaz, one of our local physicians, grew up in Zaragoza, Mexico. He knew of this sculptor's work. When he learned of the blessing of the statue for miracles, he purchased it and brought it here. He has a child who suffers from multiple sclerosis."

"Why would the sculptor sell the statue that saved his vision?" Dixon had a healthy cynicism when it came to miracles.

"Arguillo had his miracle. Why should he hold on to the statue when others might be helped?"

"How much did Diaz pay for it?" Money was probably a more realistic reason.

The priest shook his head. "He didn't tell us. He's going to be heartsick when he sees what some vandal has done."

"Are you sure it was a random act and not someone connected to the church?"

"Who else but a vandal would do such a stupid, destructive thing? There is no other possibility. No one could hate us so much."

But Dixon knew that someone could hate Dr. Diaz or Father Patrick or perhaps just Catholics in general. These were ideas she'd ask Horton about, if he ever deigned to speak with her.

As the priest drove away, Dixon walked over to the sheriff. "Excuse me, Sheriff Horton. Do you have any idea where all the blood came from?"

He turned around and assessed her. "You're Dixon Sinclair."

She nodded.

"Sorry I haven't gotten back to you. I have one deputy, and we stay pretty busy." He sighed. "What a shame."

"The blood?" she persisted.

"I can't say for sure, but my guess is that it's some kind of animal. A large animal."

"Can you test it and tell?"

He nodded. "Whoever did this put a lot of planning into it."

"How so?" she asked.

"They had to collect the blood, bring a tool that would sever the head, case the church to be sure no one was around. Father

Patrick frequently stays at the church. There's an apartment here for him. Whoever did this watched the place."

"So you don't believe this was the work of simple vandals?"

Horton tilted his head slightly as he evaluated her. "It would be premature to speculate."

"Is speculation all you have, or do you have evidence?"

She saw a professional shield slide into place. "We have evidence," he said, "but none that I'm going to discuss in the press. You take care, Miss Sinclair."

Dixon watched him walk away. He was a powerful man, heavily muscled, fit. "My deadline is ten o'clock tonight," she called after him. "It would be great if you could let me know the animal the blood came from." He didn't turn around.

✝

The Mississippi sun blazed white-hot, bleeding the color from the midday sky. Angie Salter stretched on the hot sandbar and stared at her friend from beneath the straw brim of her red sun hat. Trisha Webster was afraid of her own shadow.

Angie tossed her a bottle of suntan lotion. "Your shoulders are getting pink. I don't know why you won't take your top off. You're going to have those ugly white stripes. You want some lemon juice to streak your hair? It would look cool."

The boom box blared a song with heavy bass, the words muffled against the sandbar that stretched for half a mile down the west side of the Pascagoula River.

"Thanks." Trisha slathered her shoulders with the lotion and silently flipped onto her stomach.

Angie knew that Trisha's silence indicated anxiety. She pushed her long, blond hair back from her shoulders and held her face to the sun, the movement tumbling her hat to the sand. "The magazines say that sun is bad for you, but all the models are tan. Scarlett Johansen was bronzed at the Oscars."

"I don't want to get burned," Trisha said. "I don't want Mama to figure out we skipped school."

"Your mom won't have a clue." Angie shook out her hair. "I'm too short to be a runway model, but I can make half a grand an hour doing magazine work." She could see the wind machine blowing her hair, the makeup woman hovering, the photographer telling her how hot she looked, how much he wanted her as he clicked away. Angie knew she had the looks—boys in school fell over themselves when she walked past them in the hall. Now, she had the means to get to New York. It was going to happen. Soon.

Trisha shifted on her towel. "Don't all those girls work through one of those modeling agencies?"

"I've checked into it. I need a portfolio." Angie loved the word, the way it rolled and sounded like magic. And it would be. It would be her ticket out of Jexville. Out of the tiny little shit hole town where her only hope of ever having anything was to claw it away from someone else. Her secret burned hot on her tongue. She was dying to tell Trisha.

"Where are you going to get the money for those kind of pictures? I read where some of those photographers charge hundreds an hour."

Trisha's skepticism made Angie angry. She could do it. No matter that her mother laughed at her ambitions and mocked her. Her mother was a moron who lived with a man who was a worm. Angie heard them at night, lying in bed, laughing over one of her remarks, making fun. Beth Salter said Angie was putting on airs. Now her best friend didn't have any faith in her. "I'll get the fucking pictures, don't you worry about that."

"I didn't mean that, Angie. I just wondered how. Will Jimmy help you? Or your mom?"

"Right. If Mama had the money, she'd buy that dickhead Alton a motorcycle or something else he wanted." She hesitated. "Jimmy doesn't make enough at the store."

"Is that what all of this with Mr. Hayes is about?" Trisha glanced at the boom box.

Angie reached over and punched a button, shifting from the CD to a Mobile, Alabama, radio station. Jexville, being the hick town that it was, didn't have anything except an AM gospel station. "Mr. Hayes might help finance my portfolio. We'll just have to see."

Trisha sat up and squinted toward the yellow-brown river. "You want to get in the water? I'm hot."

"Sure." Angie opened the ice chest and drew out two icy beers. "Let's smoke a joint first."

"You got some pot?" Trisha pushed her chin-length brown hair behind her ears. "Man, Angie, how'd you manage that?"

"I've got connections." She couldn't help herself. She had to tell. It wasn't the big secret, only a tiny part of it. "I did some coke the other night."

Trisha's eyes widened. "How was it?"

"Man, it was wonderful. I mean, I felt like I could do anything. It was like I was on top of the world." Angie looked at her friend. "You'd love it. Next time maybe I'll get some for you."

"Who is the guy who gives you all that jewelry?" She pointed to the intricate gold bracelet on Angie's arm. "That must have cost at least a thousand dollars."

Angie held her arm up, and bright sunlight struck the gold. "A lot more than that." She lit the joint, inhaled deeply, and passed it to Trisha.

"This guy who gives you jewelry, does he give you the drugs, too?"

"What are you, writing a book?"

Trisha dropped the joint into the sand. "Dammit, Angie. I don't deserve that kind of shit."

Angie retrieved the joint and took a hit. "I didn't mean to be ugly. It's just that you ask a lot of personal questions."

"You can get mad at me, but your mama's gonna see that bracelet and ask a lot more questions."

"Mama's so stupid she thinks it's costume. She can't tell real gold from fake." Angie passed the joint.

Trisha hit it hard. "You know, when I think about how we'd be spending this Tuesday morning in school, I get a sick feeling. But then," she grinned, "I feel the hot sand and listen to the water, and I guess I don't care." She looked down, gathered a handful of the white sand, and let it sift through her fingers. "I wish I was going to New York to be a model. Shit, I wish I was going to Mobile to be a clerk in K-Mart."

Angie exhaled. "When I make it big, Trisha, I'll send for you. There's lots of jobs in New York. You could be anything you want. How about . . . on one of the soaps!"

"That would be terrific."

Angie took another hit from the joint. "Man, this shit is good. My head is buzzing. Put it out and save it for later."

Trisha checked her watch. "We have to be back before school lets out. Jimmy doesn't know we took his truck, does he?"

Angie flopped dramatically on her towel. "Oh, too bad," she said in a lilting voice, "Jimmy will be very, very angry." She laughed. "I can manage him."

"Listen. There's a boat coming. You'd better put some clothes on."

"Let 'em come. It's a free country." Angie watched her friend frantically stubbing out the joint. "Why should anyone care if I show my tits? If they don't like what they see, they don't have to look. Alton loves looking at them. I catch him watching me dress all the time."

"Really, put your swimsuit on. It could be anybody."

Angie sat up. "Let's run naked on the sandbar. We can shock the bejesus out of 'em."

Trisha shook her head. "There're a lot of old fishermen around here. Some of them look mean." She reached for her T-shirt and pulled it over her swimsuit.

Angie laughed. "Come on, Trish. If you don't loosen up, you'll never have a good time. Let's just give 'em a thrill. Hell, they haven't seen anything like us in fifty years."

Trisha reached for her friend's hand as Angie stood up, the sun highlighting the golden tones of her skin, her slender, perfect figure. "Sit down!" Trisha tugged at her hand. "Sit down, Angie!" There was real panic in her voice.

The blonde sank back onto her beach towel. She realized Trisha was about to cry. "Shit. What's wrong with you?"

"Daddy's friends fish up here sometimes. He'd kill me if—"

"Okay. I'll see who it is first." Angie pushed a beer into her friend's hand. "Then we'll decide if we can have some fun."

The sound of the boat grew louder. It was a big engine. Angie sipped her beer and listened. Hell, it didn't matter if she had a little fun on the sandbar. She was headed to New York City. In less than five months she'd be sixteen. Once she got a legal driver's license, there'd be no keeping her in Chickasaw County, where the only choices for a pretty girl with ambition were an old man with money or young boys who thought a joint, a six pack, and two rubbers were the ingredients of a dream date.

The boat drew closer, the engine whine blocking out the sound of the radio. Angie glanced at her friend, who'd turned her back to the water. Trisha was her best friend. Her only friend. But sometimes she acted like an old maid. When she looked back at the water, her smile was big and eager. What would it hurt to have some fun?

CHAPTER THREE

It was almost noon and hot as hell. After a near-sleepless night, Dixon wondered if she'd died and was suffering her punishment—running a weekly newspaper in a small Mississippi town split by religion, gender, and poverty.

She sat in her truck gathering herself for the fray. The unexpected closure of the Jexville Canaan Baptist Church Wee Care—the second big story in less than twelve hours involving a church—had thrown the town into an uproar. Thirty-seven working women had no one to care for their young children. Religion was big business in Chickasaw County.

Several men carrying hastily made signs supporting the closure were lined up on the east side of the church lawn. On the west side were angry women. Screaming, whining, running-wild children ping-ponged between them.

Dixon sat in the blast of the truck's air conditioner, examining her notes and watching the bedlam. Rev. James Farrell stood, arms linked with a dozen women, guarding the front door of the church. Three television camera crews were set up on the church lawn. Someone had been giving the good minister lessons in staging a media event.

Dixon scanned the crowd, making certain Tucker Barnes was photographing the fracas. Her gaze stopped on a tall, dark-haired man who was staring at her. She hadn't seen him in her two weeks in Jexville. The man made no effort to hide his interest. He looked as if he didn't belong in Jexville any more than she did.

Tucker's actions caught her gaze.

He was getting dangerously close to a big, beefy man with a high-blood-pressure red face. Tucker was young and ambitious, and in the brief time he'd worked at the *Independent*, he'd come a long way. He reminded her of the reasons she'd once loved journalism. He had yet to learn that reporting could be a dangerous profession.

Dixon got out of her truck and crossed the well-maintained lawn. The minister and his forces guarded the church steps. On one side were the angry women; on the other were the men with signs and placards.

"Go back to God's way!" one sign read. The picket line was marching, and the men were chanting, "God's plan—obey your man! God's plan—obey your man!"

Dixon saw a brown sheriff's car pull to the curb half a block down the street. J.D. got out. He had the look of a man who'd spent his youth in the military. Good posture, a casual self-confidence. He looked at her and nodded, then shifted his gaze to the dark-haired man, who was still staring at Dixon.

Whoever he was, he was a bold one. The intensity of his stare sent a ripple of anticipation down her arms. The impulse to go over and ask him, point blank, why he was gawking at her was strong. She didn't act, though. She had a paper to put to bed, and strange men, no matter how compelling, would have to wait until Thursday, when the edition was on the streets.

The general bedlam on the church lawn increased, and Dixon was reminded of traffic accidents she'd worked long ago as a photographer. She realized anew how many years had passed since she'd actually been a good journalist. She'd had plenty of opportunities to show that she was her father's daughter, but drinking had been safer and more satisfying, until the last year when she'd finally felt her spirit eroding. Buying the *Independent* was her last-ditch stand. Jexville was her mound of ashes. If her phoenix was going to rise, it would have to be here, despite the naysayers who'd urged her not to make the move.

Her misgivings resurfaced. This wasn't going to be anything like journalism as she'd known it. This was grassroots, right in the middle of a town where everyone knew everyone else. This was the kind of newspapering her father had loved—the paper as the watchdog of the community. She took a breath, fighting for calm. By god, she'd made it through the night without a drink, but she needed one now.

She walked up the stone steps. Into the teeth of angels, she thought as she faced the minister.

"I'm Dixon Sinclair, publisher of the *Independent*. Could you tell me why Canaan Baptist has decided to close its day care facility?"

Reverend Farrell's face was flushed. His blue eyes radiated a glow. Some would call it angelic, but Dixon had a feeling that he was mad as a March hare.

"I know who you are." Farrell disengaged his hand from the grasp of a thin young woman who held a toddler on her hip. "I've heard all about you." His tone was insulting.

"I understand you're closing the day care facility. Is there a reason for this action, maybe a structural problem?"

"The building is sound as a dollar. I'm closing it because God commanded me to do so." Several of the women whispered, "Amen."

"Is that a joke?" she asked, hesitating.

"I don't make jokes about God's will."

"You realize you're leaving forty-two youngsters with no day care?" Maybe it was just a media event, a platform so he could air his views.

"Last night, God spoke to me. He said our family units are disintegrating. He said our womenfolk have laid down the burden of tending their children, giving their own flesh and blood into the hands of strangers to raise and mold. He said that Canaan Baptist Church had played a role in that desecration and that I was to put a stop to it."

"That was a rather lengthy conversation. God must have been in a talkative mood," Dixon observed.

"Blasphemer," the thin woman whispered.

Farrell ignored Dixon's sarcasm. He lifted his blue gaze toward the sky. "I am blessed that God chooses to speak with me. I am blessed, as is the entire congregation of the church. We are obedient to God's will. The vandalism at the Catholic church shows how far we've fallen from God's graces. No place is sacred any more, not even God's house of worship. Look toward the Catholics, if you must. Wayward young people desecrated God's house, destroyed a statue of the mother of Jesus. No matter what we think about the Catholics and their papist ways, that tells us how far our children have strayed."

"Amen!" the women chorused.

Farrell's smile was tolerant. "Our children are growing up wild. Without the love and security of a home where their mothers cook and care for them, they are falling to the Beast."

"Reverend, some of those women," Dixon pointed across the lawn, "don't have a choice. They work because they have to. And while they work, someone has to care for their children. It would seem to me that the church is a safe setting for children."

"Women must stay at home and keep the family unit intact."

"What if the mother is the only provider for the family?"

"God will provide. He never closes a door unless he opens a window."

Dixon looked across the lawn. Spectators were cheering the picketers and the women on. If someone didn't break it up soon, there would be some dramatic photo opportunities, complete with blood. She looked for the sheriff and saw him walking, unhurriedly, toward the church. His gaze was on the minister. He did not look happy.

Dixon looked back at Farrell. The light of battle was in his eyes.

"Come, ladies, let us sing 'Onward Christian Soldiers.' " Farrell launched into the hymn, his tenor leading the women.

The sheriff came up the steps and stopped beside Dixon. He leaned down to speak softly to her. "Giving them publicity will only excite them to more of this kind of behavior." He nodded toward the church grounds. "With just one little push, this could turn into a riot. I don't want you to be the match that lights that fuse."

"I'm not here to make news; I cover it."

The sheriff turned to Farrell. "You've got quite a scene going here, James." His voice was low, conversational.

"It is a scene designed by God to show His will." Farrell nodded as he spoke, his focus now on the sheriff.

The woman beside Farrell blanched as a tall man came toward them. His white hair crested in a wave atop a handsome face. He wore a navy blue suit, tailored to fit. Although she'd never met him, Dixon knew instantly he was James "Big Jim" Welford, superintendent of education in Chickasaw County.

"What in the hell do you think you're doing, Farrell?" Welford demanded. The singing faltered to a stop. Welford ignored everyone except the minister. "Have you lost your mind?"

"When God speaks, I listen, and then I act." Farrell's angelic demeanor was spoiled by a slight frown.

Welford looked at the women. "Get out of here." They scurried like leaves in a wind. He turned to Dixon. "Who are you?"

"Dixon Sinclair, publisher of the *Independent.*"

Welford's gaze went to Farrell, quick and deadly, then to J.D. "She's the new owner of the newspaper?" He turned back to stare again. "This has all been blown out of proportion." He put his hand on her shoulder in a gentle, familiar gesture. "I need to speak with the minister here, see if I can't talk some sense into him before this thing goes too far."

"Are you affiliated with the church?" Dixon asked.

"I'm on the board of deacons." He nodded at her notes. "There's no need for any of this to go in the paper. I'll have it settled in less than an hour." He grasped Farrell's arm. "Get inside," he ordered. "Now!" He propelled the minister through the church door.

Dixon and J.D. were left. He stared at her long enough that she lifted one eyebrow.

"Looks like it's over." He pulled the brim of his hat so that it shaded his eyes. "Have a good day, Miss Sinclair."

Dixon hurried to catch up to him. "Sheriff, just a minute; I have some questions. Have you got any leads on the vandalism of the statue at St. John the Baptist?"

He studied her a moment. "Nothing for print."

"I need a comment," she said.

"Religion is Chickasaw County's claim to fame. There're eighty-seven churches in the county."

She couldn't read his expression, which was carefully neutral. "And St. John's? Is this related?"

"Only in that Farrell saw an opportunity to get on the front page."

"What about the blood?"

He hesitated. "Cow blood. Juney Moons found one of his cows with its throat cut. The blood came from the cow."

Dixon tasted something metallic in the back of her throat. "Who would do such a thing?"

"I couldn't accurately speak to that. You take care, Ms. Sinclair." He started down the steps, his gait casual, as if he were out for a stroll.

"Sheriff, why was Reverend Beatrice Smart at the church last night?"

He turned and studied her. "Because I asked her to be." He tipped his hat and turned away.

Dixon's eyes followed him until her attention was diverted to the dark-haired man, who was still staring at her. Then he turned and walked away.

✝

The fish were elusive shadows in the big, artesian-fed vat. They swam frantically, almost colliding with the sides. As they approached a wall, they swerved at the last instant, darting toward another corner.

Eustace Mills never tired of watching the fish. Some were better than five pounds, others just under two, perfect for church fish fries. He liked the bigger ones himself. The darker, gamier meat made the best-tasting stews. In his sixty-odd years on the Pascagoula, he'd seen river cats that weighed eighty pounds, granddaddy fish with dangling whiskers on a head as big as a man's. Those were fighters, fish that sought the mud bottom of the river and went deep, ignoring the hook that tried to pull them to the surface.

A fish tail broke the surface, and Eustace straightened. He limped toward the supply of hooks, knives, hammers, and pliers he kept on a picnic table beneath the tin roof of his skinning shed. He led with his right foot, the left one dragging after him. He was glad to be in the shade during the early afternoon heat.

Next to the open-sided shed a stout creosote post held a heavy board where he cleaned fish. The three fish heads he'd left nailed there the night before were gone. The board, five feet off the ground, was empty. The six-pack of beer he'd left on the picnic table was gone too.

"Eu-stace! Eu-stace, honey! Are you on the grounds?"

"Here." He looked at the table again to make certain the beer was truly gone and not just playing with him.

26

"Are you busy?"

He could tell by her voice that she was sitting in the middle of the floor. She'd have an ashtray beside her slender right thigh and tarot cards spread out by her left. He could almost smell the dark coffee she drank each morning as she read the cards.

Limping slightly, he made his way across the grassless yard and climbed the twenty-three steps to the cypress camp that he'd built on pilings driven deep into the clay bank of the river.

"I'm goin' to check the trot lines up the Leaf," he said. "I got the Chickasawhay earlier."

"You've got half the fish in the river in your vat already." She turned over a card revealing a man hung upside down. She put her hand over the card and looked up at him. Eustace got the feeling she was protecting him.

"I got to check the lines anyway. You can't just leave the fish hanging on 'em. They'll die there."

She nodded, looked into his eyes for several seconds, then took a drag off her cigarette. "We need some coffee and some other things. Shall I go into town and do some shopping?"

"Okay." He touched his face. "I need some razor blades."

"I'll be back by five. I'm going to stop by Mama's and make sure she hasn't driven Daddy completely insane. She has her massage on Tuesdays. Maybe I'll have one."

"Be careful." He turned and went back down the stairs, past the skinning shed, and on toward the Pascagoula River that glimmered reddish yellow through the dense oak leaves. When he looked back at the fish camp he saw her coming down the stairs. She wore her hair tucked up in a man's hat, utterly feminine with a red slash of lipstick. She waved once, and he turned to the water.

His boat was chained to a cypress knee. He freed the rusted lock and climbed in. The small outboard cranked instantly, and he aimed the boat north. He'd set his lines some five miles upriver, beyond the fork. The sun was hot on his head and back. He dipped his hand in the water, then ran it through his thick hair.

When he rounded the bend and came in sight of the bridge, he heard music above the gurgle of his motor. He crossed under the old bridge, moving fast and steady. The tip of the sandbar came into view, and in a few moments he passed two girls.

One was topless and sat cross-legged. She held a silver beer can out to him in an apparent toast. "Hey, old man, come on up and have a drink!" she yelled. The sun glinted off a thick gold bracelet on her left wrist.

Eustace increased the throttle.

"Hey! We're having a party. Come have a beer with us." She laughed, holding the beer high as she poured it into her mouth, some of it splashing down to the breasts she covered with her hand.

The other girl lifted her head, and brown hair fell forward over her sunglasses. She simply looked at him before she lowered her head.

Eustace notched the motor up, never looking back.

One of the girls let out a blood-curdling yell. "Tell everybody they're invited to the party! Just a little harmless fun!" she called.

The sandbar disappeared behind him, and he took the fork of the Leaf River. He worked the lines on the west bank, easing his boat among the trees that managed to survive in soil that was more water than dirt. The point of land between the Leaf and the Chickasawhay was treacherous swamp. Not even poachers wandered into it.

Once, fifty years before, Eustace had packed a lunch, stolen his daddy's best shovel and boat, and deliberately headed into that swamp searching for buried treasure. He had gone hunting fancies—and had almost died in the sucking kiss of the swamp. Now he lurked on the edge, going no farther than the river willingly took him. There were still places the river demanded to keep as her own, and he respected that. He pulled up the line he'd tied in a dying sweet gum, unhooked a five-pound cat, and moved farther up river.

An hour later he had twenty pounds of writhing fish in the big chest that centered his boat. He'd cut one spoonbill free. A snapping turtle, dead on a line, had been flung into the bottom of the boat. Blacks would pay good money for turtle meat. He headed back to the camp.

The sandbar was half a mile away, but his thoughts had already jumped ahead to the girls. They were so young. He knew they could hear his boat motor. Had probably heard it for the last ten minutes.

The sandbar loomed in front of him, nearly a mile of the whitest sand anywhere. Music vibrated off the water, the bass booming in a steady rhythm with words that sounded like another language. He eased the motor back, drifting.

He saw the blonde, basking in the sun and the beat of the music. She didn't bother covering her naked breasts. She was a bold one. The other girl had her back to him.

It occurred to him, not for the first time, that half-baked, naked girls, alone on the sand, were incentive for a fucking or a fight.

CHAPTER FOUR

J.D. Horton wasn't a man who let his demons or the opinions of others govern his actions. He lived by few rules, preferring a code of personal ethics where judgment came into play. There were truths about human nature, though, that he believed. One was that an emotionally unhinged man or woman was capable of anything. Decapitation of the statue at St. John the Baptist Catholic Church was the work of someone unbalanced, someone enraged, someone who had lost control. And that was dangerous.

Beatrice Smart had only confirmed what he'd seen in the gory splashes of blood and the power of the blow that decapitated the figure of Mary. This was not the work of teenage pranksters, as he wanted most of the county to believe. A man had done this. A strong man, and one with a burn on for the Catholic Church, a symbol of miracles, or someone in particular at St. John's.

What he knew of Father Patrick did not lend itself to warped hatred. Still, it was an avenue J.D. would explore until the physical evidence he'd accumulated from the crime scene told him differently. Based on the blow that had been struck, he believed the assailant to be under six feet. A partial shoe print in the blood was a size ten sport shoe of undetermined brand. Most important, the perpetrator had not been careful. He'd tracked back and forth through the blood repeatedly, as if he didn't care about concealing his identity, or as if he were justified in his actions.

J.D. jotted down a few notes and put his hand on the phone. Dixon Sinclair had asked for a comment, and he had something to give her.

A knock on his door interrupted him. When Robert Medino walked into the sheriff's office, J.D. already knew as much about him as his deputy, Waymon, had been able to find out. Medino was a writer for a "very important" liberal magazine that specialized in politics and culture. He was an authority on Central America, and he was staying at the Magnolia Bed and Breakfast, where he had charmed the socks—and possibly the pants—off Ruth Ann Johnson. When Waymon had talked to Ruth Ann, she'd been all a-twitter about Medino's accomplishments.

"He went to Harvard," she'd told Waymon. "Imagine that. A Harvard man here in Jexville. I asked him what he was writing about, but he said it was top secret." Waymon had done a pretty good imitation of Ruth Ann's breathless soprano. The fact that Medino was single didn't hurt, either. Ruth Ann had sampled the men of Jexville and found them wanting. A writer would make a good pet for her, at least for a while.

"What can I do for you, Mr. Medino?" J.D. asked, curious about what a writer for a liberal magazine was doing in Jexville, a town with a head count of no more than five liberals.

"It's more like what I can do for you." Medino held out his hand, reassessing J.D. "Since you know my name, you probably know that I'm a writer for *Cue* magazine. You've heard of it?"

32

The man's assumed superiority shimmered like an aura. "What can I do for you?" J.D. repeated as he took Medino's hand.

"I'm in town on a story," Robert said, unfazed.

J.D. leaned back in his chair. The man's brown eyes were alert, almost amused. He reminded J.D. of a boy poking a snake with a stick. "What kind of story would interest you in Chickasaw County?"

Medino smiled. "A good one."

J.D. didn't react. But he found that Medino was equally good at saying nothing. "Let's see, the president is coming to address the local rotary club, right?"

"Not my type of story," Medino said. "I'm more interested in the destruction of church property."

J.D. felt the muscles of his back tighten. A local story didn't normally attract the attention of a national reporter. "Why does that interest you?" He shifted so he could better examine Medino. He was a lean man, built like a cyclist. His hair was long, unkempt, his jeans worn. Even his boots showed age and wear. He dressed like the farmers and ranchers of the county, but there was something in the way he held himself that said otherwise.

"I've been following a story that starts in Zaragoza, Mexico, and comes straight this way, right down Interstate 10 East."

"Chickasaw County isn't a big destination for illegals. We have a few in the nurseries, but that's it." J.D. saw the amusement in Medino's eyes. "But it isn't migrant workers you're interested in, is it?"

"Someone is vandalizing churches. Specifically Catholic churches. Even more specifically, images of Mary in Catholic churches."

J.D. let the information settle. "And you think this person or persons did the damage at St. John's last night."

"I do."

"What would bring a roving religious fanatic to the backside of nowhere in Jexville? We're fifty miles off the Interstate."

"It's an obsession, and the statue is a work of art, created by a blind sculptor who regained his sight while working the stone."

J.D. had heard the blind-sculptor-regains-sight story, but it wasn't uncommon for religious icons to generate tall tales. "I didn't realize reporters for *Cue* got their leads from the *National Enquirer*."

J.D. waited. Medino wouldn't be able to let that pass without a reply.

"I interviewed the artist, who also happened to be from Zaragoza. He can see. It's a true story."

"And you have proof he was really blind?"

Medino frowned. "I do. Couple that with the fact that the statue is now destroyed . . ." He shrugged. "It's a sensational story."

J.D. didn't try to hide his smile. "Right. Sensational."

"I'm glad you find me amusing." Medino slouched against the wall. "The first destruction of church property was in Zaragoza about six months ago. My man is obsessed with images of Mary. He has defaced or destroyed over a dozen statues, broken fifteen stained glass windows depicting her image, and ruined over half a million dollars in church property."

"And you have proof all of these acts were committed by the same man?"

Medino shrugged. "I have very good hunches."

"If I could arrest criminals on gut instinct, Chickasaw County would have a lot less crime. Unfortunately, the law requires proof."

"I'm not asking you to do anything. I'm merely acting as a good Samaritan and telling you that you have an obsessed, anti-Catholic, woman-hating criminal in Chickasaw County. You might want to keep your eyes open, because I believe he's going to progress in his crimes."

"What, he might go after images of the disciples?" J.D. couldn't help himself. Medino was too smug.

"I don't think he'll go after more icons. The violence has escalated, and he's moved on to killing animals." Medino stepped closer. "Next, I think he'll go after a priest, or a nun, choir girl, someone like that. If not here in Chickasaw County, then at the next stop. Or the next. You could catch him here."

Robert Medino might believe it, but the idea of a lunatic traveling around the south destroying religious statuary and breaking windows didn't make a lot of sense to J.D. Then again, the damage at St. John's didn't make good sense either. Back in the nineties, there'd been a series of church burnings across the southeast. There was precedent for a religious kook, but there was also the fact that Medino was a man looking for a story. A sensational story. J.D. could smell ambition on him.

"What kind of evidence do you have?"

"Instincts and a map. Check it out, Sheriff." Medino pulled a worn map from his back pocket. "I've marked the locations of every attack against a church. When the Arguillo statue was dedicated, I figured he'd come here."

J.D. looked at the page. A black line punctuated with stars marched from a small town in Mexico to Jexville.

"I figure he's still in this area," Robert said. "That's why I'm here. When I heard about the Arguillo statue, I was over in St. Martinsville, Louisiana. He broke four windows depicting Mary—only Mary—at a Catholic church. I've been getting closer and closer to him. This is where I'm going to catch up to him."

J.D. looked at the map. "What do you intend to do if you find him?"

"Interview him. It's part of a larger story on how traditional religion is failing people. This man feels betrayed by the Catholic church, betrayed by Mary. He's furious, and he's acting out. In Louisiana, he began splashing red paint on the lower torso of Mary. Now he's using real blood, maybe to symbolize the blood of childbirth or womanhood. He's working from a lot of rage, and it's directed toward the feminine."

J.D. looked out the window of his office. "Can I have a copy of that map?" he asked.

"That copy's for you. Call the law enforcement agencies in those towns. Check it out. You'll see."

✝

The hot day had melted into an oven of a late afternoon. It was five o'clock, and heat devils still danced on Main Street. Dixon swallowed a knot of frustration as she moved the typewriter platen backward to X out a misspelled word. The newspaper was antiquated—not a single piece of modern equipment in the place, except for the computer Linda used to set the stories in type. Just as soon as she could scrape together five hundred dollars, she was going to buy a word processor. Sharing one with Tucker would be better than using her own typewriter.

It had taken all her savings to make the down payment on the newspaper, and even thinking about the risk made her hand shake and sweat touch her forehead. She needed a drink.

Instead, she focused on the reasons she'd chosen the *Independent*. Good, solid, rational reasons. Jexville wasn't just a random choice. Tentacles of the past held her here. Jexville had been her mother's childhood home, a place painted as idyllic and safe, a place Dixon had few memories of. Marilyn McVay Sinclair had grown up not two miles away on Peterson Lane in the home that had been built by Will and JoHanna McVay. Had it not been for the fact that the McVay family home was still in the family, Dixon would have been sleeping on the sidewalk. Yes, economics were a solid, rational reason.

That explained the location. The desire to own a weekly came from hope and fear. She hoped to prove herself the journalist her father always believed her to be, and she feared that she would fail. JoHanna had been only the first of the McVay women to run into trouble in this town, and Dixon felt a pulse of self-doubt. This was her last chance. If she'd chosen unwisely, the price would be too high. If she didn't grab hold of her life and stop drinking, she would die.

In the composing room Linda Moore's rapid typing halted at the sound of her cell phone's ring. Twenty-one years of marriage and three kids had given Linda a level head and a keen sense of the absurd. She was also one helluva typist and fast becoming a good friend.

Dixon looked out the window at the town closing up around her, then refocused on her story. She had to finish. Linda would be waiting on her copy, and, so far, the decapitation of the statue at St. John's and the Canaan Day Care fiasco were their biggest stories.

The telephone jangled, and Dixon cursed under her breath. The damned phone hadn't stopped. "The *Independent*. May I help you?"

"Ms. Sinclair, this is Sally West in Senator Barrett's office."

Dixon eased back in her chair. "Yes?"

"The senator sends his congratulations on your purchase of the *Independent*, and he wants to invite you to his strategy session in Jackson Saturday evening."

There was an expectant pause. When Dixon didn't respond, Sally continued. "This in no way obligates you to support his candidacy for governor."

Dixon felt herself slide into memory; time telescoped. She saw herself, hair still damp from the shower and thirty minutes late as she'd pulled her old red truck up in front of her father's newspaper office. She could see her father through the plate glass window of the *Jackson Standard*, holding a page proof, scanning the headlines. He'd looked up, his face changing from concentration to a smile that absolved her lateness.

The noise and glass had come simultaneously. The front window exploded. Ray Sinclair was lifted, and the world had become a mass of sound and pain and fire.

Dixon's hands began to shake.

"Ms. Sinclair, are you there?" Sally West asked.

"I won't be attending any strategy sessions," she said. She replaced the telephone receiver softly.

A movement outside the window caught her attention, and she turned to confront the open stare of a young black man. She could not tell his age, but his copper skin and sharp eyes were familiar, and she realized she'd seen him before. Somewhere other than Jexville. His hair was cut close, and his T-shirt bore an emblem she couldn't identify. He took a deep breath.

Dixon started to speak but realized he couldn't hear her. As she headed to the door, he turned away. By the time she got to the sidewalk, he was crossing the street more than half a block away. He looked back over his shoulder once but kept going.

He was from somewhere in her past, and the past never paid her a simple courtesy visit. She felt a hand on her shoulder and jumped.

"Is something wrong?" Linda asked.

Dixon turned and saw worry on the typesetter's face.

"Just a kid watching me. What is it?"

"One of my friends just called. Two teenage girls are missing." Linda pressed her lips together. "From what I can tell, they've been missing since nine this morning."

Chapter Five

The porch of the Chickasaw County education office was partially surrounded by azaleas that had grown nearly as tall as the roof. Sweat had collected beneath the belt of Dixon's khaki slacks, and her once-crisp red blouse stuck to her back. Thank goodness the day was finally fading into dusk.

She wiped her forehead and watched as a heavy woman with five children lumbered across the grassy square of the Chickasaw County Courthouse. The children, two of them wearing only underwear, screamed and careened across the grass as if tiny nuclear reactors had been implanted inside them. At the courthouse steps the children surrounded the woman and swept her inside, a behemoth captured and brought down by pygmies.

Dixon stared at the empty square. Life in Jexville, population 1,654, was going to be very different.

"Miss Sinclair!" James Welford walked across the peeling paint of the porch and picked up her hand. He pressed it between his thumb and forefinger. "Sorry to keep you waiting so long. This porch is hot as an oven."

Dixon felt as if he were testing her hand for depth of flesh and bone structure, perhaps to see if she'd cooked through.

She took off her sunglasses. Welford's silvery white hair looked mail-ordered from Hollywood, unaffected by the heat and humidity. She wondered if it was a toupee.

"The Chickasaw County Board of Education had a meeting scheduled for six this evening. I've been waiting for the members to show up," she said.

"We met." He never looked away.

"Your secretary told me to wait here, that I'd be certain to see the board members when they arrived." Dixon would not give him the satisfaction of showing her frustration.

"Attie means well. She must've gotten confused. We moved our meeting over to the courthouse. Turns out our coffeepot was on the blink, so when Elton Cook offered us the use of the supervisor's board room, I accepted." He shrugged. "I had no idea you might want to attend the meeting. The *Independent* hasn't sent a reporter for years. Augusta, the former owner of the paper, seemed happy going over the typed-up minutes."

Dixon pulled her notebook from the purse that was slung over her shoulder. "School board meetings are public, Mr. Welford. State law requires that the public be notified if the meeting time or place is changed."

"I'll keep that in mind for future reference." His smile stopped before it reached his eyes.

"Since I missed the meeting, you won't mind answering a few questions for me, will you?" Dixon tapped the notebook gently against her thigh.

"Not at all, but Attie will have the minutes typed up by tomorrow. You can have a copy then. And by the way, everything is settled at Canaan Baptist Wee Care. The facility will close for three weeks for some painting and then reopen."

"I'll be sure and put that in the story," she said. "As to the minutes, our deadline is Tuesday. That's tonight."

41

Welford's gaze narrowed, then he looked past her to the courthouse lawn. His expression turned rueful. "You have no idea what it's like trying to educate the children here. Chickasaw County has the highest teenage pregnancy rate in the state of Mississippi. We have students in the seventh grade who already have children. They drop them off with a relative or day care, then go on to get pregnant again."

Dixon saw no reason to beat around the bush. "I understand the board was entertaining bids on sixteenth section timber land. Were bids opened?" Bid openings were prime opportunities for graft and corruption, which was why she'd waited two hours on a deadline day.

"Actually, no." He shifted from foot to foot. "Today's meeting involved personnel."

"Hiring or firing?"

"The latter. We have a touchy situation. A young man's career hangs in the balance. We'd like for this teacher to leave without besmirching his name. No real harm has been done, and we simply want him to move along."

"What did he do?" Dixon lowered her pen.

"As far as we can determine, the teacher has become . . . involved with a young girl. For the sake of the student and the teacher, it will be best to nip this thing in the bud."

"The girl has made a charge?"

Welford's hands tensed and then flexed. "No official charges have been made."

She raised her eyebrows. "A complaint then?"

"Not in so many words."

For a moment neither said anything. "You're firing the guy, and a complaint hasn't been filed? How can he defend himself? Does he know you're firing him?"

Welford looked at his watch. "He will shortly."

Dixon stepped back. "It seems to me you don't really have enough evidence to dismiss a teacher. No charges, no complaint. Where's the cause for action?"

"I know you're used to big-city ways." He frowned slightly. "In a place like Memphis, there's a degree of anonymity. Governing bodies meet and discuss personnel, decisions are made, folks resign or get fired. Here in Jexville, it's a bit more delicate. If we can prevent this problem from getting to the stages of a formal complaint, then we'll have saved a young man's career and a young girl's reputation. This man can go on to teach and perhaps profit by the mistake he made here. But the girl has to remain. She can't leave. This is her home. Ultimately, it's the needs of the schoolchild that I base my decision on."

"What if this man is innocent?"

"Innocent? He's not innocent." Welford flushed, openly contemptuous. "Tommy Hayes was in that classroom with those young girls talking about reproduction and sex. He's leading them on, getting them thinking about sex, working them up. He's using his youth and knowledge to stir a hornet's nest. And even if he hasn't actually made advances toward the girl, then he's stupid for putting himself in a vulnerable position, staying after school with her, tutoring her. Next time Tommy Hayes will know to behave in an appropriate fashion. We don't need his kind of teacher here in Chickasaw County."

Dixon wondered if Welford's use of the teacher's name was a slip or a deliberate plant. She was developing a distinct dislike for the superintendent. "Does he have an attorney?"

"Look, I know how it might seem to an outsider. The truth is, the fat's in the fire. The best thing for the teacher is to cut his losses and move on."

As Dixon bent to make a notation on her pad, she saw movement in the dark hallway behind Welford. The woman was slender, with red hair. Dixon couldn't be positive, but she looked like Vivian Holbert, the bank president's elegant wife. Whoever she was, she disappeared through the door like a wraith. Dixon looked into Welford's flushed face. "Thanks for your time."

He patted her back. "I haven't had a chance to welcome you to Jexville." He patted her back again and leaned closer. "Actually, I find the story of the week to be that Pine Trust Bank made such a large loan to a single woman. Calvin is generally more conservative."

Dixon met his gaze. "There're no secrets in a small town. Everybody's dirty laundry eventually gets hung out."

The sun had set as Dixon walked down the empty streets to the paper. She heard the sound of a sputtering car engine behind her. When she turned, she saw Tucker in his ancient Toyota. She noted the high color on his peach-fuzz cheeks, the eagerness in his face.

"Linda sent me after you," he said as he leaned out the window. "Her friend called back. They think those two missing girls might have drowned in the river. I want to follow the story."

"You've already got one big front-page story this week with the chancery clerk charged with embezzlement. Blood lust is unattractive in a young reporter." She gave a lopsided smile to take the sting out of her words. "How long have they been gone?"

"They skipped school after first period, so probably since nine A.M. Someone saw a vehicle they might have been driving parked near a sandbar. Linda knows the part of the river they went to. It's up at Fitler where the Leaf and Chickasawhay join to form the Pascagoula. She said the currents are treacherous. Kids drown there a lot."

Dixon checked her watch. The front page had to be put to bed soon. She had decisions to make. She could go to the paper, or she could track down Tommy Hayes, the high school teacher who had just been fired for alleged misconduct. Perhaps Hayes would make a statement. Maybe he had a side to his story that needed to be printed.

"Go over to the sheriff's office and see what you can find out. See if they're getting search parties up or what. Could be the girls just decided to drive over to Mobile or down to the beach."

"You think?"

Dixon saw his sudden deflation. Tucker had been working on his master's degree in journalism at the University of Southern Mississippi when his money ran out. It had taken a sub-subhuman salary and the promise of many front-page bylines to draw him out of the USM library and into the newspaper office. She had appealed, cold-bloodedly and without remorse, to Tucker's pale blond ambition. Beneath the bookworm exterior beat the heart of a newshound.

"Check it out with the sheriff." She hesitated. "Don't let Horton send you down a rabbit hole."

"Okay. So what happened at the school board meeting?" Tucker pushed his hair out of his eyes, a gesture he made at least a thousand times a day and one he'd obviously studied in the mirror. Dixon could only hope he never went bald; he would have no defining action.

"They moved the meeting, and as my daddy always told me, secret meetings are held for one purpose: to conduct secret business . . ." She faltered, hearing the echo of an explosion. She shook her head and checked her watch again. "Make it fast, Tucker. I'm going to give a teacher a call. Time is running out. We've got to get the paper ready to take to the printer."

As she walked briskly toward the newspaper, she pondered Big Jim Welford's agenda. She was tempted to slam him with a story that would spin his head around on his neck. Public business needed to be conducted in public to give all sides a chance to have their say. If she went after Welford the way he deserved, a young girl and a teacher could suffer. It was also possible that Welford had set her up to do his dirty work for him.

The street was empty, and as she walked she listened to the sounds of a small town settling in for the night. A child laughed in a backyard. The smell of barbecue wafted through the oaks. She stopped and looked around. She could be in a small town anywhere in the south—the early September heat, the trees, the sense of day ending and evening—for families—beginning. The quiet street, lined with oaks whose gnarled roots bumped up the sidewalk, embodied the charm and beauty of the old south.

She started walking again. Only time would tell what course she should take. But the problem with hindsight was that it only pointed out that no choice was without penalty, no action without consequence.

✝

J.D. sat at his desk, a sense of impending doom weighing him down. First he'd been visited by Robert Medino. That conversation stuck in his craw, but he'd attributed it to a simple dislike of a smartass—until he'd gotten a phone call an hour ago from Beth Salter. She'd been out of control, demanding that he form a search party for her daughter Angie and another teen, Trisha Webster. The two girls had left school in the morning and hadn't been seen or heard from since. Angie had a record as a runaway, but Trisha, from all accounts, was a quiet, well-behaved girl.

From his window he could see the Chickasaw County board of education building. He watched Dixon Sinclair's conversation with Big Jim and knew trouble was brewing there. He'd made it his business to learn about Dixon, and what he'd discovered was that she wouldn't be intimidated by the good ole boys who ran Chickasaw County. She had a reputation as a drunk, but he hadn't seen any signs of it. Her eyes had been clear, her questions sharp. Dixon was a harbinger of change. He felt it in his bones.

He made another call to the Webster house, and Trisha's mother answered.

"I don't want to speak poorly of anyone, but I believe Angie is a bad influence on Trish. My daughter would never skip school unless she got talked into it. I feel sorry for Angie. She's a lost child, but I don't want her taking Trish down that road with her."

"You still haven't heard from your daughter?" J.B. asked, his sense of trouble deepening.

"Not a word. When she does get home, she's going to be grounded for the rest of the year. Are you organizing a search party?"

"Let's give them a little bit longer to show up," he said. He replaced the phone, thinking about the treacherous current of the river, especially at Fitler where the two rivers joined. He looked up when Tucker Barnes walked into his office. Tucker looked as if he were fourteen, but behind the John Lennon glasses was a quick mind.

"Sheriff, have you had a report on some missing girls?"

"We don't have an official report yet. Mrs. Salter called and said Angie didn't come home from school." He hesitated, then continued. "Mrs. Webster hasn't seen them, either." Perhaps that would prevent the reporter from calling and upsetting Mrs. Webster further. "So far, they aren't considered missing, just late."

"Are you launching a search?" Tucker asked.

J.D. considered. "It's just getting dark. I hope the girls show up before bedtime." He didn't tell Tucker about Angie's record as a troubled teen.

"If they don't come home, what'll you do?"

"Let's not get the cart before the horse," he said.

"I got some photographs of the girls from the school annual," Tucker said. He pulled two small photos from his pocket. "Is this Angie Salter?" he held out one photo.

J.D. looked at the image of the girl. She had on make-up so heavy she looked twenty-one instead of fifteen. "That's her."

"And this is Trisha Webster?"

The girl was timid. He could see it in the way her gaze didn't quite make it to the camera. Her brown hair was thick. She had the look of a follower. "That's the Webster girl." He hesitated. "If you play this story up, those girls are going to have to live with it when they come home."

"If they come home," Tucker said. "Folks are saying they might have drowned in the river."

"Folks aren't the most reliable source, Mr. Barnes. I hope you keep that in mind."

His office door opened again, and Vivian Holbert stood in the doorway, looking annoyed at Tucker. "Sorry, Sheriff Horton. I didn't realize you had someone in here."

"Mr. Barnes was just leaving, Vivian. Is there something I can do for you?"

She entered, her pale face pink from exposure to the sun. "I want to speak to you alone."

J.D. nodded at Tucker.

"I have to get back to the paper," Tucker said, closing the door behind him.

J.D. turned his attention to Vivian. He knew more about the Holberts than he cared to know. Vivian and Calvin's daughter, Camille, lived on the river with Eustace Mills, a fisherman and retired bootlegger who was nearly forty years her senior. Calvin had repeatedly tried to force J.D. to go to the river and physically remove Camille. J.D. had consistently refused, pointing out that Camille was a grown woman and could live with whomever she chose. Such logic cut no ice with Calvin. Now, here was Vivian, ready to launch a fresh assault when he had two missing girls to worry about.

"I was over at the board of education." She paused, her pale green eyes steady. "I heard that two girls are missing. I was there when Beth Salter showed up. She made an ass of herself, trying to blame the school because her daughter cut class. She says she's going to sue."

J.D. was silent. In his dealings with Vivian, he'd learned to neither confirm nor deny.

"I think Eustace did it. I think he took those girls and hurt them." She lifted her chin, daring him to deny it.

"Vivian, there's no indication that anyone took those girls. I believe they're just working out a wild hair. They'll be back by suppertime."

"And if they aren't?" Her tone was cool. "That man is a deviant. I will never understand why you protect him. He has my daughter, and Camille may be twenty-three, but she isn't capable of making that kind of decision."

"Until Camille is legally ruled incompetent, I have to allow her to behave as an adult." J.D. wanted to tell Vivian that Eustace would never hurt Camille or any other young woman, but that would just fuel the fire.

"You defend him when his actions are indefensible." She stood up. "One day, and not too far away, you'll have to admit that you're wrong about him." She marched out of the office, her high heels tapping on the floor.

J.D. leaned back in his chair. It was time to go home. If anything happened, the dispatcher would call him.

CHAPTER SIX

Dixon read Tucker's brief story on the missing girls. It had been a difficult call to make, but by eleven, when the girls hadn't returned, she'd finally settled on a small story simply saying they were missing. Her decision not to use names or photographs had aggravated Tucker, but she explained her reasons: no speculation, no panic. It was consideration for the families of the girls that held her back, not worry about the Chickasaw County authorities. As the sheriff had told Tucker, the girls would have to live down whatever was printed in the paper.

She typed out her four-paragraph story on the closed-door school board meeting and walked to the composing room to hang her copy on a hook for Linda. Once those stories were set and pasted up, the paper would be ready for Tucker to take to Gautier at two A.M., where it would be printed by an offset press. Wednesday before noon, the papers would be hauled to the post office for delivery.

She stood in the composing room, the backshop of the paper visible. When she'd bought the *Independent*, she'd gotten the old press and linotypes, dinosaurs, from a time long past in newspapering. She'd wanted them.

As a preschooler, she'd frequently gone to work with her father at his politically oriented weekly in Jackson. She'd stood on a crate beside him as he made up the heavy metal pages. Her job had been removing the old slugs of lead from the previous week's issue. She'd take the slugs to the linotype machines where they would be melted down and reset. Most of the linotype operators were deaf, and they'd laughed in a high-pitched cackle when she deposited her small buckets of lead for them.

The press had been a roaring monster that rolled forward and retracted on its bed, the steady rhythm frightening—yet also satisfying and exciting. Once a pressman's fingers had been crushed beneath the press as she watched. The pressman had gone to the emergency room, then returned to continue running the press. Getting the paper out was a matter of honor for all involved.

Shaking off the ghosts, she sighed. The *Independent*'s press hadn't run in years and wouldn't ever again. She was lollygagging in the past. She returned to her desk, picked up the phone, and dialed. There was one last lead to follow. A wary male voice answered on the first ring.

"This is Dixon Sinclair. May I speak with Tommy Hayes?"

There was a pause. "He isn't home."

"When do you expect him back?" She tapped the eraser on the pad as she listened to dogs barking in the background.

"He was supposed to be back at four."

The man's voice sounded worried. He was hoping she was the cavalry. Wrong story—she was the Big Bad Wolf. "I'm the publisher of the *Independent*, and I'd like to speak with Mr. Hayes when he returns. Would you take a message for him?"

"Why is the newspaper calling Tommy?" the young man demanded. "Has something happened? He should be home by now."

Dixon hesitated. "Please ask Mr. Hayes to call me when he returns," she answered.

"It's that bitch Angie, isn't it? He should have had her expelled."

"Angie?" Dixon fumbled on her desk for the story of the missing girls. One of them was named . . . she found the copy that Tucker had turned in. Angie Salter. "What does Angie Salter have to do with this?"

There was silence, then the telephone hummed in her ear. Dixon swiveled her chair to face the front window. Dust motes swirled in the slanting golden sunlight, and she thought of the story her father had told her when she was a child. When the day died, the dust motes turned into tiny fairies, creatures brought to life by the fading sun to dance for an instant in the blue hour before the fall of night.

A brief, fierce dance of death.

Outside, along the half-mile strip of Main Street, the lights were on. The pink mercury vapors were the only concession to "town." Jexville didn't exactly welcome the night with celebration, but it didn't struggle against the darkness with shafts of neon, either. It gave up gently with a locking of shop doors and the glow of kitchen lights and televisions.

She went to the composing room and reread Tucker's story on the missing girls. The connection between Tommy Hayes, a just-fired teacher, and a missing girl, who might be the source of his problems, was disturbing. Her gut told her to play it big, but she left it as it was. If she trusted her gut, she'd end up back in the bottom of a bottle.

✝

Awake in the moist embrace of the night, Dixon lay on her left side. In the moonlight that filtered through the bedroom window, the far wall was a pale coral. The beaded board paneling had been a bitch to paint.

In the darkness a vehicle shushed past leaving isolation in its wake. The house on Peterson Lane, with the woods around it and the small creek behind, remained untouched and secluded. She'd lived her adult life in the hustle of cities. Now she found the woods comforting but wasn't sure why.

Beside the bed the gauzy curtain fluttered as if blown about by the unexpected cry of a bird that swam through the humid night. The gentle question of a hoot owl came from somewhere in the woods behind the house.

Dixon wasn't sure whether it was the awful heat and humidity, anxiety, or a noise from the woods that had awakened her. She listened for a moment, but there was nothing except the owl and the autumnal rustle of the leaves, a branch brushing lightly against the screen on the window.

She rose from the bed and walked across the room, pulling the nightshirt away from her sticky skin. She fought the uncooperative windows closed and flipped on the old air conditioning unit that droned so loudly it blocked out the night sounds.

Ignoring the letter on her bedside table, she checked the clock. It was nearly dawn. Tucker would already have driven the black asphalt highway to the printing press in Gautier with this week's edition of the *Independent*. Leaning back into the pillows, she forced herself to savor the sense of accomplishment. The front page was solid, and the editorial page had some teeth. It was a good start. The only thing that troubled her was the story on the missing girls. That and the letter.

At last she snapped on the light and lifted the letter to read again her mother's angry words.

Dear Dixon,

Since you won't return my calls I have no other recourse but to write. The warden at the prison has called me again. He said you were there, asking to talk with that murderer. I demand that you stop this foolishness. Your father is dead. By going to the prison, you make that horrible day alive for me and for everyone else who suffered so. You must stop this reckless behavior, for your own sake as well as mine. I view the purchase of that weekly newspaper as another reckless act. You are bent on self-destruction. You and your father . . .

Dixon lowered the pages, but the words had already scalded her. She hadn't meant to upset her mother, had never intended that her mother learn of her recent trip to the Mississippi State Penitentiary at Parchman to visit the man who'd been sentenced to life for the murder of her father.

The phone beside the bed rang, and she snatched it up. "Hello."

"Dixon, are you okay? You sound like you're hatching that telephone."

Dixon recognized Linda's voice. "I was dreaming, I guess. What's going on?"

"They're gearing up a search for those missing girls. They'll be leaving the sheriff's office at dawn." Linda cleared her throat. "I'm afraid something has happened to those girls."

Dixon swung her feet to the floor. The pages of her mother's letter fluttered beside her toes. "How'd you find out?"

"They called Frank to serve on the search party, but he can't miss work. They've got an inspection at the shipyard, and he's in charge."

"Sheriff Horton is leading the search?"

"He's the man."

"Will he let a reporter tag along?"

Linda's voice was soft, as if she were being careful not to wake someone in the house. "I don't know him well enough to say, but ask him. J.D. will probably be glad to have you along. He was the chief source of gossip until you moved to town. You've sort of taken the heat off him."

"I'll bet." Dixon felt along the floor for her slippers.

There was silence before Linda spoke again. "Don't let on that you heard about the search from me. I don't care, but it would make it hard on Frank."

Standing, Dixon glanced at the clock. She just had time for a shower. "Listen, Tucker's in Gautier. He can't get back in time, so I'll have to go. Can you and Tucker handle getting the paper over to the post office?"

"No problem. Just remember that you owe me."

"I get the feeling I'm going to owe you a lot more. Thanks."

"Dixon." Linda hesitated. "Angie's a kid with a lot of troubles. Plenty of them she makes for herself. Still, she's a kid. Folks around here like to judge a person, and once the verdict's in, there's no second chance."

Dixon knew what she was asking. "They're juveniles, Linda. If they're into something, we'll have to be very careful with the story."

"Angie thinks she's tough, but she's been lucky." She sighed. "She wouldn't agree with that, but she has. Look, be careful. There're places in that swamp where you really can disappear."

✝

Dawn broke hot and hazy, the sun fighting to penetrate the dense atmosphere that seemed at least 90 percent water. Eustace sat in the old, brown Adirondack chair and sipped the hot coffee. He'd slept little. Throughout the night, Camille had thrashed and moaned. Waking her would have done no good, so he'd lain beside her, soothing her with a gentle hand on her back or a whisper.

Camille's nocturnal episodes were less frequent now, but they worried him. She lived with demons, and though some had evaporated along the banks of the river during the year she'd been with him, others remained. They tormented her, invading her sleep and even her waking moments. She never talked about them or the past. She had made it clear that both topics were off limits. Because he was afraid he'd lose her, he had complied. But, when the demons came, her face would draw together, shutting him out, and he felt as if he'd die of loneliness.

He took a swallow of his coffee and looked down the river. A caravan of trucks and cars slowly moved onto the Pascagoula River Bridge. Eustace sat up straighter, shifting his coffee cup to the arm of the chair. There were at least a dozen cars. Once the road had been a federal highway, but now it was mostly abandoned. Large portions of the land around the river had been purchased by the Nature Conservancy, preserved against man's uncontrollable desire to destroy the wilderness. Access to much of the swampland had been restricted, and that was fine with him. He liked it best when he had the river to himself.

"Eustace."

He turned at Camille's voice. She was a vision in her flimsy nightshirt, her red hair hanging nearly to her waist in thick curls. She smiled tentatively, as if she'd done something wrong in the night. "I'm sorry I kept you up."

"You didn't," he lied.

She touched his face. "I did." She kissed him. "What are you going to do today?"

"Maybe hang around here. I need to work on a few boat motors." The truth was, he didn't want to leave her. The vehicles on the bridge meant that strangers were about. Camille had never learned to protect herself. She was like a child, willing to talk with anyone, assuming that strangers meant her no harm.

"I want to go to the place where we're going to build the kiln," she said. "I want to start work on it."

"I thought you'd planned to do something with your mother." He hated Vivian and Calvin, but he would never interfere with Camille's relationship with them.

"I don't want to. I'm not going to."

He knew that she wouldn't call them. And he would get the blame for it.

"There's a man in the woods." She was looking across the water to the west bank of the river, to the place they'd planned to build her kiln to fire her ceramics.

Her words chilled him. Besides the fish heads and beer, things had gone missing from around his camp. Food, a knife, towels, and a beautiful table runner that had been Camille's grandmother's.

"Are you saying you've seen a man in the woods?" he asked. He had to be very specific with Camille, and it was possible that she was referring to her nightmares.

"In that old sycamore tree. I felt sorry for him. I thought we could take him some food." She pointed to the bridge. "What's going on?"

He knew better than to press her. She'd withdraw, thinking he disapproved or found fault with her. "I don't know. That's more cars than I've seen on that bridge in fifteen years."

"What are they doing?"

"I'm sure we'll find out soon enough."

"Come inside. I'm going to make some breakfast."

Eustace rose and walked beside her. Some days she forgot to eat, so he took it as a good sign when she thought of breakfast. Whatever she decided to cook would be fine. If she asked him to eat nails, he'd do it.

CHAPTER SEVEN

The old iron bridge that spanned the Pascagoula River moaned beneath the weight of the caravan. From her seat in the back of J.D.'s Ford Explorer, Dixon examined the iron structure that had played such a prominent role in her family's past. As the truck lumbered slowly over the rutted, dangerous span, she stared at the river that looked as if it had fallen asleep and forgotten to flow on to the Mississippi Sound. The river's appearance was deceiving. The current was both strong and treacherous.

One of her relatives, Alfred Dunagan, had been involved in the controversial plan to build the Fitler Bridge back in the early 1900s. He and his wife had drowned when the ferry capsized crossing the river during a storm; the story was family legend. Neither Dunagan nor his partner, Jacob Senseney, had lived to see their dreams sculpted into concrete and iron.

The state legislature had recently promised a flood of state and federal money into Chickasaw County to preserve the old structure. The Fitler Bridge, unwanted and damned a century earlier, was now a historic landmark.

The caravan halted on the single-lane bridge when the lead car dropped through a pothole and came to rest on its rear axle. Dixon heard car doors slamming, voices, even a few snorts of laughter as the men clustered around the crippled car. Ranging in age from early twenties to sixties and dressed in jeans that bagged at the knees or army camouflage, they were tribal. Their relationship with the land and the river—a relationship she wasn't willing to designate as love because of the harsh usage they gave both—bound them together more tightly than marriage vows or lust. She remembered Linda's story of the man who had surprised a robber in his home. "Take anything you want," he'd said. "Take it all. You can even have my wife as long as you leave my huntin' dog."

Climbing out of the Explorer, Dixon stretched, her body stiff from the beating she'd taken over ten miles of washboard road. The lead car, a 1992 Grand Prix, was so deep in the hole that the rear wheel spun free in empty air. J.D. Horton knelt beside it.

He'd shown neither surprise nor dismay when she appeared at the courthouse ready for the search. Clear blue eyes had given back only her own reflection, and he'd assigned her a seat in the Explorer, not giving her a chance to ask any questions.

Horton was examining the stuck car's axle. Among the men, he adopted a good-ole-boy attitude, but it wasn't his natural mode. Or if it was, world travel and a twenty-year stint in the marines had given him polish. She wanted the answer to the question everyone in Jexville had asked—why had J.D. come back to Chickasaw County? He didn't fit in any more than she did. He could have made a lot more money almost anywhere else. He wasn't married. He had no children. Why Chickasaw County?

Speaking of not fitting in, the tall man she'd seen at the day care fiasco stuck out like a sore thumb. He seemed less interested in her today, but she noticed a notebook tucked into his back pocket.

She walked to the rail and watched the river. It sneaked past the bridge without a hair of discernable movement. A small log surfaced, wallowing up as if to gasp air before being sucked back under and away. It was a chilling giveaway that the current was at work. If the girls had drowned, there was no telling where the bodies would eventually float up. She just might have let herself in for a very long, hot, uncomfortable day. And Tucker had wanted this story.

"You okay?" Deputy Waymon Semmes looked amused as he came up. "You look like you might jump. I thought maybe you were gettin' spooked." He laughed. "I told J.D. this wasn't no place for a girl. Them swamps are haunted."

"Next time I do a poll on a woman's place, I'll be sure and give you a call."

Waymon grinned. "I'd like that. When do you think you might do that story? Will you use my picture?"

Dixon managed not to smile. "Sure, a mug shot. We'll do it soon. Real soon." She turned and pointed west. "Is that the tip of the sandbar?" She could see, nearly a mile away, where the Leaf and Chickasawhay Rivers flowed together into the broader, murkier Pascagoula. Right at the fork, on the west bank of the river, a pristine sandbar humped out of the water and disappeared around a bend.

"There's a path that cuts through the woods, but it's a walk. I hope you brought some mosquito repellant." He swatted at his neck.

"I'll be fine." She smiled. "Who's the guy over there?"

"Him? Name of Robert Medino." Waymon tried for nonchalant. "He's a writer from a big-city magazine. He's staying in town, working on some kinda story. He was in yesterday, talking to the sheriff and all. J.D. said it was a top-secret story."

Dixon wanted to ask what kind of story, but she didn't. She focused instead on J.D. as he took a position midway in the caravan.

"Okay, men, Ms. Sinclair, Joe's staying here with the cars until the wrecker can come and get him out of the hole. Then he'll move the other cars down off the bridge, so be sure you leave your keys. We're going on to search. Waymon will take some of you south. I'll take Ms. Sinclair, Jay, and Cooney. We'll search the sandbar and the woods—"

"What about me?" Medino asked. "I want to help."

J.D. didn't move. Dixon felt the tension between the two men.

"You come with me," J.D. finally said. "I want to be sure you don't get yourself killed in the swamp."

The men broke up, tossing their keys to the owner of the stranded car, taunting him good-naturedly as they passed. Their footsteps echoed on the old bridge. The span was level with the tops of the trees that grew along the banks, and Dixon recognized sweet gums, willows, pines, cedars, scrub oaks, and the live oaks that dominated with their grace and beauty. The trees were draped with the lacy fringes of Spanish moss, a beautiful parasite. It was not so different from the Pearl River that looped and wiggled around Jackson, where she'd grown up.

At the foot of the bridge, the men separated. She followed J.D. down a pig trail into the woods. Medino followed her, making no effort to talk, though she felt his gaze. Cooney and Jay brought up the rear; she knew that J.D. had arranged things so that she and Medino could both be watched. He didn't trust their wilderness skills.

Dixon realized that the woods were much denser than they appeared from the bridge. Stepping beneath the canopy of tree branches, she felt the temperature drop at least ten degrees.

J.D. set a brisk pace. The trail was narrow but clear. In places the thick vines and leafy trees closed over them. Where the sunlight filtered through, it was dappled, but many areas were in constant gloom, the ground thick with rotted leaves that hushed their footsteps. Dixon tried not to think of past assignments where tragedy had lurked beneath a layer of leaves and branches.

The two faces in the school photos floated before her. Angie Salter was pretty and hard; it showed in her lipsticked pout. Trisha Webster had the look of a timid rabbit. They were a recipe for trouble.

"Keep your ears open." J.D. spoke softly. "There are wild boars out here, and they can be mean if you 'rouse them. Especially if they've got a litter." He moved on, barely rustling a leaf with his passage.

"Sheriff?" It was Medino.

"What?"

"How did the girls get to this sandbar? There wasn't a vehicle around. Have you found the person who gave them a ride?"

The question and its tone, just short of sarcastic, hung unanswered in the air.

By the time they reached an opening in the heavy curtain of trees, Dixon was panting with exertion and heat. She'd once been athletic, but the years of anxiety and drinking had taken a toll. Sweat trickled between her breasts and down the small of her back.

J.D. turned to look at his search team. "Okay, now fan out. I'll take the position by the water, Ms. Sinclair beside me, Medino at the edge of the woods. The sandbar is half a mile wide in places. Cooney, Jay, you take the north trail back and then start down the road." He checked his watch. "If you haven't found anything, head back to the bridge at ten." He glanced at each of them. "Be careful not to destroy any evidence. Look for anything. Footprints, beer cans, potato chip sacks—anything to indicate how those girls spent their time. If you see something, put it in these." He handed out evidence bags. "Be sure you don't touch it. Latent prints can be on any surface. Use those rubber gloves. Okay, let's go."

The men headed out, and Dixon was interested to see that Medino did as he was told without comment. J.D. studied the sand in front of him, and she studied him. After a moment, he asked, "You sure you're up for this?"

Dixon had no choice but to nod. She'd asked to come along.

He went to the water's edge and signaled her to keep pace with him as she covered the center of the sand bar.

From the bridge the beach had looked pristine. Walking along it, Dixon found the remains of a hundred camp outs, evidence of old fires and parties. Glass and aluminum were everywhere.

About a hundred yards away, She saw the sheriff closing in on a blue ice chest. Beside it a circle of silver cans winked in the sun. Vibrant red and black lettering told of their recent deposit on the white sand.

Dixon's hands went to the camera that dangled around her neck. She lifted it, began to shoot, then walked over to J.D.

Using a handkerchief from his pocket, J.D. opened the chest. Three full beers bobbed in the melted ice water that gave a breath of cool to Dixon's face as she leaned over it. She clicked off a shot.

J.D.'s voice was hardly more than a whisper. "Dammit it all to hell. When I get my hands on Waymon I'm going to break his neck."

"What did he do?" Dixon hadn't noticed the deputy doing anything untoward. He wasn't even in sight.

"It's what he didn't do," Horton said under his breath. He spoke louder. "Sometimes he just doesn't think of the consequences."

Dixon focused on the sand, which had been dimpled by early-morning dew. Prints of bare feet, small and high-arched, were still visible. There were also bigger footprints from hard-soled shoes, possibly work boots, not the athletic style she would expect from a young boy. The prints made a chaotic pattern around the ice chest and disappeared at the water's edge.

"Cooney!" J.D. called in a voice that bounced off the water. "Cooney! Can you hear me?"

"Yo!" The answer came back muffled by the thick stand of trees.

"Go back to the patrol car and get some plaster molds!" He looked at Dixon, and for a moment she saw regret in the angle of his mouth.

"You think something has happened to the girls?" She was surprised at her feeling of dread. For so long, she'd been numb to the ramifications of the stories she covered. Then again, for so long she'd been drunk.

J.D. was studying the sand where a girl's prints, one foot bare and the other in a shoe, went into the water and didn't return. She snapped a photo and heard J.D. sigh as he reached into the river and pulled something out.

"What is it?" she asked.

"A sandal." He looked toward the river. "Looks like she walked right off into the water and disappeared. Waymon should have had sense enough not to leave those girls stranded."

"What did he have to do with this?"

"The kid who owned the truck called and reported his vehicle missing. He told Waymon the story, I guess about three o'clock. The kid suspected the girls had come here to the river, and he got Waymon to ride him out here. They found the truck, and the kid used his key to drive it off. He was pissed, said he was going to get fired from work because of Angie taking his truck. Waymon followed him back to town."

"Your deputy didn't check on the girls? Did he or the boy see them from the bridge?"

J.D. shook his head. "No. And they didn't look. They thought it was a big joke to leave them stranded out here on the sandbar. Of course, Waymon didn't bother to tell me this until three o'clock this morning, when he got a call from Beth Salter and realized the girls didn't go home. Which is why we're searching now."

Dixon eyed Horton. The tracks had obviously told the sheriff a more detailed story than she could read. "Do you think the girls went in the river and drowned?"

J.D. rubbed his mouth with the bank of his hand. "We're going to be out here a while."

CHAPTER EIGHT

Dixon rested against the trunk of a sweet gum and tried not to let her imagination get the better of her. Trisha Webster and Angie Salter were not on the sandbar or in the nearby woods. The slender evidence they'd found didn't make a lot of sense. It appeared that the girls had simply vanished, possibly beneath the muddy water.

The sheriff had ordered the river dragged. So far the draglines had found a battered trunk, several trees, fishing nets, a sack of garbage weighted with bricks, part of an old cement mixer, three tires, and a sunken boat that was on the verge of complete disintegration.

Laughter caught her ear, and she turned to the bridge, which was lined with spectators who had come to see if the river would give up a body. There was almost a festive air, and Dixon wondered again at the callousness of the human animal. She had seen the same reaction time and time again, folks stopping to examine the carnage of a wreck or watch a neighbor's house burn. So far no television crews had arrived. She caught a glimpse of copper skin. The young man she'd seen outside the newspaper office stared at her, then vanished into the crowd. A moment later, she saw him on a bicycle peddling across the bridge. She watched him until he disappeared into the trees.

With a flick of her wrist, Dixon used her notebook to splatter a blood-fattened mosquito on her thigh. West Nile, a mosquito-borne virus, flitted through her mind. Movement on the sandbar caught her eye, and she looked up to see several of the searchers converge on the sheriff, whispering urgently. The volunteers ignored her and Robert Medino as long as they stayed out of the way. Medino ignored her, too. He remained aloof, scuffing through the sand or writing in his notebook. He was handsome in a dark, unkempt way, the exact opposite of Horton, who was blond and well groomed.

She gingerly shifted her weight. Her bladder was about to burst. There was no help for it; she was going to have to walk into the woods and pee. Remembering that a tiny side trail cut north, she started out for it. Winding deeper and deeper into the woods, she almost passed the trail, which sloped down to the site of underground springs.

The swamp fell silent as she stepped off the path and into the layers of leaves. In real urgency now, she hurried down a slope, then stopped at the vista before her. Bream darted among the tree roots in dark pools ringed by cypress knees. It was a place of wild beauty.

She turned left to avoid a bog. The trees closed around her, a thicket of huckleberry, palmetto, and scrub oak. She looked in all directions but saw only trees and leaves, patterns of light and dark. She unzipped her pants and squatted, concerned momentarily that she'd held it for so long that she couldn't go.

A slip of white paper, stuck in a briar next to her caught her eye. It was a receipt from Circuit City for $149.93. The fresh crispness of the paper so deep in the woods intrigued her. She slipped it into the pocket of her jeans.

It was hot as hell, and not even a breeze stirred a leaf. She thought of the icy beer floating in the chest and wondered if J.D. considered it evidence. She could only imagine his face if she were to ask if she could drink it. He wouldn't be amused.

She started back the way she'd come, stopping for a moment at the spring-fed pools. They looked like something out of a fairy tale, but chances were the water contained more than one moccasin.

"Hey! Sinclair! Where in hell are you?" J.D.'s voice sounded close.

She hesitated. The woods were thick, and it would be more sensible to go back the way she'd come. But that was the longest way, and the sheriff sounded so close. "Horton?"

"Where are you?"

"I'm coming."

"We don't have time to start a search for another person." He sounded angry.

She tripped on a root but regained her balance. Using her hands she pushed through the undergrowth. Directly in front of her was a wall of bullace vines laden with the delicious grapes. She picked a handful and popped them into her mouth, expertly sucking out and discarding the seeds and thick skin as she hunted a way through vines. At ground level she found a break and began to crawl. On the other side, she looked up into a dark, cool haven.

It took a moment for her eyes to adjust, but her nose was quicker. The ripe smell of the bullaces gave an exotic scent, sun-heated with a hint of fermentation. It was a faintly sexual odor, filled with promise. The vines had grown up and over the lower branches of a huge oak. The result was a tentlike room, high-domed, created out of lacy vines and leaves. Sunlight filtered through the dense vegetation, giving a wash of dim green illumination. She stepped deeper into the enclosure.

Beside the oak tree was a wooden bench. She walked toward it, her hand automatically reaching for the camera that dangled at her waist. She whispered softly, "Holy shit," and started snapping photos.

A rough altar constructed of cement blocks and boards was covered with an embroidered white cloth. Even in the dim light the colors were radiant. Dixon recognized the extraordinary labor that had created the tableau. Stubs of candles melted into the bases of tin cans adorned either end of the altar, and an offering of withered flowers formed a centerpiece. Beside that was a worn rosary and a rough imitation of a crucifix whittled from a cypress knee. Next to the beads was a pink-and-purple bikini top. Dixon stared at it, unable to think of a single explanation for it. A single *good* explanation. She backed away.

"Sinclair! Goddammit!" J.D. wasn't far away.

Dixon stumbled across the enclosure. "Wait!" Her fingers searched the vines for a place she could force through, but the web was impenetrable. "Horton!" She waited five seconds. "Horton!"

"By God, Sinclair, if I have to come in there after you, I'm going to arrest you."

She concentrated on his voice. She tore at the vines, at last finding a place where they yielded. "Horton," she called.

As she ducked through the opening something snagged her foot. She kicked to free herself and felt it give. She stumbled backward with it dangling on her shoe. Even in the dim light of the vine room, the pink-and-purple fabric was still bright, only a little dirty. She picked it up. A bikini bottom. Bright, sassy beachwear. Scraps of fabric tied together at each hip. She held the cloth with the tips of her fingers. There appeared to be a stain on it, maybe mud or blood.

Dixon swallowed. "Horton, you'd better come in here."

"I don't have time for this." J.D.'s words were accompanied by the snapping of tree limbs as he plowed through them. "I can't baby-sit the damn press and manage a search. I can't . . ." His tirade faded when he saw her, half hidden by the vines, the bikini bottom in her hand.

"What is it?" But the knowledge was in his voice, his eyes locked onto the material. He held out an evidence bag, and she released the suit into it.

"It hung on my foot when I was trying to get through the vines. In there." She lifted the vines to allow him entrance. "You need to see this. The top is in there, too."

J.D. pulled a flashlight from his belt and swung it side to side as he ducked beneath the vines. A dozen empty cans that had once held beans and Spam and potted meat were scattered in the clearing. When the light struck the altar, he held it there. Then he shifted the light and looked at Dixon's face. "Are you okay?"

She pushed the light down. "Yeah." She looked at the evidence bag. "I'm okay."

She heard the rustling of leaves. When she looked up, she expected to see Waymon. Instead, Robert Medino pushed through the vines. His sharp gaze took in everything.

73

"You need to leave," J.D. said.

"I was right." Medino was excited. "He's here. And he's got those girls. Two of them. I knew he'd progress to the real thing. I warned you."

J.D. grabbed his shirt. "This may be a reason for celebration for you, but if those girls are dead, it's going to be a tragedy for their family and friends. I suggest you keep that in mind."

Medino pushed the sheriff's hand away. "You should keep in mind that I'm not some local you can push around." He smoothed his shirt. "I'm not glad the girls are dead. And you should look at this as an opportunity. You can catch a killer. You'll be doing interviews on *20/20*."

"You really think a television interview equals the lives of these two girls?" J.D.'s fists clenched at his side.

Dixon put a hand on J.D.'s arm, lightly restraining him. The gesture was automatic. She realized that after only two weeks in Jexville, she, too, viewed Medino as an outsider, but an altercation with him wouldn't help a thing.

"Let's go back to the beach," she said.

Medino pulled out his notebook. "I've been tracking this man. The sheriff scoffed at my idea, and now he has two dead girls on his hands."

"They aren't dead until we find the bodies," J.D. said.

"They're dead," Medino said. "They're dead, and we all know it. Look at this stuff." His hand swept toward the altar where the sunlight sifting through the vines caught the crude crucifix. "He's a psycho, just like I said. Those girls are dead because no one would listen to me."

CHAPTER NINE

J.D. stood on the spit of land where one bare footprint led into the river and disappeared beneath waters now golden orange in the slant of the afternoon sun. He looked upriver at the circling boats. More than thirty hours had passed since the girls were last seen. He stared out at the water, keenly aware of the quiet that surrounded him.

He knew the hush that had fallen over this section of the twisty river. He'd heard it before—the presence of death.

In a dense jungle filled with a green so intense it blistered the back of his retinas, he'd heard the silence that preceded death's appearance. It had been a day as hot as anything Mississippi could deliver. Marines all around him cursed as they made their way up a hill. Without a hint of warning, the day lost volume. His buddies stumbled and cursed, their faces tired and furious at the upper-level betrayal that had put them in a country where no official war had been declared, where the troops they'd been sent to help were murdering women and children, even nuns. Around them the tropical forest was alive with birds and the quick, elusive creatures of Central America. Then the birds hushed. Death drained all sound, sucking it away before rising up out of the lush vegetation, exploding with a vengeance that cut J.D.'s friends into ribbons. Sound returned with the screams and cries of the injured and dying.

That had been the first time.

J.D. had heard the hush of death again in a dark El Salvador City alley, where he stood with a drunken buddy, a black kid from Chicago who argued in his flat, clipped speech. "You can't sell a ten-year-old girl," Mike had insisted to a dead-eyed man with the facial features of the Mayans.

"Come on, Mike," J.D. had told his friend, pulling him along by the uniform sleeve. "We can't do anything here. Not now." They were being watched by El Salvadorian soldiers, men with guns who didn't care who they killed.

His friend had tugged free, walked back to the pimp, and grabbed him by his shirt, lifting him against the wall. "I'll be back," he said, "and when I do, I'm going to cut your gizzard out, you piece of shit."

The noise of a city in the throes of night had suddenly disappeared. For two seconds there had been total silence, then the click of the knife blade and Mike's soft grunt of surprise. J.D. had known in that split-second vacuum that his friend would die. Nothing he did or said could stop it. Mike was a dead man, and there was no turning away from it. Even as J.D. leaped forward, the noise came back in a hot rush. The pimp screamed a curse and fled as Mike sank to his knees, his brown eyes still disbelieving, his big, calloused hands holding in his guts.

J.D. looked out at the river, aware that sound had returned. He heard the murmur of Dixon's voice as she spoke with Medino, and he heard his deputy approach.

"The volunteers are ready to go back to town," Waymon said.

J.D. nodded. He'd called technicians from the state lab to work the scene around the altar and had a call in to Parchman Penitentiary for some tracking dogs.

"Looks like the national reporter is trying to make time with the local press," Waymon said.

J.D. turned to look at the sandbar, where Dixon chatted with Medino. Her hair was damp with sweat, and he could see the outline of her breasts beneath the clinging sleeveless cotton shirt.

"She's not hard on the eyes," Waymon said. "Too bad she's a reporter."

"Yeah," J.D. said. "Let's go. We'll come back tomorrow with the dogs."

†

From the back seat of the Explorer, Dixon watched the sheriff's head. J.D. Horton was not typical of her experience with law enforcement. Linda, who knew the ins and outs of everyone in Chickasaw County, said that loss and the sheriff's experience in Central America had changed him.

How could it not? People unaffected by violence were the ones sitting on death row—at least the ones who had been caught.

One man now on death row, Willard Jones, had been there for eleven years, ever since his conviction for the murder of Ray Sinclair. Even in the blistering heat, Dixon felt a chill. She had visited Jones at Parchman, and she had begun to doubt the verdict. Doubt was guilt's partner in the destruction of happiness, and Dixon suffered. Jones's execution was only four weeks away. He'd exhausted every appeal. Dixon understood that it was her waffling belief in Jones's guilt rather than her visits to him that upset her mother. When a man was to be executed in an act of Biblical justice, there was no room for doubt from the family, who were supposed to feel vindicated.

"Sinclair, I'd watch out for Medino."

Horton's advice was unexpected, and she didn't respond. She studied his neatly cropped hair. Thick and fine. Even driving, he had the upright posture of a military man.

The press and law enforcement often ended up at odds with each other. Both were bonded to tragedy. Both sought justice, and Ray Sinclair had believed that newspapering was the greater weight in the scale of justice.

"Miss Sinclair." Waymon turned around in the front seat so he could see her. "What do you think about that reporter man?"

"He's got some impressive credentials," she said.

"Like what?"

"He's educated at Harvard. He works for one of the most prestigious magazines in the world, with heavy emphasis on culture and politics. He won a Pulitzer for a story he did on abortions in Mexico—"

"He's one of them folks like to come in and stir folks up." Waymon frowned. They bounced off the bridge and onto the dirt road.

"That's a journalist's job, to make people think and see different sides of things."

"Don't need none of that in Chickasaw County," Waymon insisted.

"I disagree, Waymon. Chickasaw County needs a good bit of stirring up." Dixon saw Waymon frown. The deputy wasn't as dumb as he liked to pretend. "Mr. Medino has a theory on the disappearance of the girls and why he believes this psycho has taken them."

"Did Medino elucidate his theory?" Horton asked.

Horton might not have gone to Harvard, but he could toss around some ten-dollar words. "It had to do with Mexico, a fallen Catholic, a man who is conflicted with his image of women and his lust for them. Medino says the man has taken the girls because he thinks he wants to save them. Then he feels sexual desire for them, and once he's had them, he'll have to kill them."

J.D. pulled the SUV to the side of the road. "Waymon, find Ms. Sinclair and yourself a ride to town in another vehicle. I have something I need to do."

Dixon got out and stood in the hot sun. Horton didn't look back at her. He drove off, thick dust churning from beneath his wheels.

✝

Jouncing over potholes, J.D. turned down the rutted lane that led to Eustace Mills's bait shop and fish camp. Live oaks older than the state shaded the grassless yard. He parked and got out of the SUV, his face turned up to the camp. The tranquility of it always struck him anew. Some twenty feet up on pilings, the cypress structure looked like a strange airborne church nestled in the gnarled arms of the oaks. J.D. had a sense of coming home.

He wanted to talk to his old friend. Eustace was a man of logic. The two of them would sit under the oaks and drink a few beers and talk through the disappearance of the two girls.

J.D. walked through the trees. The place was quiet. Camille's car was by the house, and he could see Eustace's boat at the landing and his old truck parked behind a shed. Eustace had to be there.

"Lots of excitement, J.D." Eustace's voice came from the direction of a lightning-blasted tree trunk.

"How's it going, Eustace?" he said when the fisherman walked out from behind the tree. Blood covered Eustace's oversized hands. A glistening hunk of blood-soaked skin hung from the pliers he carried.

"Did you find the bodies?"

J.D. didn't answer immediately. "So you think they're dead?"

"That's the talk all along the river. Two girls missing. Have the draglines brought anything up?" Eustace looked up toward the camp, where Camille walked out, sat down on the top step, and lit a cigarette.

"Not yet." J.D. concentrated on Eustace's face as his friend watched Camille.

Eustace wiped one hand on his filthy shirt. "Any idea what happened?"

J.D. noticed the bruises and scraped knuckles on Eustace's right hand as he leaned a hip against the SUV. Since Camille Holbert had driven her Mercedes SL500 out of her rich daddy's driveway and into the swamp and parked it beside Eustace's camp, the fisherman hadn't invited him inside. Today would be no different. "Like you said, some folks think they drowned." Eustace knew the swamps better than any man alive; he was up and down the river several times a day, and he was observant. "You didn't see the girls, did you?"

"No." Eustace motioned for the sheriff to follow him. "You want to talk, I've got to finish this fish. A man's comin' by for thirty pounds, cleaned and skinned."

J.D. followed him, noting that his limp was more pronounced than usual. J.D. looked back at the redhead smoking on the steps. She was a good thirty-five, maybe forty, years younger than Eustace. She looked like a child.

There had been wild talk about Camille. Her name had been linked with a host of younger men, boys really, but as far as J.D. knew, none of them had ever confirmed the gossip. When she left a man, she sealed his lips, and that was a talent in a town where counting notches was a public competition.

Eustace pointed to a picnic table with benches beneath an open-air shed. J.D. took a seat while Eustace finished pulling the skin off a five-pound catfish he'd nailed to a board. J.D. looked away at the sound of the skin tearing free.

"Have you seen anything unusual on the river?" he asked.

Eustace shook his head. "I was up the Chickasawhay almost to Leakesville. Anybody coulda come and gone." He paused to wipe his sweaty forehead with his arm. "I'm not surprised they're gone. My bet is, if they aren't dead, they ran off with somebody. They'll be home when they finish scratching their itch."

Eustace picked up a net and went to the vat where the artesian water bubbled. Struggling briefly, he pulled up another catfish. The creature thrashed coming out of the water, its gray sides slick, scaleless. Eustace lowered it to the concrete floor beside J.D.'s boot. Stepping on the net to pin the fish in place, he lifted a baseball bat and brought it down with a smack on the fish's head. The fish stilled.

Careful not to touch the whiskers, Eustace freed the fish from the net and picked it up. Selecting a huge nail, he drove it through the fish's head and hung it on the board.

Eustace worked smoothly, quickly, with an efficiency of movement that J.D. admired. The knife flicked below the head, and Eustace began to peel the skin off with pliers.

When he finally spoke, it was to ask a question. "Why didn't those girls' folks start hunting before now? If it'd been my girls, I'd have been out on the river yesterday."

J.D. looked at the dusty toes of his boots. "Angie Salter has been known to get into a little trouble and then come home with her tail tucked between her legs. It wasn't until I found out her boyfriend retrieved his truck and left the girls stranded in the woods that I got worried."

"So the boy was there." Eustace looked at J.D. "What about him?"

"Jimmy Franklin's got an air-tight alibi. He was in class all day, and my deputy was with him when he 'repossessed' his truck. Jimmy drove straight to work at Delchamp's. The manager vouched for him. Didn't leave the store."

"Maybe the girls hitched a ride," Eustace suggested.

J.D. recalled the set of prints, one foot bare, that led into the water. "No prints leading off the sandbar."

"So you're thinking if they left, dead or alive, they left by water." Eustace netted another fish. "It's hard to say about the boats. I hear motors. Some are distinctive. Others . . ." He shrugged. "I haven't seen anyone on the water that made me stop and think about 'em. Truth of the matter is, since I put in the air conditioner for Camille, we turn it up at night and I don't hear things like I used to."

"Anybody unusual in Fitler?" J.D.'s gaze drifted to the artesian vats, which were cold as ice and where Eustace kept beer chilling. It had been a long, discouraging day.

"Nobody I took notice of. There's some beer down in the vat if you want one."

"No, not right now." J.D. worried the edge of the table where some animal had chewed. "I found a place. Sort of strange. Some boards fitted across blocks with a cloth on it, some candles. An altar." He waited.

Eustace lowered the pliers and turned to look at him. "Folks don't just happen through Fitler any more. Especially not someone holding religious services in the woods. Where was this?" He nudged the net with his foot. "Catch me another fish."

J.D. picked up the net and went to the vat. Beneath the clear water the fish swam in a frenzy. He wondered if, isolated in water, they heard the terrible silence that preceded their death. "About half a mile off the sandbar, up a hill. Dense woods." He lowered the net, scooped out a two-pounder and took it back to Eustace. He described the cloth and candles in more detail as Eustace skinned.

"I can't help you there," Eustace said, not looking up from his work.

J.D. walked to the SUV and came back with the plastic bag holding the long cloth he'd taken from the altar. He unbagged it and held it up. "Does this look familiar?"

"Nope." Eustace bent to his work.

Something moved near the house, and J.D. turned. Camille was running toward him, her eyes excited.

"J.D., where'd you get that?" She reached for the cloth, her cheeks flushed and her breath coming quickly. "Eustace said someone stole it off the clothesline."

J.D. felt the beat of his heart, as if his chest had suddenly grown hollow. He'd been thirteen when he first met Eustace, and it was Eustace more than anyone else who'd saved him from the path of self-destruction on which he'd been bent. In all of those years, he'd never known Eustace to lie to him. Never. Until now. He looked into Eustace's eyes. "Stolen off the clothesline, huh?"

Eustace didn't say anything.

"Someone's been slipping around here," Camille said. "They've taken a sheet and some pants and a shirt." She took the cloth out of J.D's hand. "I'm sure glad to get this back. I use it to lay out my tarot cards." She looked up from the cloth. "And the thief took some food and beer. And a pair of Eustace's boots." She smiled. "But he doesn't mean any harm. He's just scared and hungry."

J.D. held Eustace's gaze. "I guess this doesn't qualify as unusual?"

Eustace didn't look away. "I figured it was some kids sneaking around, jerking my chain since I can't hear 'em because of the air conditioner. Truth is, I forgot about it. Camille, he's got to take that cloth with him. It could be evidence."

"You need to give me a list of everything that's missing. Everything." J.D. dropped all expression from his face. He held the evidence bag open so Camille could drop the cloth in.

Eustace shook his head, the furrows in his brow deepening. "You know as well as I do that anybody could have come down the river, or up. They could have come in from 57 or 98. If someone took those girls, they could be halfway to China by now."

"What girls?" Camille asked. "I saw all those cars and trucks on the bridge. What's wrong?" She looked to Eustace for an answer.

"Two girls are missing. They may have drowned."

She shook her head. "That's terrible. The river is dangerous. Eustace says I can't ever go swimming unless he's right with me."

"That's good advice," J.D. said. It was time to go. "Eustace, sometime tomorrow do you think you could go over a map and point out some of the deeper holes on the Pascagoula? And maybe a few places where if you wanted to hide, it might be a good place?"

Eustace took his arm and began to move him gently down the drive. When they were out of Camille's earshot, Eustace said, "Don't put no bad pictures in her head. She has nightmares."

"Eustace, something has happened to those girls. I'd keep Camille out of the woods if I were you."

"That's not easy to do. She likes to go by herself. She says the spirits of the Indians come there to talk to her."

Camille had been institutionalized in an expensive private clinic in Louisiana. Visiting with Indian spirits didn't seem to be a good sign. They both turned at the sound of a vehicle approaching. Eustace spoke first. "I think they're looking for you."

"I'll get rid of them." J.D. walked forward to meet the white minivan that pulled toward the camp. The peacock on the side indicated that it was the NBC affiliate out of Mobile.

J.D. turned around and watched Eustace walk back to his camp. Camille saw him and waved. J.D. was chilled by the gesture. It was as if her arm floated up in water.

CHAPTER TEN

Long ago, Dixon had learned that a good editorial page in a newspaper served as a voice of reason, but according to her father, it was also a carrot and a stick. The letters-to-the-editor section should churn with dissenting opinions. An editorial could praise the actions of a public official or damn him. Ray Sinclair had prided himself on editorials with teeth.

She sat at her typewriter, wondering if an editorial on the state sunshine law were the best choice. Although Big Jim Welford, with his high-handed tactics, had aggravated her, the secret school board meetings were not the story that weighed most heavily on her mind.

Seven days had passed since Trisha Webster and Angie Salter had disappeared. The only evidence that the two girls had been on the sandbar were a few beers, some footprints, and the bikini that Mrs. Webster had identified as Trisha's. Dixon knew that an editorial about the missing girls would sound like blame.

Willard Jones was one week closer to his execution. Doubt about his guilt ate at her, and the morality of the death penalty would make a knock-down editorial. But Jones's crime, if he'd committed it, was in the middle of the state. He held no interest for readers of the *Independent*.

That left the school board's penchant for secret meetings. The board had held another secret meeting, and Tommy Hayes had been reinstated. Dixon had heard that Hayes had hired a Gulfport lawyer. The young teacher had not gone quietly, and the school board, facing more legal problems over the disappearance of the two girls, had backed off. In essence, Hayes had been charged, hung, and resuscitated without ever having a trial.

Dixon picked up the photographs of Trisha and Angie. Since the river search a week ago, there had been five others, with dogs, horses, four-wheelers, jeeps, and a psychic whom Beth Salter had brought from Pensacola. God, Beth Salter was a nightmare. She'd ranted and accused and laid the blame for Angie's disappearance everywhere except at her own doorstep. She was more interested in lawsuits and laying blame than in finding her daughter.

It didn't seem possible that the two girls had disappeared without a trace, but no one had seen or heard from them since first period at school the past Tuesday.

Dixon thought again of the river, with its deceptively quiet surface. The girls had been taken. By the river or by someone. What would a kidnapper do with them? They weren't girls whose families could pay a big ransom. But they were pretty girls. Sexy girls. Perfect prey for a predator. The thought of Robert Medino's theory about a religious zealot chilled her.

The bell over the door jangled, and she looked up to find Medino standing just inside the door.

"What's the lead headline?" he asked. The smile that followed was calculated.

"Too early to tell," she said. "We could have a breaking story before we quit tonight. Where have you been all week? I haven't seen you at any of the searches."

"I had to finish up a story in New Orleans." He shook his head. "Those girls won't be found. At least not alive."

"What makes you so sure?" Dixon remembered the way the sheriff had looked at Medino. Not contemptuously, exactly, but close, tempered with suspicion.

"I've been tracking this guy since last spring. I've devoted months to this story. This statue that he decapitated here, it's sort of the culmination of his obsession. At least with statuary. Now he's moved on to flesh."

"And his obsession is?" Dixon didn't have time to shoot the breeze with Robert Medino, but she couldn't help herself. He was smart and articulate, and he had the fire of a good story in his eyes. He had a high opinion of himself, but Dixon found that appealing; confidence was an attractive quality.

"The Virgin Mary."

His serious expression stopped her from laughing. Medino wasn't a man who would enjoy being laughed at under any circumstances. "So how do you figure he hooked up with those two girls? Angie Salter, from all I've heard, wouldn't qualify as a virgin." She thought about Tommy Hayes and Welford's insinuations.

"If I have this man pegged correctly, he views women as either/or. Either a slut or a virgin. This obsession stems from something in his past, some church-related incident."

"I didn't realize you had a degree in psychology." Dixon took care to keep her needling complimentary.

"I've done a lot of reading and a lot of talking to several authorities. Dr. Jonas Brennaman of the Center for Human Wellness, folks like that. That's one thing about working for *Cue*: people find the time to talk to me."

"I can see where it would be a real asset." Dixon had known national magazine reporters. They had access to people. The rich and famous wanted good press. "And your theory is that this religious fanatic has moved from statuary to flesh?"

"It's not that simple. I've been following him for months. I've seen the progression of his anger. That's what drives him. He's torn between his belief in the sanctity of the female and her terrible sexual power over him. He wants to be loved and nurtured, yet he wants to screw her. When he first started destroying church property, it was only images of Mary where she was praying. He'd leave the ones of her with an infant or with the saints. As his desire grew, so did his anger." He shrugged. "He can't win, and that frustration has grown over the past months. It's the virgin/whore complex taken to the ultimate extreme. I'd guess his mother figures prominently into this. It was inevitable that he'd move against a woman-child. If the sheriff had listened to me, those girls might still be alive."

"It isn't every day that a religious nut case strolls into Chickasaw County. So how does he travel?"

"I'm not certain. Could be a car, or it could be by bus."

"How did this guy find out about the statue in Jexville?"

"He reads. I'd be willing to bet he's well educated. Possibly church educated. That statue, because of the blind artist, got a lot of media attention. I believe he's traveling 1-10 East. My guess is that he's going to head to St. Augustine, where the Spanish first brought priests into the New World. I expected him to do something dramatic there, but he's upped the ante here in Jexville."

Dixon nodded. "It's an interesting theory."

"It's more than a theory." Robert leaned closer. "This is going to be a big story. Huge. Maybe a movie. Why don't you help me?"

"Why are you doing this?" National reporters weren't in the habit of offering a portion of the pie to locals.

"Folks around here don't like me, except for maybe Ruth Ann. She likes me okay, but she doesn't know anything. No one will talk to me about these girls. I need a local to bring them to life. You could do that. No byline, but a credit at the end of the story."

He wanted this story badly. She could almost taste his desire for it. He'd spent months already working on it. She nodded. "Okay. I'll help you, but not today. I'm on deadline, and I have to get back to work."

"Later in the week let me take you to lunch. After deadline. I've rented a room in a charming B and B, the Magnolia. Do you know it?" He didn't wait for an answer as he opened the door. "It's like stepping back in time, a theory of mine about Southerners. You people have managed to cling to the things that are important. Graciousness, good manners, and . . . trust. I'll be back later in the week. After deadline."

He went out the door, turned to look at her once, then walked away.

Linda Moore walked through the saloon door that led to the back shop. She went to the front window and leaned for a last glance at Medino's disappearing back. "Who the hell was that?"

"The Writer from the East—that's all caps."

"That man is trouble. Trouble with a capital T." Linda swung around to face her. "He's got a way with words, but I wouldn't be a bit surprised if he isn't the one abducting young girls and making up theories to cover his own tracks."

✝

J.D. stood at the edge of the river about twenty yards from the landing that marked Eustace's camp. With the summer rains over, the water level was down. He'd been lucky, weatherwise. For the past seven days there had been no thunderstorms, only the heavy dews that silvered the early mornings. That luck couldn't hold out long, not in September. A massive low was moving in from the west, and he figured he had one day, maybe two, before Chickasaw County would be drenched.

"Sheriff, are you waiting for Eustace?"

Camille's voice was soft and cultured, the product of private schooling and summers in Europe. He shook his head. She'd been watching him for a while from her porch, but he hadn't acknowledged her, and she'd managed to slip up behind him. Camille was an odd duck, on the verge of either brilliance or insanity.

"Eustace has given me all the help he can. We've sent divers into every deep hole from here to Cumbest Bluff." He didn't look at her, uncomfortable with his half-truth. No matter how he cut it, Eustace came up as a possible suspect. There was no real evidence to link him to it, except proximity and lies. And his peculiarities, one of which was Camille.

"Eustace says I can't walk in the woods anymore." Her statement was tentative, not quite a question, not quite a confession.

J.D. turned his back on the river and looked at Camille. He was startled, as always, by her beauty. She was the most delicate human he'd ever seen. Her skin was painfully white, her eyes big and pale green, wide open with innocence—or maybe drugs the doctors had given her for depression, anxiety, and a host of other problems. He knew enough about women with money to know that ordering Camille to stay out of the swamps would be stupid.

"Eustace wants to keep you safe. I'd listen to him, Camille. Once we find those girls, this will all be over with and things will get back to normal."

She hesitated, staring at the ground. "I saw someone in the woods this morning."

J.D. kept his tone quiet. "What did you see?"

She searched his face, and J.D. knew she was hunting for a sign that he intended to tell Eustace she'd been in the swamps. "I drove over the bridge. There's a place across the river that's special to me." She looked at her bare toes digging into the sand. "Usually I just take the skiff across the river, but Eustace has been locking the boats up lately." She looked up at him. "You can't tell Eustace I went over there. I promised him I wouldn't go to my place until this whole mess was finished. You promise you won't tell?"

"I won't tell him unless I have to, Camille. But it's important that you tell me. Those girls may be alive somewhere in the swamp. If someone has them, what you saw could make a difference." He looked up at the sound of Eustace's old truck coming through the oaks.

Camille heard it too. She swallowed. "I saw a man. He was in a tree, looking down at me. At first I thought I'd imagined him, but I didn't. He's real. He's been in the area for a week or so."

"What did he do?" J.D. wasn't certain whether to believe her or not. Camille's mental problems were legendary in Jexville, but the townspeople had a way of blowing everything out of proportion, especially when it was vicious and cruel.

"He looked at me." She shrugged. "He watched everything I did."

"What was he doing?"

"Hiding."

"What were you doing?"

"Listening to the spirits. They want me to make water designs in my pottery, to show the flow of the river. The river is . . . what it means to be free."

"Free?"

"Of obligation, of guilt, of remorse, or thought, or regard for the future. The things that drive humans insane." She smiled. "I'm an expert on the things that make a person insane."

J.D. nodded. She might be crazy, but he understood her. In fact, she was more lucid than most people he talked to. "This man you saw, what did he look like?"

"He was crouched in a big sycamore, so it was hard to get an idea of his size, but he had the darkest eyes. They were like black pebbles washed by a strong current. And he had dark hair, very straight but not cut neatly. Hispanic. Youngish. Maybe thirty, maybe older or younger; it's hard to tell with an olive complexion. They don't age the way I will." She touched her cheek as if she suddenly felt a wrinkle. "I'll be old by the time I'm forty, unless I develop a relationship with Mama's plastic surgeon."

"Stay out of the sun," J.D. offered, trying not to appear too eager. "When he was watching, did he do anything that frightened you?"

She shook her head. "No. That's what I wanted to tell you. He isn't dangerous. I mean, he isn't here to hurt anyone. I would have felt danger from him if he meant to hurt me. He just watched. He never moved at all, except his eyes. I've never seen a human hold still for so long."

"Where was he?"

She hesitated. "My place is secret. I've seen all those men hunting for the girls, stomping through the woods. They don't respect the land or the river."

"How about if I promise to go myself? Alone." J.D. looked at the camp. Eustace had finished unloading and was heading their way. After seven days of coming up empty-handed, Camille was giving him something solid—if he could get her to tell him. "Camille, please."

"I'll show you," she said, then turned away and ran toward Eustace.

J.D. watched the flash of her long, slender legs. Young-girl legs that showed muscle and bone. She was an elfin creature with a hint of something untamed in the way she moved. When she got a couple of feet from Eustace, she launched herself at him, hitting him solidly enough that he staggered under the impact but caught her and whirled her around.

"What's the latest?" Eustace asked J.D. as he walked over. He lowered Camille to the ground and hugged her against his side.

"Nothing new since Orie Webster identified the bikini bottom and top as Trisha's." Eustace knew the rest. Dale's bloodhounds had tracked back and forth from the sandbar through the woods and all the way to the county line without finding a trail. Cadaver dogs from Pensacola had sniffed the river from a mile up both forks and halfway down to Cumbest Bluff. The highly trained shepherds had never even caught a scent. It looked as if the girls had left the sandbar by water but were no longer in or on the river.

"Come up to the shed and have a beer," Eustace said. "You look done in."

"I thought we might take J.D. to my secret place," Camille said. "He knows the swamps. He can say if it will flood or not."

Eustace stared hard at Camille. "I know it doesn't flood there, Camille. I told you that. J.D. doesn't know—"

Camille pulled away from him. "Please."

Eustace stared at the river, then looked suspiciously at J.D. "Sure. Let's go. We can take my truck."

Eustace and Camille got in the cab, and J.D. climbed over the tailgate and took a seat on a wheel cover against one side. He wasn't disappointed in Eustace's driving, which was too fast for the bad roads. Eustace had a reputation for vehicular recklessness, and not even the wreck that ruined his leg had slowed him down. J.D. braced with his hands and tried to avoid taking the punishing ride with his spine.

They crossed the river at a dangerous clip, then Eustace spun the truck to the left, barely missing a tree. In the cab Camille began flailing at him with her fists, forcing him to slow so he could defend himself.

J.D. could hear the force of her blows as they rained on Eustace's shoulder and head, and he wondered at the strength contained in her lithe body.

"I don't have to take this shit from you or anybody else," she yelled. "Damn you to hell and back. I've lived with abuse, and I don't have to anymore. If I want to be bruised up and terrorized I can go back home." She was crying as well as yelling. "I can go live on Mama's houseboat at Cumbest Bluff!"

Eustace slowed and stopped the truck. He caught her wind-milling arms and pulled her against his chest, tucking her head beneath his chin. She struggled, but he held her tightly, whispering.

J.D. looked past the tailgate. It had been a mistake to push Camille into this. She might have made the entire thing up. She had a big imagination. This lead was probably just a waste of time and an imposition on an old friendship already under strain.

The truck started forward, this time slowly, and J.D. forced his body to relax. He'd see this through and have a talk with Eustace later. The trail dead-ended, and they got out and walked. After ten minutes of pushing through thick undergrowth, Camille stopped.

"That's a magnificent tree, isn't it?" She pointed to a sycamore that seemed to touch the clouds. "Eustace said someone planted it at least a hundred years ago."

J.D. looked at the big tree. It was an old one. Small privets and brush had grown up around the base, and deep in the tangle of green was the brown of fallen leaves. He walked around the tree, looking for signs that someone had scaled it.

The bark was slick and silvery and showed no marks of disturbance. As he came around it for the second time, sunlight glinted off something deep in the undergrowth.

J.D. walked over and carefully picked up the beer can with his handkerchief. Old Milwaukee. It was the brand Eustace drank, and it was new. He backed up and stared at the tree, feeling both Eustace and Camille watching him.

"The kiln will be over here," Eustace said, indicating that J.D. was to follow.

"Just a minute." He stared at the tree, wondering if Camille had actually seen anyone in it. It was a perfect place to hide and watch. No one would think to look up in the trees. He could have moved from tree to tree and outfoxed the dogs.

"You got something?" Eustace finally asked.

"I'm hoping this is one of the beers stolen from your camp, and I'm hoping I can get a set of prints off it." J.D. held the can out to Eustace. "Do you mind waiting a minute?" He was climbing the tree before he even finished the question. As he got higher, he felt a cooling breeze from off the river. Peering through the lush leaves, he could see the opposite bank of the river and, almost out of sight, the landing where Eustace's boats floated, easy pickings for anyone with larceny in his heart.

J.D. started down the tree. When he got close to the ground, he grabbed a branch and swung down. He felt his old friend's gaze leveled at him.

"Have you seen what you really came to see?" Eustace asked.

J.D. hesitated. "I'd like to see where you're going to build the kiln."

Eustace nodded once but didn't move. "What will you do if you don't find any prints on that can but mine?"

"Keep looking." J.D. wanted to tell his friend that he didn't suspect him, but Eustace would know he was lying. J.D. suspected everyone; that was the curse of his life. That was what life had taught him.

"Folks in town won't forget that I tore up my leg runnin' moonshine. They already know I sell beer and whiskey and that you don't do anything about it. They figure I'm doin' something bad out here with Camille." Eustace's look asked Camille if she, too, suspected him.

"Honey, I was showing J.D. the tree because there was a man in it earlier today." Camille went to Eustace and put a hand on each side of his face. "Look at me, Eustace honey. I didn't want you to know I'd been over here. I didn't want to worry you." She was talking fast, the words tumbling and jarring into each other. "He was up in that sycamore, watching me, but I know he isn't a bad man. I wasn't afraid of him at all. But I knew you'd worry. That's why I pretended to show J.D. the kiln. Don't be angry, Eustace. Please." She withdrew her hands from his face and covered her ears, hugging her head down to her chest. "Please, I can't stand feeling like I've done something to hurt you. Please."

Camille's need for Eustace was so open, and the only thing she could do to protect herself was hunker over and hide in her own arms. Living that raw and open, it was no wonder she had to go off for treatment. Camille had never learned to develop the protective shields that everyone else put up. Her pain was palpable, and J.D. wanted to turn away from it.

Eustace put his arm around Camille and drew her close, kissing the top of her head. "It's okay. No harm's been done.

Don't fret over it, girl." He shielded her against his chest as he turned to J.D. "You ready to go?"

J.D. nodded. He held the can lightly as he fell in behind Eustace and Camille. He looked back at the tree once. Had Camille really seen someone, or had she made up the entire thing to protect Eustace?

✝

The mercury vapor lights that lined Main Street had just buzzed into life when the front door of the newspaper office opened. Two women Dixon had seen but never met came in. One was Calvin Holbert's wife, Vivian. The other was Reverend Beatrice Smart.

"What can I do for you ladies?" she asked, standing up at her desk. She had seven more headlines to write and five cutlines for the photographs Tucker was printing.

"I'm Beatrice Smart," the brunette said. "This is Vivian Holbert. She wants to offer a ten-thousand-dollar reward for information leading to the return of the missing girls."

Dixon nodded. "That's a very generous thing to do."

"I don't know these girls," Vivian said, her sun-pinkened face flushing darker. "I just feel that someone should help. Money is what I can do."

"A reward is a good idea. The families of the girls aren't in a position to offer anything. This is a wonderful gesture."

"No, it's just that I have a daughter." She looked down at the floor. "I'd give anything to make her safe."

Beatrice put a steadying hand on Vivian's shoulder. "I'm the pastor at the Methodist church, and what I'd like to do is take up a special collection at the Wednesday service to add to the reward. I'm going to ask all the churches in the county to participate."

"Another good idea," Dixon said. "This will be a real community effort."

"Would it be okay if the reward is anonymous?" Vivian asked. "Calvin and I don't want our names attached. We're lucky to be able to do this, but some folks might think we're trying to show off."

Dixon looked up from her notebook. "I think it's kind and generous and you deserve credit, but if you want it anonymous, that's fine by me."

"Good. Don't use our names. The money is already deposited in a special account. Anyone with information should call the sheriff's office. If you could put a story in the paper, then people would know."

"Front page, top of the fold," Dixon said. She caught a hint of sadness in Vivian's penetrating eyes. It was gone in an instant, but it was enough for Dixon to recognize that the woman suffered.

"I saw you the other night, and I've meant to get by here and introduce myself," Beatrice said. "Life is just too busy. Would you like to have some coffee tomorrow, after the paper has gone to the post office?"

"Sure," Dixon said. "That would be nice." The minister knew about the newspaper's deadlines and schedules. "Where?"

"How about the Hickory Pit? Good coffee and even better lemon meringue pies."

"My second favorite," Dixon said. She liked the minister. She had an openness that Dixon didn't normally associate with persons of the cloth.

"And apple would be your first?" Beatrice asked.

"You must have a little bit of the psychic in you," Dixon said, surprised.

"Just a good ear for gossip," Beatrice acknowledged with a wry smile. "You've had apple pie three times in a row. Folks take notice of attractive publishers."

Dixon felt the first flush she'd experienced in a long time. "Folks pay attention to strangers."

Beatrice's smile faded. "Obviously not enough attention, or those two young ladies would be home by now."

CHAPTER ELEVEN

Walking down Main Street, Dixon passed the plate glass windows of the Hickory Pit and noticed that the diner was almost empty. The businessmen and farmers had gone back to their chores, leaving the three waitresses in their bright red shirts to sit for a moment at the counter to gossip and rest their tired feet.

Dixon entered, slid into an orange vinyl booth, and asked for a glass of iced tea. The minister had called at noon, setting a late luncheon meeting for one-thirty. She'd also said that Vivian would be accompanying her.

She wondered about Vivian. Dixon had obtained the loan to buy the newspaper from the president of Pine Trust Bank. Approving the loan, Calvin Holbert had mentioned that Vivian had no use for muckraking journalists. Dixon wasn't in Vivian's social circle, and neither was Beatrice Smart. So what was Vivian's purpose in joining them for lunch?

The waitress brought her tea. Dixon had just finished stirring when Beatrice and Vivian walked into the diner. Vivian was stunning in a white pantsuit that hugged her body. She had to be at least fifty, but she didn't look a day over thirty-five. She was a woman who invested in her body, and the dividends were high.

"I hope you don't mind my horning in on your lunch," Vivian said as she slid across the vinyl seat. "I spoke with the sheriff this morning. He's had twenty-seven calls from the story about the reward in the paper."

"That's wonderful." The moment lunch was over Dixon would check with J.D. "Did he say if any calls seemed promising?"

"J.D. doesn't share information with me," Vivian said, her full mouth tightening. Now she looked her age. "You could say that J.D. and I have issues. He rather despises me."

"Vivian—" Beatrice said.

"Oh, don't try to hush me. Ms. Sinclair should have an idea what kind of man J.D. Horton is. He comes across so proper and law-abiding, so determined to do the right thing. There are two types of law in Chickasaw County, Ms. Sinclair. One for most folks and one for J.D.'s friends."

Dixon put more sugar in her tea. Whatever was eating at Vivian had hold of her good. "What did Horton do to you?" Dixon asked.

"It's more like what he didn't do. My daughter has been abducted." Vivian's voice rose. "That swamp creature has taken her and cast a spell on her."

"Vivian," Beatrice said, "you sound unbalanced when you talk like that. People won't take you seriously if you exaggerate."

Dixon noticed that the waitresses had stopped talking and were looking at them.

"Eustace Mills is a swamp creature, and—" Vivian began.

"This isn't the time," Beatrice interrupted.

"No, no." Vivian held up a cautionary hand to the minister. "It's okay, Beatrice. Ms. Sinclair needs to hear this. She might decide to do a story on Eustace and force the sheriff's hand for me." Vivian turned to Dixon. "Eustace Mills, a former bootlegger and criminal, has lured my daughter into the swamp to live with him in sin. I can't say that the man has taken her against her will; she went on her own. But Camille is young and not stable. She's fallen in with a man who supplies her with liquor and God knows what else." Tears shimmered in her eyes. "Our daughter's innocence has been stolen. There's nothing we can do to bring her home. J.D. Horton absolutely refuses to lift a finger. He says Camille is old enough to make her own decisions. That man, Eustace Mills, has taken a restraining order out against me so that I can't even step foot on his property to see if my daughter is eating properly. She has emotional problems, and he's keeping her there."

"If he isn't holding her against her will, I don't know what Sheriff Horton can do," Dixon said. She picked up her tea and took a long sip. "Do you ever talk to your daughter?"

"She refuses to listen to a word I say."

Dixon caught a glance from the minister. "I know it must be hard to have to sit back and watch a child choose her own path."

"I'm worried for her safety. I'd be willing to bet another ten thousand that Eustace Mills did something horrible to those girls. He's a deviant. He lusts after young women. He's a sick, sick man who has the idea that he's above the law. He's the one the sheriff should be looking at for these abductions."

"Vivian, I know you're upset, but you could be charged with slander for such talk." Beatrice's tone was calm but firm. "Please stop this."

"That's why I offered the reward," Vivian continued. "I can't do anything for Camille, but perhaps we can help find these two girls, unless they're dead and buried in that awful swamp."

Beatrice signaled the waitress. "Iced tea, please."

"I'm okay, Beatrice," Vivian said. "I know I shouldn't get so wound up." She looked at Dixon. "Beatrice has been working with me on a professional basis, to help me learn to accept things that I find unacceptable. She told me I shouldn't come for lunch. She was afraid I'd upset myself, and I have."

"I'm a licensed therapist," Beatrice explained to Dixon.

"Beatrice is a tremendous help to me. To all the people who'll let her help." Vivian took a deep breath and sat straighter. She found a tiny smile. "Bea is right. We should talk about something else. Ms. Sinclair, tell me about yourself. I hear you worked in Memphis. It must be hard coming to a hick town like Jexville."

"I hope to make Jexville my home," Dixon said.

Vivian smiled. "It'll be a shock for the good-ole-boy system, to have a female publisher chewing their butts."

Beatrice asked, "What do you do for fun, Dixon? Vivian is a champion water skier."

Dixon was relieved at the shift in the conversation, but she hadn't thought about a hobby since she was in high school. "I don't think drinking qualifies, so I guess I don't have any."

"Vivian worked for several summers in Florida. Cornelia Wallace skied there, but it was before Vivian's time, I think."

"That's right," Vivian said. "I learned to ski when I was five. I always swam like a fish, and I loved skiing. I kept up the practice," Vivian said. "Believe it or not, it's quite a workout, and it beats the hell out of step aerobics or a NordicTrack. You'll have to come with me sometime."

"Do you work, Vivian?" Dixon asked.

"I was trained as a surgical nurse, and I was very good at my job. But when I married Calvin and we came here, to Jexville, this town made it impossible for me to continue with my career."

"How, exactly, did that happen?"

Vivian smiled. "You don't understand how a woman could be forced to give up a career, do you? You're thinking that nobody could force you out of your job. This was twenty-five years ago, Ms. Sinclair. Calvin took over the bank, and as the bank president, he became an important local figure. For his career to advance, he needed a wife. This day and age, a woman can be a wife and have a job, but not the kind of wife that Calvin required." She lifted one eyebrow. "I'm a hard worker in civic areas. I'm president of the garden club, publicity chairman of the arts organization. I'm a Girl Scout leader, organizer of the Christmas parade, head of Room Mothers for Better Schools." She laughed softly. "I haven't been inside a hospital since I had my tubes tied."

"Do you miss working?" Dixon asked.

"I made the choices allowed me as Calvin's wife. I don't regret a single one. My life has been fulfilled, except where my daughter is concerned. And that's the bottom line. I've suffered because of Camille. I've lost her as surely as the Salters and Websters have lost their daughters. Except there's a chance Angie and Trisha will come home. I don't have that hope for Camille." Her voice hardened. "At least not until that old man dies."

✝

The telephone in the Chickasaw County Sheriff's Office rang constantly. The lure of ten thousand dollars had loosened the tongues of close to fifty callers, almost all of them crackpots or crackheads. J.D. had returned every call and sent Waymon to talk to three of the callers, though the leads they offered were mostly imagination. One caller claimed to have seen the girls at the high school hiding in the bathroom. Another saw them hitchhiking on Highway 98. Those had been a waste of time and effort. Another call, though, had set him thinking, especially with the forensics report he'd just received. An anonymous caller, a soft-spoken black woman, had said she'd picked up a hitchhiker and given him a lift up Highway 98 West. She said the man was Mexican but spoke a little English. He'd gotten out at a beer joint near Fitler, on the Greene County line. The man hadn't talked much, but he'd been intense, according to the woman, and he'd never said his name. But J.D. thought he knew it. He just had to make sure he didn't rush to any conclusions.

He picked up a copy of the *Independent*, refolded it, and put it on his desk. He couldn't help glancing out the window at the superintendent of education's office. He could only imagine the conniptions Big Jim was having over the editorial in the paper. Dixon Sinclair had verbally kicked him in the balls. At long last, the superintendent had gotten into a pissing match with someone who wouldn't back down.

J.D. found Dixon an interesting woman. He wasn't certain about her motivation, but he knew that she'd come to Jexville to prove something, at least to herself. J.D. never trusted delicate snooping to Waymon, and he'd checked out Dixon's past himself. He'd read the files on her father's murder and on the conviction of Willard Jones, a man who still professed his innocence. Jones had an appointment in the gas chamber in less than three weeks, and if his execution were carried out, his guilt or innocence would soon be a moot issue. After the explosion that killed her father and destroyed his newspaper, Dixon had been hospitalized for several weeks. She'd left the hospital and moved to Nashville, then to Charlotte, and finally to Memphis. Her reputation was solid, if not exciting. Then she'd dropped out of journalism for a year and resurfaced in Jexville.

Dixon's mother, Marilyn McVay Sinclair, had been a local beauty queen turned photographer. When Marilyn married Ray Sinclair and left Jexville, her parents had moved to Jackson, too. They had been a well-respected but aloof family. Dixon was living in the old McVay family home on Peterson Lane, an isolated place, but probably a good location for a writer. No one would interrupt her.

J.D. remembered the way Dixon's cotton shirt had clung to her breasts at the river. Her long hair, curled with humidity, had been dampened on her forehead. He could see in her eyes that she was haunted by something. But it wasn't his problem, and he wasn't taking on the role of rescuer. He'd learned that he couldn't save anyone, maybe not even himself.

He put aside thoughts of Dixon and picked up a manila folder. The forensics report on the beer can he'd found beneath the sycamore tree had come back. There were three sets of prints. Eustace Mills's, some that didn't match to any in the system, and those of Francesco Chavez, which had been a lucky hit. The Mexican native had been arrested six months ago in the small Texas border town of Eagle Pass for vandalism. The charges had been dropped, but the fingerprints had remained on file. That, coupled with the anonymous call reporting the hitchhiker and Camille's description of the man in the tree, couldn't be ignored.

It galled J.D. to admit it, but it was beginning to look as if Medino's theory had some teeth. Chavez was in the area, or at least a beer can with his prints was. Not just in the area, but where the girls had disappeared.

From the Texas file, J.D. had learned that Chavez was a native of Zaragoza, Mexico. He was an only child, and other than the arrest for vandalism, he'd never been in any trouble. But how did he get to Chickasaw County, and why had he come?

J.D. rose slowly. His back ached, and his feet were tired. He'd been in the swamps every day for a week, searching, hunting, praying that he'd find something that would lead him to the girls, and that—miracle of miracles—they would be okay. Death sat on his heart, but he clung to the slim chance they were alive. He'd hunt until that chance didn't exist any longer.

He needed to talk to Camille and Eustace. His old friend hadn't been honest with him, and that cut J.D. Eustace was a loner and a man who operated by his own code of conduct. It was a strict code, but it didn't include telling the truth to figures of authority, and J.D. knew he had to keep that in mind. Eustace had lied to the badge, not the man.

He'd just picked up his keys to the patrol car when he heard a tap on his office door. "Come in," he called.

Beatrice Smart stepped into his office and closed the door softly behind her. "I'm concerned for Vivian," she said, her face a mirror of her feelings. "She's obsessed with the idea that Eustace has taken those girls. She has a gun. She told me so. As unstable as she is, I'm afraid she might go down to the swamps and try to kill him."

Dealing with Vivian was low on the list of things he needed to do. "I'll go and talk with her," he said. "Thanks for telling me."

"I'm not trying to tell you your business, J.D., but I'd talk to Calvin. Get him to turn in the gun. If she only has her mouth, she can't do real damage. The gun worries me."

"You're positive she has one?" It was possible that Vivian had lied just to sound dangerous.

Beatrice nodded. "I saw it. She had it in her purse at lunch today. Looked like a .38."

J.D. picked up his keys. He would swing by the bank before he went to Eustace's. "Thanks, Beatrice. I'll take care of it now."

Beatrice hesitated in front of his desk. He put his keys down and softened his posture. "Is there something else?" Beatrice had had a rough time in Jexville. Though the Methodist church was the most liberal in town, the congregation had been affronted at the idea of a female minister. They had adjusted slowly, but there had been ugly scenes, and her car had been egged and her house pelted with rotten tomatoes. She had hung tough, though, and finally worn down the resistance. Or so he hoped.

"I know you have a full plate, J.D., but I've been getting phone calls."

He felt his muscles tighten. "What kind of phone calls?"

"I can't distinguish the caller, whether it's even a man or a woman. They just say that I'm a godless bitch and that I'm going to pay."

"Have you tape recorded any of these?" he asked, keeping his tone casual.

"No. If the answering machine picks up, the caller hangs up. There have been a number of hang-up calls." She bit her bottom lip and kept her gaze on the floor. "I thought all of this was over."

"I did, too," J.D. said. He came around the desk and put a comforting hand on her shoulder. "I doubt it's serious. Just another person who doesn't have the grit to confront you face to face, but to be on the safe side, have you thought about a dog? A big dog."

She looked up and smiled. "You're teasing."

He shook his head. "Not in the least. I have a friend whose dog had a litter about two months ago. They're a chow-shepherd mix, and he says they're smart as a whip. It wouldn't hurt to have something in the house that barks."

She studied his face. "You're serious."

"Two girls are missing. I have a reporter here from out of town who says they've been abducted by some religious zealot. The statue at the Catholic church was decapitated. There are a lot of things going on around Chickasaw County that indicate trouble afoot. I'd feel better if you had some protection."

"I'll speak to John about it."

"I know your husband is trained in firearms. Do you have a gun?" John Smart's army record was impressive. Two purple hearts and bronze and silver stars for action in Desert Storm. He was a quiet, steady man who spent his days as a woodworker. Beneath that quiet was a man who could defend his home and family if the need arose.

"We don't believe in violence," Beatrice said. "We—"

"I don't either, Beatrice, but if someone tries to hurt you, I'd rather see John take action."

"You're scaring me, J.D."

"That's not my intention, but it might not be a bad thing. I'll talk to Waymon about setting up a tap on your phone line at home and at the church. One way or the other, we'll take care of it. Now, I'd better go see about Vivian. Just answer me this, Reverend. Why is it that the only people who own guns are the idiots who shouldn't?"

J.D. was rewarded with a smile as he ushered Beatrice out of his office.

CHAPTER TWELVE

With the newspapers labeled, sacked, and hauled to the post office by deadline, Dixon had given Tucker and Linda the rest of Wednesday afternoon off. The rhythm of the weekly was like a great wave, building gradually on Thursday and Friday, towering to a peak on Monday, and crashing to shore on Tuesday. By Wednesday, everyone was exhausted.

As much as Dixon was tempted by the thought of her cottage on Peterson Lane, she forced herself to trudge to the board of education offices. Jim Welford was going to be furious, but she wanted him to know right up front that his fury didn't intimidate her. The secret meetings were a serious issue, and she wasn't about to let it drop.

Attie Wilson, a perfectly manicured woman in her early sixties, informed Dixon that Jim Welford was in an urgent meeting and couldn't be disturbed. She feigned complete indifference when Dixon asked for the minutes. She got the folder, handed it over, and resumed typing.

Dixon flipped through the neatly typed pages, then closed the heavy folder. "Ms. Wilson, I need to speak with Mr. Welford."

Attie didn't look up as she continued typing. "What is it?"

"There aren't any minutes for the two secret meetings. The last minutes recorded are for August 28."

Attie's fingers slowed, then stopped. "No action was taken at the last meeting. I only record the official action."

"But Mr. Welford told me they fired a teacher. He said the minutes would be recorded. There's not even a notice that the meeting was held."

Attie glanced at the door that led to Jim Welford's private office. "If official action was taken, it would be recorded in that book. Unless it's in the minutes, it didn't happen." Attie pushed back her chair. "Excuse me, I have to see if Mr. Welford and Mr. Holbert would like some coffee." She tapped lightly at the door before she disappeared inside. When she came back out, she left the door cracked open. She walked past Dixon without looking at her. "I'll be gone about fifteen minutes."

Dixon stared at the secretary's retreating back, then turned to the open door, where Holbert's voice could be clearly heard. Whatever her reasons, Attie was giving her an opportunity. Dixon stepped closer to the door.

"Calvin, you have to keep Vivian away from here."

"I try, damn it. She's completely obsessed with the idea that I'm screwing some cheerleader."

Big Jim's voice was low and firm. "Keep her away from me. She came in here last week acting like a shrew. She was calling you all sorts of names and threatening to go to the newspaper with her accusations. She's a loose cannon."

There was a pause. "I can't control her any longer."

"You'd better. Now, I don't care what you do or who you do it to, but if you were involved, in any way, with that Salter girl, you'd best clean up after yourself."

"What do you mean?" Calvin sounded worried.

"Pay off the mother. Pay her well and quickly. She's not as stupid as she acts. On his salary, Hayes can't afford cubic zirconium, and that girl was wearing some expensive stuff."

There was another pause. Big Jim spoke again: "Look, the girl was a slut. Just don't let this shit get all over you, because I don't want it spreading to me."

A chair scraped across the floor, and Dixon hurried from behind the secretary's desk. She passed Attie and gave her a nod of thanks as she went down the hall and outside to her truck, her heart hammering.

Three minutes passed before Calvin Holbert hurried out of the superintendent's office and headed across the porch.

From her vantage point, Dixon assessed the man who controlled the county school board and the only bank in town, and who had enough discretionary funds to offer a reward that was larger than the base income of many Chickasaw County families. A man who had a penchant for young girls.

Holbert was in his early fifties and had never been handsome, but he exuded confidence. Head up, bright tie, dark suit, he was the big fish in a small pond. Mr. Brisk-walking Success.

She got out of the truck and was gratified to see his smile fall away.

"How long have you been here?" he asked.

"A while." She thought of her father and felt a surge of confidence. It was a heady sensation. "I'm having a little trouble finding the minutes from the school board meetings. I was hoping you might be able to help me."

Holbert started walking away, but not before Dixon noticed sweat on his forehead. "Mr. Holbert!"

"Jim's in charge of the minutes." He kept walking.

"Mr. Welford is too busy to see me. I thought perhaps you could give me a brief summary of that meeting. The readers of the *Independent* are very interested in what's going on with their public schools. And their school officials."

Calvin Holbert stopped. "The residents of Chickasaw County wouldn't know we held school board meetings if you didn't make such a stink about it." He flushed. "You'll get the action of the board when we get ready to give it to you."

"I shouldn't have to quote state law to you." Dixon fell into step beside him.

Calvin swung around to face her. Sweat trickled into his neatly trimmed sideburns. The corners of his mouth were hard indentions. "You obviously know your statutes, but I know banking. As I remember, you don't have a cushion on your loan, Miss Sinclair. I took a risk on you when I agreed to it. There's not any room for you to mess up. Keep in mind that a bank can be lenient on a loan, or very rigid."

Calvin hadn't bothered with a subtle threat; he'd gone for her spine. "My financial status, though interesting, isn't part of my story. Did the board fire Tommy Hayes? Yes or no."

"You'll have to check the minutes. I don't trust my memory for such details." He turned away.

Dixon stepped in front of him, forcing him to stop or push her into Finley Street. "There are no minutes. None. I get the impression the school board hopes to pretend that meeting never occurred. My question is why. Is there something about Tommy Hayes and his alleged relationship with Angie Salter that troubles you?"

He blanched at Angie's name. "If you were truly concerned with this community, as you stated in your editorial, you would understand that two young girls are missing. Pursuing this matter won't do their families any good. Now step aside." He used his shoulder to brush past her. He stepped into the street, ignoring the car that braked and swerved to avoid hitting him.

"Sorry, Mr. Holbert, I didn't see you," the driver called, waving him on across the street.

Dixon watched him disappear beneath the oaks, swallowed by the shadows cast by the trees. The scent of his cologne lingered after him.

✝

The yellow crime scene tape fluttered in the breeze. Eustace paused, looking at the cascading bullace vines. He was alone in the woods. Camille had gone into town, another trip to placate Vivian and Calvin, to show them that she was whole and free to do as she pleased. But it wouldn't matter to the Holberts. They couldn't think of Camille with him except in the context of prisoner. In some ways, they were right. He had cast a spell on their daughter, a simple spell of acceptance. Camille had nothing to live up to with him. That was what bound her to him. He loved her unconditionally, just as she was.

The crime scene tape fluttered again, beckoning him closer. Eustace lifted it and stepped under. J.D. had finished his work, but no one had bothered to remove the tape. The vines were thick and laden with wild grapes. Some had fallen to the ground and begun to ferment. When he'd been a young man and his leg was whole and strong, he'd gone to the woods with

Peggy and picked grapes for her father to make wine. Eustace could hear their laughter, echoing back to him across the years. It had taken so little to make the two of them laugh. Simple things, the joy of the sun and the prospect of a bit of skinny dipping in the river were enough. Peggy had loved life. At seventeen, she'd tasted none of the bitterness. Perhaps her drowning had been a blessing. She'd been spared a lot of hurt.

Eustace sighed and stepped into the vines. He didn't like to think of the past. It was all such a long time ago. There were times he wasn't certain any of it had really happened.

He let his eyes adjust to the dim, vine-shrouded space. He didn't fully understand his reason for coming here, to a place sacred to a man accused of abducting the two girls. Eustace had no quarrel with the man just because he worshipped in the woods. Formal religion had left Eustace cold. The high-dollar beliefs of the folks in town were of no use to him. His leanings were simple and in conflict with what he knew of the Protestants. He drank without shame or remorse. Making love with Camille was one of the rare joys of his life, and no amount of religious rhetoric could ever make him believe it was a sin. What he felt for Camille was holy and pure. She was like the river, always in motion, secrets held deep, sometimes hot and sometimes cold. If Eustace worshipped anything, it was nature, and Camille was the closest thing to nature he'd ever found in a human being.

He had only to look into her eyes to see the work of a greater being. He had accepted the task of protecting her, and he thought that was why he'd come to the shrine in the woods.

He'd seen Camille and the Mexican in a tableau that made his chest ache whenever he thought of it. He'd seen them only that morning at the kiln site, when he'd followed her. She hadn't known he was watching. Camille had touched the man with a gesture so tentative and gentle it was as if she were trying to tame a beast.

He'd hidden in the bushes, ashamed, listening with the intensity that had kept him alive in an environment that didn't allow for carelessness. Camille's voice had drifted back to him. He couldn't distinguish what she was saying, just the lilting comfort in her tone. Camille put her hand on the man's chest. She made a noise that communicated sorrow. The man had touched her hair, lifting it up as if he'd never seen anything so flame-colored and precious. Camille had knelt and looked up at him, her hand still on his chest. Eustace had felt a rage so consuming that only the boiling sound in his head was audible.

Unable to bear anymore, Eustace had fled, knowing he would never ask Camille about the meeting. Knowing he was too afraid of the answer. But he'd come to this sanctuary to find answers. What could this man, this possible murderer, offer Camille? It must have something to do with this place. Camille lived in a world where spirits were as real as the people around her. Somehow, this man shared something with Camille.

The idea terrified Eustace because of the web of implications. Where were the girls? What had the man done with them? What would he do with Camille? Eustace couldn't help wondering exactly what Camille knew about the disappearance of Angie Salter and Trisha Webster. She knew something. He was sure of it. He'd seen her hiding something in her underwear drawer the day after the girls disappeared, and when he'd asked, she'd lied to him. Later, he'd looked and found an expensive gold bracelet. One he'd never seen. But he had remembered the glint of gold on Angie Salter's arm as she'd taunted him from the sandbar.

Eustace stepped into the gloom of the trees, caught in the scent of grapes. He closed his eyes, trying to organize his thoughts and calm his fears. He'd lied to J.D., on more than one occasion now. His latest lie was serious. Eustace had been tailing the Mexican, following him through some of the thickest swamp, sighting him from a distance. But he had made no effort to capture him. Instinct told him not to, and Eustace relied on his gut rather than rules and bargains. Even with his friend J.D.

If the Mexican were responsible for taking the two girls, he needed to be apprehended. But not if it jeopardized Camille in any way. Vivian and Calvin would jump at any chance to take Camille away, even if it meant putting her in a mental institution or prison.

Getting justice in Jexville could be difficult. Emotions were at a fever pitch over the missing girls. Camille could easily be dragged into the fray. The Mexican, a stranger, might end up on the end of a lynch rope, and there would be no sympathy for anyone who'd befriended him. Such things had happened in Chickasaw County, and not so far in the distant past.

The musky scent of grapes filled Eustace's nostrils as he stared at the rough wooden plank that served as an altar. Fresh flowers were on it. The blooms were droopy but not dead. Eustace picked up a carving of a deer. There were an opossum and a raccoon, too. The carvings were finely crafted, detailed. The man was bold. He'd come back to his sacred place as soon as the authorities were gone.

Eustace sensed someone behind him. He turned.

The man, bare-chested, stood twenty feet away. Eustace, who could hear a squirrel climb a tree fifty yards away, had not heard him approach. In the man's right hand was the sharp skinning knife that had gone missing from Eustace's shed. On his hairless chest were marks, scars. The skin was ugly and welted, as if it had been burned. Eustace swallowed. He stepped closer. The marks were crosses of all sizes, and they were burned into his chest. Eustace couldn't take his eyes off them. Then he saw the pewter cross, hanging from a chain around the man's neck. Camille's cross. The one she always wore. He felt sick when he couldn't remember the last time he'd seen it. He felt her slipping away from him.

Eustace knew there came times when a judgment had to be made. That was what life was about—making a choice, then sticking by it without complaint. He'd crippled himself because he made a choice one cool fall night. He had been hauling a load of moonshine when a deputy pulled behind him, blue lights flashing. Instead of stopping, Eustace had floored the accelerator. Every day of his life he'd paid for that decision, but he'd never complained. Not once. Not to anyone.

Eustace knew he could try to kill the man. He was close enough, and even though he was at least thirty years older, he could take him if he could get his arms around him. It was the getting to him that troubled Eustace. His bad leg would slow him. But one question held him back.

Where were the girls? Eustace had seen them when he'd come back down the river. After docking, he had gone up to Leslie's Grocery for some beer and had helped Otis Hobby fix his truck, lingering in the shade of the store to drink a cold beer and listen to Otis tell a few jokes. When he'd come home, Camille had been gone in one of the boats. He hadn't given it a thought then. Hadn't even wondered where she was. Freedom was the breath of life to her, and though he sometimes worried for her safety, he never tried to hold her back from wandering the woods and river on her own. But Camille had come home an hour later, splattered with mud, her dress torn. She'd been dazed and withdrawn, and since then her sleep had been troubled. When he'd asked her what was wrong, she'd said, "Death is of the spirits. A gift."

He thought of that now. "Death is of the spirits." Now he faced the man who may have introduced Camille to death.

The light was poor, but when he looked up into the man's eyes he saw satisfaction. Eustace decided to capture him and make him tell where the girls were. Then he would kill him. If Camille were implicated in the girls' disappearance, the man would never live to tell it.

Eustace lunged. Just as he reached out for the man, his foot hung in a vine. He hit hard enough to knock the wind from his lungs.

He struggled in the carpet of leaves, thrashing. He knew he had to keep moving or the man would stab him. Rolling quickly, he looked up.

The man was gone.

He rose, frantic. The vines wouldn't turn him loose, and he clawed at them, memories of Camille's hand touching the hideous scars fluttering in his brain.

At last Eustace broke free. The woods were empty. He ran to the river, where he'd tied off his boat. The bank was empty. Only the river lazed by, so calm on the surface and so turbulent beneath.

Chapter Thirteen

Chickasaw County High was a long, low building that reminded Dixon of a place where poultry was imprisoned until fat enough for market. A straggle of rose bushes, surrounded by hundreds of cigarette butts clung to life at the front door. She stepped inside and made her way down the silent hallway. The place smelled like bad plumbing, dirty gym socks, and sweat, a mix that brought back a rush of memories and a vague sense of anxiety. She didn't have permission to be on school property and figured she couldn't get it. But Tommy Hayes had given her the dodge for over a week, and she was determined to talk to him, especially in light of what she'd learned from Calvin and Big Jim.

She looked through the small glass window of each door as she made her way down the hallway lined with metal lockers. At the end of the hall, she found the biology class. Hayes sat on a stool as he addressed his students.

Dixon tapped lightly on the door. When she opened the door and walked into the classroom, he froze. The dark circles under his eyes, his pallor, and the trembling hands he shoved in his pockets were at odds with the freckled, open freshness of his face.

Hayes looked toward the door, panic on his face.

Dixon didn't give him a chance to run. She closed the door and glanced around the room. "Mr. Hayes, I need to talk to you."

Before Dixon could say anything else, the bell rang and the students rushed out. Dixon and Hayes were left facing each other.

"You had no right to come in here." The teacher was angry. "Those kids are having a tough enough time. They're children."

"I've been trying for a week to talk with you. You have a connection to the missing girls. Angie Salter almost cost you your job."

"I don't want to talk to you, and I don't have to." Hayes walked to the open door.

"What's going on with the school board? First they vote to fire you, and then no action is taken. It's as if I never had a conversation with Jim Welford where he as much as said you were corrupting your students."

Hayes turned away. He went to his desk and lifted a sheaf of paper. "I have quizzes to grade. I'd like you to leave."

"Why didn't they fire you? Does it have to do with Angie Salter's disappearance?"

His chair tumbled to the floor with a loud echo as he whirled to confront her. "I don't know. I've never been told I was fired. Look, I need this job. This is my first contract, and if I'm dismissed, it's going to be hell to get on at another system, especially if there's the taint of inappropriate behavior hanging over me. If I can complete this year, I'll gladly pack my things and get out of this sick, God-forsaken place."

"Tell me about Angie." Around them the school had grown silent. The students had fled like escapees. "Tell me about her," Dixon insisted.

He slammed his palm on his desk top. "She wanted an A. She made an F. I wouldn't change her grade, but I told her I'd help her, you know, if she really wanted to learn. She wasn't stupid, but she was lazy. She thought she could get anything she wanted by shaking her ass. She got really mad when she realized I meant for her to study and told me she'd fix it where I wouldn't ever be able to bother her again. Well, she almost has."

Dixon heard footsteps. They stopped outside the biology room and a man's face peered in.

Hayes strode to the door. "Get out of here," he said. "It's the reporter."

"I'm not leaving." The man stepped into the room.

Dixon had never seen him, but she knew he had to be the man she'd spoken with on the phone.

He looked from Hayes to her. "My name is Craig Baggett. This is about Angie, isn't it?" Anger tightened his mouth. "Tell her, Tommy. Tell her the truth." When the teacher remained silent, the other man turned to Dixon. "Angie was trying to blackmail him for a good grade."

"She seems a little young for such a ploy," Dixon said.

Baggett snorted. "Right, she was such a baby that the same tactic worked on the principal at the middle school. That's how she finally passed the eighth grade, or at least that's what she said. She'd sit on the tailgate of Jimmy's truck while she was waiting for him and brag about the guys she'd done and how she could get anything she wanted. How good she was. You can ask any of the students." He wiped his hand across his mouth as if to rid himself of a bitter taste.

Baggett had been at Hayes's home, and now he was defending him. She was curious about their relationship, but she was more curious about Hayes's connection with Angie Salter. Whether Baggett knew it or not, he was talking motive for murder. "Was Angie still seeing the principal?"

The young man shook his head. "Not from the gossip. She'd met some guy with money. She had this expensive gold watch. It was a . . ."

"Cartier," Hayes supplied.

"And diamond earrings," Baggett added. "Big ones. She said they were a carat each. She had other jewelry, too. Tommy couldn't afford that kind of stuff even if he wanted to give it to her. Which he didn't." He looked out the window at a gang of boys dressed in football uniforms jogging toward a practice field.

Hayes nodded. "Someone was giving her expensive gifts. When I wouldn't give her a better grade, she said she'd settle for a boom box." He pointed out the window. "I wasn't in a position to give her either. Now, Craig has to go to work and so do I."

Baggett glanced at Hayes. "You might want to check out who was beating Angie. I saw her after school last week, and she had bruises on her."

"Who was hitting her?"

Baggett shook his head. "I don't know. Ask her boyfriend, Jimmy Franklin."

Hayes picked up his papers. "We're leaving."

"One more question. Were you at the river the day Angie disappeared?"

Hayes held her gaze. "I drove down to Biloxi and hired Johnny Grelot as my attorney." He pulled his wallet from his back pocket, retrieved a card, and handed it to her. "Call him. He'll verify I was there."

✝

J.D. sat on the edge of the Victorian sofa and held the dainty coffee cup in a hand almost twice as large as the china. Steam rose from the hot coffee.

"I was hoping Calvin would be home from the bank," he said.

"Not for a while." Vivian crossed her legs in the chair beside him. "You look worn out, J.D. I just wonder how you can come here considering all the times you've refused to help us get Camille back."

J.D. put the untouched cup on the table. Vivian had insisted on the coffee, even though he'd declined. She was watching him now, enjoying his discomfort. "I do need to talk to Calvin about something that pertains to this family," he said.

"Don't tell me! You've finally come to your senses, and you're going to physically remove Camille from those swamps."

J.D. shook his head. He bitterly regretted coming to the Holbert house without calling first to make sure Calvin was home. "No, I came to talk about keeping Camille safe. Camille and the other folks in town."

"Oh, goody!" Vivian clapped her hands. "Please tell me how you're going to accomplish that. I guess it's a little late for the Webster and Salter girls."

J.D. looked out the window at the expanse of immaculate lawn and the road beyond that. There was no sign of Calvin's car, even though it was after six o'clock in the evening.

129

"All sarcasm aside, Sheriff, how do you propose to keep us all safe when that maniac swamp man is on the loose and two girls are missing, probably dead? Tell me the truth, have you even questioned him? Does he have an alibi?"

"Do you honestly believe Eustace would harm those girls?" J.D. had never believed Vivian's complaints that Eustace was dangerous, or that he practiced mind control on Camille, or that he still ran moonshine. Vivian lied to achieve the result she wanted—in this case, getting Camille away from Eustace.

"I believe it with every bone in my body," Vivian said. She uncrossed her legs, the silk of her pantsuit making a noise like a soft zipper. "I believe it because it's true."

"What proof do you have?"

"Those girls are the latest. They were on the river and now they're gone. He took them and he killed them. If anything happens to my daughter, I'm going to hold you responsible."

Arguing with Vivian was a waste of breath. "Camille is free to leave Eustace at any time. If it's any consolation to you, Vivian, I saw her recently and she was fine. You see her all the time when she comes to town, which is fairly regularly. Ruth Ann Johnson saw her in the beauty salon and said Camille looked better than she has in a long time. Rested."

"Ruth Ann isn't a reliable witness and you know it."

J.D. shifted on the sofa and checked his watch again. It was going on six-thirty, and still no Calvin. "Would you mind calling Calvin to see if he's coming home any time soon?"

"He won't answer the phone at the bank or his cell phone. It's one of his little idiosyncrasies." She leaned forward so that the front of her suit opened, exposing the creamy expanse of her breasts. "Are you afraid to be alone with me, Sheriff?"

Tempting him was a new game for Vivian. J.D. wanted to sigh, but he didn't. "Vivian, do you have a weapon?"

She frowned. "There are knives in the kitchen—"

"A gun."

"Is there a law against an honest citizen's owning a gun?"

"No, but it would ease my mind if I knew it was locked up somewhere."

She laughed. "Are you afraid I might hurt myself or someone else?"

"Both," he said.

"Put your mind at ease," Vivian said. "Calvin took it away from me."

J.D. stood. "That's all I wanted to know."

"Calvin won't be home for a while. Are you sure you have to run off?"

"Yes, ma'am," J.D. said, walking to the front door. When he stepped out into the still warm evening, he felt a sense of relief. Vivian was like a large cat toying with her prey.

To Vivian, everyone was prey.

CHAPTER FOURTEEN

The sky above the river was fuchsia, purple, and gold. The Pascagoula River shared the sky's fiery palette, and, as the light faded, the river turned silver and then black, merging with the dense tree line on the opposite shore.

"Eustace, honey, why are you sitting out here all by yourself?" Camille asked as she approached the boat where he sat.

His rifle was covered with a tarp, and Eustace felt a moment of guilt. Camille trusted him to do the right thing. "I was just thinking," he said.

"Oh, I don't like the sound of that," Camille said with a forced laugh.

He felt her hand on his back. Her warm fingers slid around his chest, and she held him tightly.

"Camille, is something wrong?"

She shook her head against his back, but he felt her tears. He held still, waiting for the storm of her emotion to pass. She was volatile, and it might be nothing serious that was upsetting her.

"What is it, Camille?"

"Mother is such a bitch."

Eustace felt a familiar stab of hatred. Vivian and Calvin weren't satisfied with their twenty-three-year-long attempt to destroy Camille. They kept on and kept on, nagging and trying to force her back to a world that gave her only torment and pain. They couldn't—or wouldn't—see how happy she was. She'd found her freedom in the woods along the river. She'd found herself in his arms, and he would do whatever was necessary to save her. Even if it cost the lives of those two girls.

"I love you," he said, the only words that might comfort her.

"Mother says she's going to call the governor to have me taken away," Camille said.

She took a deep breath and tried to gain control, but Eustace could feel the warm tears splashing against his back.

"Camille, you know I never break my word, don't you?" he asked.

"Yes."

"I make you this one promise. No one will ever take you from these swamps unless you want to go."

"How will you stop them?" she asked.

"Don't you fret about that. Should you ever want to go, I'll be the first one to help you. But if you want to stay, not the governor or the president or Jesus Christ himself will be able to take you away."

She lay against his back, her cheek pressed to his spine. He could feel her breathing calm as she relaxed. Finally she spoke. "Eustace, will you make me another promise?"

"What's that?"

"If they come for me, promise me that you'll kill me before you let them have me."

He closed his eyes. "Camille, it won't come to that."

"Promise me." She rubbed against him. "Old folks sometimes make pacts where one will kill the other if they get sick. That's all I'm asking. I'd rather be dead than go back to them." Her fingers were kneading into his back like a baby kitten nursing its mother.

"Camille, you're stronger than you think."

"Those girls are gone, Eustace. The Indians called them below the river, just like the legend you told me. Remember how you said at night I could hear the Indians singing their death song as they walked beneath the water. It was like that. I saw the bubbles rising from beneath the water."

Black fear touched Eustace. "Did you really see those girls, Camille?"

"On the sandbar. I saw them. One of them was naked. She was acting like a whore."

He could hear his heart thump in his temples. "How did you see them? Did you take one of the other boats?" He'd wanted to keep the skiffs locked and chained, but he hadn't been able to do it. He hadn't wanted Camille to feel that he didn't trust her, to be a prisoner to his fear that she would drown in the river if the skiff overturned.

"Yes, I went up the river. I went to the kiln site and then up the Leaf to look for those turtles again. The yellowish ones with the wavy shells. If I could just touch the shells, I'd know how to make the pattern in my clay pots."

Eustace turned and gripped Camille by the arms, forcing her to look at him. Her eyes were dreamy, fevered, intense.

"When did you see the girls?" he asked

"Before they disappeared." She smiled. "They were so young. They made me feel old."

Eustace forced his fingers to relax. "Do you know what happened to the girls?" he asked softly.

"Someone took them." She gazed beyond him at the water. "Look, there's a pelican. I haven't seen one all summer. I was afraid they were dead."

Her face was as joyful as a child's. Eustace wanted to weep. "Camille, this is important. Do you know who took those girls?"

Her brow furrowed. "There's a man living across the river, but he's nice."

He sighed. "What's his name?"

"He never said. He knows about the girls, though. I told him how they had to leave."

"Had to leave?" He could feel his heart pounding now.

"They were bad girls. They were going to make trouble."

"Did the man tell you that?" She looked confused. "The man you met in the woods. The one with the scars. Was he the one who said the girls were trouble?"

"How do you know about the scars?" She was wary now, backing away.

"Camille, what did he do to those girls? Were you involved?" He spoke roughly, harshly. He'd frightened her, and for a second he didn't care. He grasped her shoulders.

She struggled against him. "Let me go. God damn you, let me go. I'll cut out your gizzard!"

"Camille, tell me what you did." He held her firmly. "Tell me what happened to those girls."

"Let me go, or I'll hurt you!"

Eustace moaned as he crushed Camille to his chest and held her until she stopped flailing. She sobbed against him. "Promise you won't let them take me," she said. "I can't stand it when they touch me."

He held her as he stared out into the black water and the night. "I promise," he said at last. "I promise, Camille."

✝

Main Street was empty, its asphalt stretching to the end of town and dropping away into darkness down the hill. Dixon was exhausted. She'd gone from the high school to the library and spent the last few hours on the Internet researching everything from Catholicism to Satan worship. She'd tracked down newspaper stories about desecration of church property and located the sites on a map. Robert Medino had not exaggerated—at least not the route of the desecrations or the fact that the assaults seemed to be targeted against images of the Virgin Mary. Her instincts told her that Angie Salter and Trish Webster weren't coming home.

She walked back to the newspaper office, unlocked the door, and went inside to get her purse. The message light on the answering machine was blinking, and she hit replay.

"Ms. Sinclair, I have to talk with you."

The soft voice unsettled her. There was intimacy in the tone, a secret—and urgency. She stopped the tape. In the silence, she was aware of her heartbeat. Rewinding, she started the segment again.

"Ms. Sinclair, I have to talk to you."

The urgency unnerved her.

"There are things you have to know. Things that might make a difference. My father is innocent. He's going to die unless—" The mechanical beep of the machine ended the message.

The caller was male and black. The answering machine was kept in the composing room, and Dixon peered around the swinging doors to the front office, which reflected the emptiness of the street beyond. A young black man had stared at her through that very window. She remembered his face. Was this Willard Jones's son? A child, like herself, who would do anything to turn back time?

Dixon stared out the empty window. A jury of twelve men and women had proclaimed Willard Jones guilty of building and planting a bomb in the newspaper offices of Ray Sinclair. The motive had been retribution for a series of articles her father had written condemning a black political leader, Grady Duelly, as a charlatan and cheat. The black community had been outraged over the articles, which enumerated the payoffs, deals, nepotism, and corruption that Duelly had been involved in. Ray had been accused of trying to tarnish Duelly simply because he was black.

Dixon had always felt that it was a weak motive for murder. After two conversations with Jones, she had serious doubts that he'd planted the bomb. But if not he, who?

Who? That question had tormented her for years now, disrupting her sleep, invading her mind a hundred times a day. Who would want to kill her father?

The need for a drink came hard and strong. Her mouth began to water, and she knew that in a minute her hands would begin to shake. It had been five weeks. The first week she'd done at Well Haven, a clinic. The last four she'd done on her own, determined to live without a crutch, either a bottle or an attendant. Sometimes she could go a day without thinking of a drink. Sometimes.

She replayed the aborted message a third time. There was no number or any way to contact the young man. She'd have to wait for him to make the next move. If it wasn't soon, it would be too late for Willard Jones. His execution date had slipped a day closer.

She hit the play button again, hoping the young man had left another message. Instead she heard Robert Medino's voice.

"Deadline is over, and I want to have dinner with you tomorrow night. Say seven, if that's a good time for you. Let's drive to the coast and check out some of the casino action, then grab something to eat. If this is acceptable, call me at the Magnolia. Be sure and leave a detailed message. Ruth Ann is very interested in everything you do."

She would deal with Medino in the morning, when she was fresh. Now, all she wanted was to have a drink. But she convinced herself that she could drive home, crawl into bed, and sleep.

✝

The stream's current carried her along, and Dixon closed her eyes and let the dappled sunlight shift black and red against her eyelids. The water was artesian-fed cold, and the clay bottom of the small stream was slick. The pool where she swam was clear and deep, surrounded by thick woods. It was a place of peace and contentment.

Someone long ago had partially dammed the creek behind her house, creating the swimming hole. As Dixon floated close to the makeshift dam, she stood in the chest-high water and began to walk back upstream. Trees grew down to the edge of the water. It would be a simple matter to get an old tractor inner tube and tie it to a tree. That way she could drift in the current and never go anywhere. Moored. She liked the sound of the word.

It was just after seven in the morning, and she'd decided to swim, stop by the Hickory Pit and get some breakfast, and then go in to work. She hadn't slept well. She'd dreamt of the card suit of clubs and a black carriage drawn by two gray horses with black plumes. She'd been hunting for someone, someone she'd lost at the edge of a river, someone she loved. It had been a vague and upsetting dream.

She sank up to her chin in the cold water and closed her eyes. Just another few minutes and she'd leave.

She realized that the woods had grown still, and she squeezed the water from her hair and listened. A stick crackled, sounding loud and sharp. Dixon froze. Her clothes were on the bank, not ten feet away. She glanced into the woods, feeling naked and vulnerable.

The copper-skinned boy slid out from behind a tree and stood in a shaft of sunlight. The look on his face shifted from nervousness to fear as he realized that she was naked.

"It's okay," she said. "Let me get my clothes."

He was poised, ready to flee. He held no weapon, but his fists were clenched. There was only the sound of the stream.

"I want to talk to you," she said. "About Willard Jones."

In the stillness, she heard the waffling sound of a siren. It seemed to shift in and out of the woods, and Dixon wondered if she were imagining it. But the boy heard it too. He glanced around, then looked at her, his mouth open as if he meant to speak, and turned and ran. Even when the thick trees hid him, she could hear him moving through the underbrush. She stared at the spot where he had stood, then moved toward the bank and retrieved her clothes. Not bothering with underwear, she tugged the jeans over her wet legs and grabbed her top. She was still buttoning her shirt as she started running toward the house, toward the sound of the siren.

Dixon broke from the woods just as the brown sheriff's cruiser pulled under the four oaks in front of the house. Panting, she stopped.

Waymon turned off the siren and got out of the car, moving with slow deliberation. He spit beside his boot, a brown stream of deadly accuracy, and walked toward her, eyes hidden by sunglasses. "J.D. sent me to fetch you. They found one of the girls."

CHAPTER FIFTEEN

Dixon clutched her camera as the aluminum boat sped up the Pascagoula River. They passed the sandbar, now gleaming white in the silver light of the rapidly approaching storm. They were working against time, and Dixon felt the pressure. J.D. had sent for her because she could take pictures. He wanted crime scene photos before the rain came, and there was no way a state lab photographer could get there in time.

The man who piloted the boat said nothing, and whenever Dixon looked back toward him, he avoided eye contact. That, in itself, cautioned her to prepare for the worst.

They came to the fork where the Chickasawhay and the Leaf flowed together to form the Pascagoula and veered left, up the Leaf. Vegetation grew thick on either side of the river, a jungle. This part of Mississippi was considered pine flats, but parts of it oozed into tropical. J.D. and the tracking teams had searched relentlessly. Every dry inch. An old fisherman had discovered the body.

In the distance she could see several fishing boats pulled to the east bank of the river. There was no bluff. This was land that often belonged to the water. Her pilot angled the boat and ran straight in at the shore, cutting the motor at the last moment. Dixon stepped out onto what passed for dry land, a sort of muck that pulled at her shoes. Five or six men were huddled near the boats, and when she started toward them, they shouldered in, excluding her. She continued past them, looking for J.D.'s tall figure.

She saw him waiting and walked as fast as the muck allowed in his direction.

"It's bad," he said.

She took a breath. "The rain won't hold off for long."

He nodded and turned to lead the way into the woods.

A staggering odor struck Dixon after only a few steps. J.D. heard her falter and turned, offering his clean handkerchief.

"It won't help much."

She took it and tied it over her nose and mouth, detecting the faint scent of mint chewing gum in the folds. Dixon nodded that she was ready.

J.D. parted a frond of bay leaves, and Dixon stepped into a small clearing. A swarm of flies burst from the body that hung from the branch of an oak. Dixon stumbled as she took in the mutilation. The head was a blackened lump rising above a body draped in a filthy white sheet. Hands and feet dangled. A slight breeze gently turned the body, and the rope that held it creaked as more flies, interrupted in their work, buzzed around it.

"My God," she said, forgetting the camera.

"She's been dead a while," J.D. said softly. "She was dead before she was gutted and burned."

Hands unsteady, Dixon lifted the camera and began to shoot, taking care to move around the body and get every angle. She made certain to photograph the mud, which bore traces of undefined footprints.

There was no way to tell if the body was Trisha's or Angie's. Insects had done their work, and the remains had been burned. Dixon tried not to think of the girls as she worked the scene, taking brief directions from J.D.

A fat plop of rain struck her head. She moved in closer. There was no time to think, to feel. There was only the click of the camera, the roll of the film. She finished a roll, handed the camera to J.D. for a reload, and picked up the second Nikon she carried, this one loaded with color film. The light was fading fast. She repeated the sequence of shots, then moved in for close-ups. The rain had begun to fall in big drops that exploded on the leaves around them.

"Hurry," J.D. urged. "Get the hands and feet."

Dixon switched the lens and stepped closer. She was breathing through her mouth, avoiding the smell as much as possible. Mosquitoes buzzed around her head, biting at her ears and the part in her hair. The girl's hands hung at eye level, and she lifted the camera to the face. It was a ruin, but there were a few straggles of dark brown hair. Trisha Webster. She felt the sickness swell and a stinging in her scalp that signaled distress.

J.D. stepped beside her, his hand touching her shoulder gently. But instead of speaking words of comfort, he slowly lifted the sheet.

Dixon gagged. The abdomen was a mass of open corruption.

"Dixon." J.D.'s voice was sharp.

She swallowed, lifting the camera again. The lens gave her some distance. The body was naked, the flesh of the legs less damaged. The fire had been concentrated on the head and upper torso.

J.D.'s hand came into the viewfinder, pointing at the top of the left thigh.

Dixon saw it then. A cross had been cut into the flesh.

✝

Eustace stood on the porch of his home, looking in through the leaded window of the door. The fragments of glass showed a river curling lazily between banks of trees. Camille had designed the pattern, had cut the glass and shaped it, giving the river a perfect yellow-mud color and the trees an electric color. Now, though, the hues of the glass were muted by a gray sky. A major storm was brewing. The first drops of rain blew past him and splattered on the glass.

Eustace remained on the porch as the rain built to a crescendo on the tin roof above his head. Through the glass he could see Camille bend gracefully at the hips as she leaned toward the sink, washing something.

Eustace pushed the door open. He stood for a moment on the threshold, chilled by his rain-dampened shirt and the air conditioner that hummed from the open bedroom. He went to the refrigerator and, though it was only eight in the morning, took out a six-pack. Popping the top on a beer, he watched her.

"You're angry with me," she said without looking at him.

"No. I'm not." He wasn't. He was terrified for her. Camille had become involved in something that could cost her what she valued most, her freedom. He'd spent the morning trying to figure a way out of it for her. He could kill the Mexican. He could even kill the girls, if they were alive somewhere. But he couldn't protect Camille from herself.

The swing of headlights arced through the living room windows. Eustace looked down at the drive, where a brown sheriff's car lurched into the yard. He felt a tremor of fear.

"Who is it?" Camille asked.

"It's J.D. and the reporter," Eustace said. He walked outside into the rain, taking the stairs without regard for his leg. Ignoring the patrol car, he went to the fish-cleaning shed. He tossed the remaining beer on the picnic table and sat down facing the river. Drops of water hung in his hair, and his clothes were drenched. He heard the low sound of an ambulance siren. He looked back; J.D. and the reporter were walking toward him, both sheltered by a tattered umbrella. The woman looked pale and sick. J.D., too, looked bad, and both were wet.

He knew before they spoke. "You found one, didn't you?"

J.D. nodded. "The Webster girl."

Eustace noted the way the reporter focused on the river. She looked as if she were on the verge of being sick but was fighting it hard. He remembered her mother, Marilyn McVay, a woman so pretty that the boys in high school had been afraid to talk to her. Dixon had that same beauty, but it had been eroded, maybe by grief, he thought.

"Where'd you find her?" he asked.

"Up at Hathaway's Point," J.D. looked at his dirty hands. "She was moved there in the last twenty-four hours."

"And the other one?" Eustace asked, fighting to keep his voice calm. If the Webster girl was dead, the Salter girl probably was too. With luck, that would leave only the Mexican to implicate Camille.

"No sign of Angie Salter."

J.D. didn't have to add that he believed the girl dead. Eustace could read it on his face. On the reporter's too. He pushed the beer toward J.D. and the woman. "Help yourself. It's a little early, but sometimes it's just time for a beer."

Neither of them made a move, and silence fell. "You say the girl was at Hathaway's Point?" he asked, trying not to show his worry.

"Right out on the point. Hanging from a tree." J.D. stopped when the reporter turned away. "Eustace, we need some help. Camille saw this Hispanic guy."

"No." Eustace's hand tightened on his beer. "I won't have Camille upset. The answer is no."

J.D. looked past Eustace to the house. He stood up, arching his back as if he were stiff and sore. "Eustace, I don't need to point out to you that Camille's an adult, and as such, she's going to have to tell me no herself."

Before J.D. could step into the rain, Camille appeared on the porch. Eustace saw her through the gray drops that blended into a grayer sky. The rain wasn't going to let up. Eustace stood. He willed Camille back into the house. He saw her hesitate, then take three steps down. He closed his eyes and prayed.

"Eustace," she called. "Are you still mad at me?"

He felt something crack inside his chest. "I'm not mad."

A smile spread across her face, and she started to run down the stairs.

Eustace saw it in slow motion. Camille's feet hit the yard, and then she was running toward him, her long legs flashing beneath her skirt. She was in his arms, laughing and kissing him, not at all concerned that J.D. and the reporter were watching her.

"Camille, do you think you might be able to describe the man you saw in the sycamore tree to a sketch artist?" J.D. asked her.

She frowned and grew still in Eustace's arms. "Why?"

"If we had a picture of him, we might be able to catch him."

She burrowed into Eustace's neck. He put his hand on her waist and gave the gentlest pressure. He was telling her to hold on. Don't talk. Don't say anything.

"I didn't see him that well," she said.

Eustace patted her back.

"It would help us a lot if you could remember," J.D. said.

"I'll think about it." She moved away from Eustace, casting him a sly smile as she did so. "I'll think about it, won't I, Eustace?"

"Camille, this is important."

"She said she'd think about it." Eustace had to figure a way to make Camille understand that she must not talk. Everything depended on her keeping quiet.

"Are you okay?" J.D. asked Eustace.

"Never better," he said.

"I'll be in touch," J.D. said. "Dixon, let's head back to town. I've got some calls to make."

CHAPTER SIXTEEN

Reports lay scattered across J.D.'s desk. He stared at them, trying to make sense of the information he'd gathered. It would be some hours before he had the autopsy report from Dr. Howell, and he was finding it difficult to fit together the pieces of Trisha Webster's death.

He thought about Dixon. She'd been sick at the body site, but she'd waited until she finished the photos and then gone off into the woods alone. He respected her need for privacy, and he thought for the first time that they might share more than a geographic location.

His thoughts returned to Trisha Webster. The girl had been dead for some time. He knew that much. She'd been buried and then exhumed so her remains could be hung, gutted, and burned. It was a graphic crime scene.

Outside J.D.'s office, Waymon was loud on the telephone, as usual. J.D. got his hat and keys and walked out into the hot afternoon. He walked down the street, hung a right at Main, and continued to the red brick newspaper office. Dixon had said she'd develop the photos right away.

When he walked in, he saw that Linda Moore had been crying. She knew both girls, and he felt a fresh pang for all the suffering to come.

"Do you know who did this?" she asked. "You have to find him."

"We're still waiting on some evidence." He wanted to say something reassuring, but he could not allay her fears or reassure her that justice would be done.

"Angie's dead, too, isn't she?" Linda asked.

"I don't know for certain." But he thought he did, based on statistics and experience.

"Find the sick bastard who did this and kill him," Linda said, reaching for a tissue to wipe her eyes. "Don't bring him in. Kill him in the swamp like a rabid dog."

"Justice is going to be an empty word for Orie Webster," he said, "and a lot of other people, too."

"Justice may be empty, but revenge will give the families some solace."

Linda was wounded and lashing out. He knew that nothing he said would help. "Where's Dixon?" he asked.

"She's in the darkroom." Linda put a hand over her eyes and rubbed. "She's been waiting for you."

J.D. tapped on the darkroom door and entered a small space lit by a red light. Photographs spun in a tub of constantly circulating water. The eight-by-ten black and white images floated to the top and swirled away.

"I made contact sheets, and I printed the ones I thought you might want," Dixon said. "I'm not on the county payroll. I just thought I could expedite this one little thing. I want whoever did this to be caught."

The darkroom was small, and he stood so close to Dixon that his hip brushed hers whenever he moved. He reached for a photo in the wash and pulled it up dripping. It was a close-up of the cross sliced into Trisha Webster's leg.

"Robert Medino was right, wasn't he?" Dixon asked.

J.D. looked at the picture. This mutilation was beyond his ability to comprehend. "Whoever did this has some problems with religion. This is a ritual of some type."

"Have you talked with Medino?" Dixon asked.

"I haven't had any appetite for gloat." He chanced a quick glance at her but didn't see any reaction. "I was hoping he'd take his theory and march on down I-10. I guess that was a foolish wish. Have you gotten to know him any better?"

"Not yet."

But she must want to. She'd be interested in another reporter. Journalism, like law enforcement, was a strong bond.

"When will you have the photos finished?"

"This evening. They should be dry about seven. Shall I bring them by the sheriff's department? The color won't be back until early tomorrow. I FedExed them to a private lab."

"If you could bring by what you've got, that would be great," he said.

"Do you have any leads on this guy?" Dixon asked.

J.D. reached into his back pocket and brought out an envelope. "I have this. A mug shot of him. His name is Francisco Chavez. Fingerprints on a beer can from the river matched some prints in Eagle Pass, Texas. He'd been picked up on a charge of vandalism at a church six months ago."

Dixon examined the photo under the red light. "Will you give this to the Mobile media?" she asked.

"I have to," J.D. said. "It's almost a week until the *Independent* is printed. I need immediate action. If the guy in the picture is the killer, television could be our best way of getting help from the public."

"I understand. But you'll save an interview for me, right?"

Her words made him smile. She did understand. "For you and you alone," he answered.

✝

Dixon saw the lighted cigarette arcing slowly on the front porch swing. Robert Medino's rental car was parked beneath the oaks. It had been after eight when she left the sheriff's office, and Robert's offer of a trip to the Gulf Coast had slipped her mind until well past the dinner hour. She'd called the B&B, but he'd been gone. Now here he was, on her front porch.

The cigarette tip brightened, and Dixon found the idea of a cigarette tempting. She got out of her truck and walked to the front steps. "I'm sorry I didn't call," she said. "Things got busy."

"So I heard. The sheriff ought to cut out his deputy's vocal cords. Waymon has been running his mouth." Robert patted the swing beside him. "Have a seat and tell me all about it." There was the slosh of liquid in a bottle. "I heard you were partial to Jack Daniel."

Dixon remained on the top step. " 'Partial to' is a Southern phrase. Are you quoting someone in particular?" Most likely Ruth Ann, who ferreted out gossip like an armadillo after a grub.

Robert stopped swing and stood up. "I didn't mean to imply anything. Maybe I've had a little too much whiskey on an empty stomach."

He sounded contrite. "If that's a hint for food, you've come to a pitiful place. I've got stale bread, corn flakes—no milk—and Diet Coke."

"Actually, I came to see what you know about the dead girl and how she died. If you won't have dinner with me, at least let's work together as journalists."

Dixon was surprised at the surge of disappointment she felt. That, more than anything, made her realize how lonely she'd been. "You need to eat something. Alcohol dissipates in the flames of carbohydrates."

"Why would you think I want the alcohol to dissipate?"

Dixon rolled her eyes and unlocked the front door. "The mosquitoes will eat us alive out here. Come on inside. Keep in mind I wasn't expecting a personal visit."

"I've been told I can be quite charming in person."

"Do people lie to you a lot?"

He laughed, so close behind her she could feel his breath in her hair. "I'll turn on the air conditioners. It'll cool down pretty quickly."

Robert followed her to the kitchen, but when she turned to fill the coffee pot with water, he touched her arm. "No coffee. Nothing. Just talk to me."

His eyes were brown flecked with gold. He was very close to her.

"About what?" she asked, taking a step back.

"I heard the body of Trisha Webster was in bad shape. Mutilated."

Had he come for information? She didn't think so. J.D. would talk to him, if Waymon hadn't already.

"It was bad. Really bad." She waited until their eyes locked. "How about we swap information? I tell you what I know, and you tell me all about your theory."

"Okay." He went to the cabinet and got two glasses. From the freezer he got ice cubes, and then he poured two shots of Jack. He held a glass out to her. "I'll make a wild guess and say the Webster girl was kept alive for a while before she was killed. She was sexually assaulted, either before or after she was dead—I'm not sure about that yet—and then some ritualistic symbol or act was committed. Something like burning the body, or hanging—that's ancient ritual in purest form."

Dixon held the glass. It had been five weeks. Five hard weeks. The whiskey smelled warm. She could almost taste it. Almost taste the cigarette that went with it. "You're right. Waymon is a serious gossip. How much is a guess, and how much do you know?"

"The body was hung and burned. That's all I know."

"She was gutted, and a cross was cut into her thigh."

"What order did it take place?" He knocked back his drink and poured another.

"I'm not certain. The forensics aren't back."

"Will you be able to get them from the sheriff?"

Dixon felt a wave of apprehension. "J.D. would give you a copy of the report if he thought he could trust you—"

"He won't ever trust me." Robert shook out a cigarette and offered it to her. "Never. But he likes you. I watched him at the river last week. He definitely likes you."

Dixon felt her neck redden as she declined the cigarette. "You said this type of killing is ritualistic. What culture? The gruesome nature of Trisha Webster's body doesn't lend itself to even a very loose interpretation of the word *culture*."

"Fire for purification. Vikings. American Indians. East Indians. Just about any culture that uses funeral pyres." He shrugged. "If you really think about it, embalming and preservation of mortal remains is far more grotesque than burning. Most purification beliefs spring from the theory that fire frees the spirit. The mortal flesh is reduced to ash, and the spirit is free to ascend."

"What about hanging?"

"Another type of ritual. Not purification, though some American Indian tribes did hang their dead in trees." He sipped his drink, his eyes on her untouched glass. "Hanging is more symbolic of the executioner. It's a statement coming from him. He's putting his handiwork out there on display."

Dixon leaned forward on her elbows. She held the bourbon in one hand, catching the light in the amber liquid. "You sound very certain the killer is a male. Could it possibly be a woman?"

"The Webster girl was about five-seven, a hundred and twenty pounds. The blonde was smaller. I just figured it would take a man's strength to haul a hundred and twenty pounds of dead weight out of a boat and then hang it from a tree. A woman could do it, certainly. But it would take a very strong woman." His gaze moved over her body. "You could probably do it. If you were really pissed off."

"Thanks, I think." Dixon put her glass down. "How did you know the body was taken to the hanging site?"

"J.D. Horton isn't a stupid man. If that girl had been along the edge of the river, Horton would have found her long ago. Even if she was buried. They had cadaver dogs that would have found an obvious grave. My guess is that those girls were stashed somewhere and then moved."

"And why is this person doing this?" she asked.

"The man has some intimate connection with the figure of the Virgin Mary. He's destroyed her image in towns all over the South. It was only a matter of time until his behavior shifted from image to living person. I think he views those girls as the embodiment of the female virgin. I'm not sure exactly how it hooks up, but he ultimately feels he has to destroy them because of what they represent."

"That is scary as hell," Dixon said. "So now that he's killed once, he'll likely kill again."

"That's usually the way it works. I wouldn't give the Salter girl much of a chance." Robert sat back from the table. "You look beat. That's not a personal comment but one journalist telling another that some sack time is high on the priority list."

"I feel as if my arms and legs are filled with cement."

"I'll be heading to my magnificently decorated room. I have more pillows than Cleopatra in her palanquin." He hesitated. "Will you be okay?"

Dixon nodded. "I'm too tough for the stew pot, so I guess the cannibals will leave me alone."

He shoved the bottle to her. "Keep it. For next time."

CHAPTER SEVENTEEN

Dixon snatched the telephone on the sixth ring, almost falling out of bed.

"Who is this?" Her body was tangled in the sheets, and she'd dreamt that she was tied to a chair while people watched her through a small window.

"Hello," she said again. She held the phone tightly as she scanned the room where nothing was familiar and a scraping sound came from the window.

"Dixon?" Her mother's voice was threaded with worry. "Are you okay? Is something wrong?"

"I was asleep." Dixon swung her legs out of bed and snapped on the light. The night had been an inferno of hellish images and suffocating anxiety. She had not been asleep but in a state of helpless limbo where the demons of her subconscious jumped from their cells and ran wild.

She walked to the window and flipped the blinds to reveal a morning shrouded in fog. The scraping noise was an azalea rasping the screen.

"I'm worried about you." Marilyn said.

"I'm fine," Dixon said automatically. She felt naked, talking to her mother as she stood in her underwear at the window. She picked up a pair of dirty jeans.

"The newspaper looks good. Teasie brought a copy of the *Independent* to me yesterday. She had a doctor's appointment here in Jackson with Dr. Winguard. She said she was worried half to death for you. I can see why, too. You're right in the middle of everything, just like your father. Teasie said half the town thinks you're marvelous and the other half wants to tar and feather you."

Dixon held the telephone against her shoulder, pulling on the jeans while she listened. As she tucked in the pockets, her fingers found a crisp slip of paper. When she pulled it out, she realized it was the sales slip she'd found on the river more than a week before.

"That's probably the most accurate statement Teasie ever made," she said, trying to refocus on the conversation. "But I would have said twenty-eighty." She forced lightness into her voice. "My approval rating's higher than I thought."

Her mother's laughter reminded Dixon of summer afternoons.

"I love it when you laugh, Mom," Dixon said.

"I'd laugh more if you sold that paper. You could teach, Dixon. It isn't big money, but neither is a weekly paper. You could work on a campus for twenty hours a week instead of putting in a hundred and twenty."

"If I worked on a campus, I might also find Prince Charming, someone brilliant and dedicated, and settle down to give you those grandchildren you want." Dixon didn't really mind her mother's nagging.

"I want you to be happy, Dixon." She hesitated. "Are you drinking?"

Dixon sagged. Her mother had called to see if she woke up drunk. "Not yet," she said with a bite. "If that's why you called, you can hang up now."

"Lana's pregnant. She's due in April."

"That's wonderful," Dixon faltered. "I guess Raymond's delighted. I know how much he wanted a child."

"They're both very happy." There was caution in her mother's tone.

"Me, too, Mom. I can't wait to have a baby niece or nephew. It's about time one of the Sinclairs kept the line going."

"Raymond and Lana haven't been getting along all that well. Sometimes a child makes matters worse." Her mother spoke carefully. Her primary focus in life, since her husband's death, was her children. Raymond was the son who never disappointed.

"Sometimes a child makes things better." Perhaps a child would make Raymond grow up. He was devoted to his engineering career—and his ski vacations and mountain climbing, his boats and travels. A child would center him or sink the marriage. Lana, too, would have to shift her focus from her legal career.

"I was never happier than when you two were little and your father was working as the political columnist for the *Charlotte Observer*. Those were the best days."

Dixon heard the longing in her mother's voice. Marilyn McVay had been a photographer. A good one. She'd given up her career to raise her family. But she'd never whined about that decision.

"Look, Mom, I'm doing something important, and I haven't felt that way for a long, long time. Moving to Jexville has been good for me. I just want you to know that."

"Life isn't all about career, Dixon." Her mother sighed. "I wanted you to have a girl's name, but your father was so proud of you. He insisted on giving you a family name."

Dixon glanced at the clock. It was 6:48. Her mother hadn't called at daybreak simply to tell her about the baby. "Mom, is anything wrong?"

Another hesitation.

Dixon felt her heart rate increase. "Mom, what's happened?"

"I got a telephone call Sunday night, Dixon." There was silence. "The man asked a lot of questions. About the past. About the execution. He wanted to know if I planned on attending."

"Who was it?"

"He wouldn't give his name."

"Mom, don't answer any more questions. If anyone calls, give them the number of the paper here."

"Dixon, I know you think your father's death was some type of conspiracy." When Dixon didn't answer, she continued. "I figure you've been poking around again and you've managed to stir up a hornet's nest. I haven't forgotten that you went to Parchman to visit that man. I've told you, when you stir the nest, someone gets stung."

"I don't know who called you, but I'll find out. I'm calling the phone company and ordering caller I.D. for you. Promise me you'll let them hook it up."

There was a long pause. "I hate those gizmos. There'll be wires running all over the house. Something else to dust."

"Promise."

"Okay. Only because I'm curious."

Dixon smiled and felt her heart rate slowing. "I love you, Mom."

"I love you too. Dixon, don't keep poking. I'm begging you."

"I love you, Mama." Dixon replaced the phone. She sat on the side of the bed in her jeans and bare feet and thought about the bottle of Jack in the kitchen. Her hands were shaking. She stood up and started to remove her jeans. The receipt she'd found fell to the floor.

It was only a short drive to the Circuit City in Mobile.

✝

J.D. dropped Visine in his eyes and closed them against the burn. The night had faded, yielding to a gray dawn that could bring only more bad news. Dr. Jose Diaz had been expected back in town last night, but he'd been detained in Rwanda, where he was doing volunteer work for children. J.D. needed to talk to him.

The good news was that the mug shot of Francisco Chavez had made the ten o'clock news on three television stations in Mobile, and calls had begun to come in. None useful. Yet. A lead would eventually pan out, but eventually might be too late for Angie Salter, if it weren't too late already.

He rifled through the paperwork on his desk and picked up the black-and-white photos of Trisha Webster. Cause of death had been an overdose of crystal meth. Her heart had stopped. Her body was so badly damaged and decomposed that the pathologist couldn't determine if the meth had been administered with a needle or inhaled. The cut to the thigh and the disemboweling had been done post-mortem.

The telephone rang, but he ignored it; Waymon was at his desk. Besides, J.D. had nothing to say to anyone. His focus was on finding the sick motherfucker who'd killed and then

160

burned a teenage girl. The phone rang again and he wearily snatched it up, anticipating a reporter. "Horton here." The gruesome murder had begun to attract the national media. It was going to be a shit storm, but one he intended to turn to his advantage. If the pervert who took the girls was anywhere in the area, J.D. was going to get him.

"J.D., John said you called."

J.D. loosened his grip on the telephone. He had called Beatrice Smart two hours earlier. He needed some professional advice and Bea, with her blend of religion and psychology, was a good source. "I hate to involve you, Bea, but this is beyond me."

"It's okay. I'll help if I can."

"I'll tell you the crime scene, and maybe you can give me some insight into this guy and what he may do next."

"I'm not a profiler; I'm just a psychologist."

"I'd take your intuition any day." He filled her in on everything he had, plus Medino's theory and the description of the body. When he was finished, he waited as silence filled the phone line.

At last Bea spoke. "I'm confused. Trisha Webster dies of a drug overdose, but then her body is treated with a kind of ritual that implies a person to whom God and Satan are very real. The hanging and burning are ritualistic. Whether it's Satan worship or a sacrifice to God, it is worship. Most people who believe in God also believe in Satan, or vice versa." She hesitated. "But the drugs are off kilter somehow. It's as if the killer had two personalities."

"The man I'm looking for may have defaced church property, specifically images of the Virgin Mary. If it's the same man, he's been on a spree for better than six months."

"That's helpful," Bea said. "But it still doesn't jibe with the drugs."

"Put the drugs aside. What do you get from the body?"

"Based just on that, I'd say the killer is someone so conflicted that he or she has moved beyond the ability to discern between archetypes and the reality of human form. I believe that Trisha and Angie represented temptation or sin or something that would be damning to a Christian. What confuses me is that, traditionally, the approach to sin is to forgive, to redeem the sinner. There is no redemption in death."

J.D. wished for something stronger than coffee. "So you're saying this religious fanatic wouldn't have killed the girls?"

"Not with crystal meth. At least, that's my take on it. J.D., I'm a minister who offers marriage and family counseling. My experience isn't with serial killers."

J.D. sighed. "This complicates things, Bea."

"I'm only connecting the dots you've given me based on my understanding of theology. Certainly there would be no murder if Christians followed the teaching of the religion. We both know that isn't the case. I'm just saying that it's a big leap from decapitating a statue to murdering a teenager."

It wasn't what J.D. had expected to hear.

"Thanks, Bea."

"I wasn't much help."

"Maybe more than you know."

CHAPTER EIGHTEEN

The last vestiges of morning fog were burning away in the shallow fields that lined the old blacktop county road. Cotton had made a return to the pine barrens, as well as soybeans and peanuts. Dixon had chosen a back-road route rather than four-laned Highway 98, the most convenient corridor to Mobile. Her mother's phone call had stolen any chance of sleep, and she needed the drive to put physical distance between herself and Jexville. Between herself and the swamp where Trisha Webster had surely died a horrible death. And where Angie Salter might yet be suffering.

In avoiding the murder, though, she found herself trapped in the past. As she drove past a dairy farm, she remembered her father's large hand holding her small one as they had toured a dairy. She'd been four or five, but Ray had taken time to expose her to the world. He wanted her to know where the milk she drank came from and to understand the balance of agriculture in a world where family farms were already verging on extinction. He had been shaping and molding her sensibilities in the guise of a field trip.

Not once since their father's death had her brother, Raymond, spoken of what had happened. He'd attended the trial, sitting poker stiff in the row behind the prosecution. Each day, he'd fled the courtroom, refusing to talk to anyone, even her. Once the trial was over, Raymond would not acknowledge that his father had been murdered. If he mentioned Ray's name at all, it was linked to a family memory.

Now, with the execution looming, he refused to talk about Willard Jones. On the few occasions when Dixon brought the subject up, Raymond had simply hung up the phone. Not in anger, but with finality.

Dixon contemplated a fencerow sagging under the weight of kudzu, leaves silvered with morning mist. Since moving to Jexville, there had been times when she felt that if she stood still too long the vines would slip up and cover her.

She reached the outskirts of Mobile and headed to the shopping center where the red block of Circuit City appeared to plug into the empty parking lot. While she waited for the store to open, she examined the sales slip she'd picked up in the woods, feeling a twinge of guilt that she hadn't shared her find with J.D. yet.

It wasn't much of a lead and she was no detective, but the receipt's crispness meant that someone had dropped it in the woods around the time the girls were on the sandbar. A witness. Or the killer.

She got out of her truck as a red-jacketed clerk unlocked the front door and was the first one inside. In a matter of fifteen minutes, she had the information she sought. She felt as if a weight pressed on her chest as she walked to the parking lot and got in her truck.

Tommy Hayes had purchased a boom box at 8:47 on the evening of September eighteenth. The girls had disappeared on the nineteenth. Dixon had found the sales slip, crisp and clean, in the woods on the morning of the twentieth.

✝

By the time J.D. reached New Orleans, it was almost ten o'clock. He parked in the airport lot, went directly to the ticket counter for Southwest Airlines, and booked a flight for San Antonio. His law enforcement identification and lack of baggage eased his way through airport security, and he was on the plane and in the air in less than an hour. He paid for the spur-of-the-moment trip out of his own pocket and brought little with him except identification and the articles he'd printed off the Internet.

Alan Arguillo had created the sculpture of Mary that had been destroyed at St. John the Baptist Catholic Church in Jexville. Arguillo and Francisco Chavez were both from Zaragoza in the state of Coahuila. It was a long shot, but J.D. could not sit around waiting for Dr. Diaz to return or Angie Salter to be found.

In San Antonio, he rented an Explorer and drove to Eagle Pass. From there he crossed into Mexico and Piedras Negras, a border town filled with vendors, restaurants, and music. Once out of town, he bumped over the rutted dirt road to Zaragoza.

In the marines, he'd spent some R and R time in Mexico and knew there were places of lush beauty. Zaragoza was not one of them. The town consisted of seven thousand people on land not suited for agriculture and an unpaved main street that sloped gently down to a central business district where farmers and craftsmen sold their wares.

He found the police department two blocks off the main drag, parked, and went inside. He didn't expect help, but he didn't want to rile anyone either. If a strange law enforcement officer arrived in Jexville, he would expect a courtesy visit.

The police station was unair-conditioned and hot. Three officers in uniform sat behind desks and seemed glad of a diversion. Miguel Sanchez was the man in charge, and he waved J.D. into a chair with a smile as they exchanged introductions.

"What brings you to Zaragoza?" Sanchez asked.

J.D.'s relief at Sanchez's fluent English must have shown on his face.

"I was educated in San Antonio. I came home to help my family," Sanchez said

"I'm looking for an artist. Alan Arguillo."

"Many people seek out this man. His work excites the imagination."

Sanchez showed some finesse, J.D. thought. "Yes," he said. "We have a sculpture in my town."

"And you want to buy another?"

J.D. hesitated. It was one thing to come to a small town seeking an artist. It was another to look into the past of a man who might be a killer.

"No," he said. "I'm actually looking for a man named Francisco Chavez. The artist may know something about him."

"And you suspect the police don't?"

"Do you?"

"The name Chavez is an old one in this village. One that brings many questions. Has Francisco done something wrong?"

J.D. noted Sanchez's use of Chavez's first name.

"I'm not certain."

"You're here, all the way from Mississippi. You must be fairly certain."

J.D. could read nothing in Sanchez's dark eyes. "We have a murdered teenage girl and one missing. Arguillo's statue of the Virgin Mary was decapitated and splashed with cow's blood before the two girls disappeared. Chavez was arrested in Eagle Pass for breaking windows in a Catholic church. The level of coincidence is a little too high for me to ignore."

Sanchez leaned back in his chair. "Francisco left here about eight months ago, after vandals struck at three of our churches."

J.D. felt his pulse increase. "Did Chavez commit the acts of vandalism?"

"We don't know. We found prints, but his were never on record here. He was always a quiet kid, a few years younger than me. I knew him in school, and I would have sworn that he would never make trouble for anyone, especially not the church. He was there every afternoon. He followed Father around like his shadow."

J.D. remembered his conversation with Beatrice Smart. The person who killed, hung, and burned Trisha Webster had a very real relationship with God and Satan. "Chavez was a religious child?"

"Excessively. In the first years of school, he told the teachers he would become a priest. I think he was trying to make up for his mother's shame."

"Shame?"

"After Francisco was born—he was illegitimate—Maria Chavez gave up all attempts to live a decent life. *La punta*. She serviced the soldiers. The boy saw all of it. He was taunted in school."

"Is his mother still alive?"

Sanchez considered the question. "She wouldn't talk to you. She speaks no English. It would be a waste of your time, and she is very sick now. She has the blood illness."

"She has hepatitis?"

Sanchez shook his head. "It is AIDS."

"Do you believe Francisco destroyed the church property?"

"The only windows broken were those depicting Mary. I had heard from the priest that Francisco had cursed the Blessed Virgin." He shrugged. "If I could match the prints, I would know for sure, wouldn't I?"

"Maybe I can arrange that when I get home," J.D. said. How about a map of where Mr. Arguillo lives?"

"That I can help you with." Sanchez drew a sheet of paper and a pen from his desk drawer and sketched a quick map. "You will enjoy your talk with Alan. He is an interesting man. Especially interesting since he regained his sight."

"So that really happened?"

"Indeed. I know this for a fact. He was blind. He worked by feel on the statue. He was obsessed with the work. The moment he struck the last blow of the chisel, his sight returned."

"Was he born blind?"

"No. He could see perfectly until about three years ago when he fell and struck his head on a stone. He was instantly blind."

"No one ever considered that the nerves to his eyes might have regenerated?" J.D. was skeptical of miracles.

"At the exact moment he finished this statue of the Blessed Mother? The exact moment?" Sanchez smiled. "It is easier to believe in a miracle than such a coincidence. But let Alan tell you. He will make you understand."

J.D. left the police station. Dust boiled out behind the wheels of his rented SUV. He drove with the windows down, the sun baking his left arm. Lethargy crept over him, and the thought of a roadside nap was tempting. But he didn't have time. Angie Salter didn't have time.

J.D. wondered at the killer's murdering Trisha first. Had it been because she cried? Because she didn't fight back? Because she wasn't willing? Those questions gave him hope. Angie was tough. She was a manipulator, and she was a fighter. She would do whatever was necessary to stay alive.

He passed a cluster of trees he didn't recognize, and the land rose. From the crest of the small hill, he saw the Arguillo ranch in the distance. The fields were irrigated. Nothing else could explain the green amidst the parched brown of the landscape. The house was adobe style, part of it so old it was packed and dried mud. Flowers bloomed all over the yard.

He knocked at the door and waited, wondering if the household was asleep in the midday heat. He heard footsteps and stepped back a little.

"*Señor?*"

The woman was striking. One single strand of gray ran from her right temple; the rest of her hair was luxurious black. Her dark eyes were bright with curiosity.

"*Señor?*" she asked again.

"I've come to speak with Alan Arguillo," J.D. said, holding out his badge and identification. "I'm from Jexville, Mississippi."

"Ah, the statue," she said in English laced with a Spanish accent. "It was a miracle, that statue."

"There is a young girl missing in my town," J.D. said. "Another girl is dead."

She frowned. "Why do you come here? What can we do to help something so far away?"

"Talk to me."

She shrugged. "My husband is not well. Do we need him?"

"If he isn't too tired, I'd greatly appreciate his help."

"Come in," she said, stepping back and leaving him to follow her as she walked through the dim, cool recesses of the house. She stopped at a closed door and knocked.

"Alan, there's a law officer here to see you. He's from the States."

"Come in." The voice was deep and rich.

J.D. stepped around the woman after she opened the door and withdrew into the hallway.

"Don't tire him," she whispered before she walked away. "I will prepare some refreshments. Some wine and cheese."

J.D. stepped into a room furnished in southwestern colors, a man's room with a tooled leather saddle on a rack, the bridle with silver workings hanging beside it.

"A lawman from the States?" Arguillo said as he came forward and extended his hand. "How can I help you?"

J.D. shook hands, feeling the strength in the sculptor's fingers. He was an old man, in his seventies if his face didn't lie, but he was virile and strong. "*Señor* Arguillo, do you know a man named Francisco Chavez?"

Friendliness dropped out of the wrinkles around the man's mouth. "I have nothing to do with Chavez."

"I'm sorry to bring up a topic that upsets you, but this is a matter of life and death. A girl is already dead. Another is missing. You may be able to tell me something."

"Chavez is a devil." Arguillo's sea blue eyes didn't blink.

"Tell me about him."

Arguillo walked to a grouping of chairs. "Please, sit." He took a seat and waited for J.D. to take one. "Francisco worked for me for a year. He wanted to learn to sculpt wood. Not stone but wood. I taught him every day. He was an apt student."

When Arguillo didn't go on, J.D. spoke. "Surely that isn't the end of the story."

"One day I heard Selmacita screaming. It was after I lost my vision. Francisco was gone, but he had destroyed all of his creations. He burned them, and then he ran away. He had talent and ability, but he is not a creator. He is a force of destruction. He is filled with *el Diablo*."

"Did you know him well?"

"I knew enough. His mother became a whore. She had little choice. She became pregnant with Francisco, and she would not tell the name of his father. Her family cast her out. She had no way to make a living." The sunlight coming through the window deepened the lines of the old man's wrinkles. "The life of a single mother is not easy, especially in a town where religion is the ruling force. Maria was a remarkable girl. She posed for me once, for a painting. She had a luminous quality, like a saint. It was very hard for her, and one reason I took on Francisco was for her sake. She was ashamed." He fell silent and sat in the sun. "I am an old man now. I should have done more. We all should have."

"What more could you have done?"

"Hired Maria to work here, given her employment so that she didn't have to sell herself. Her shame marks us all, because no one lifted a finger to help."

"Why do you suppose that was?"

He chuckled, a sound of remorse. "God made her too beautiful. She was a threat to the women and a temptation to the men. When her family turned her out, no one else would help her. She was cursed by her beauty."

The door opened and Selmacita entered with a tray. She assessed her husband and then J.D.

"Some wine and cheese," she said. "Refreshments, but no more serious conversation. My husband is tired."

CHAPTER NINETEEN

Eustace sat in the boat and waited, his eyes hooded. Across the sandbar, the woods were a dense blur of foliage. The past, or the future, could be hidden in the there. It was a place of secrets.

He'd chosen the boat for speed. If he saw the Mexican, he was going to kill him and then do his best to get away before he was discovered. He'd weighed it out. Killing the man would destroy the last hope of finding the Salter girl. Letting him live and be captured could end up costing Camille her freedom.

Eustace replayed the Tuesday morning when he'd seen the two girls on the sandbar. They'd been drinking, and one of them, the blonde, was looking for trouble. He saw her young, firm body and the way the sand stuck to her thighs and glistened in the sun. He could still hear her taunts. She was not worth the tip of Camille's little finger.

The sound of a boat motor sputtered in the distance, and he sat up and turned his head to hear better. It was large, not just a tin-boat fisherman. Something serious. It was time to go. He didn't want to be seen anywhere near the place he'd trap the Mexican.

Eustace used the paddle to move the skiff around the sandbar, out into the river. He slapped angrily at a mosquito on his neck. As the speedboat cleared the curve, he recognized Corley Mizelle, but he didn't know the tall, dark-haired stranger who stood like the captain of a man-of-war.

The two men exchanged some words, then Mizelle headed toward Eustace at a clip that wasn't safe.

"Hold up, Eustace," Mizelle said, swinging the boat just before they collided. Eustace's skiff bobbed in the speedboat's wake.

Eustace ignored Mizelle and asked the man, "Is there something I can do for you?"

"My name is Robert Medino. I'm looking for Eustace Mills."

"You've found him," Eustace said, aware that Mizelle, never one to keep his mouth shut, was silent.

"I want to hire you to guide me into the swamps," Medino said. "I believe the man who killed those young girls is still in the swamp, and I think, with your help, we can find him and bring him to justice. We might even save the second girl."

"You think we can accomplish what the sheriff can't?" Eustace was irritated at the man's arrogance.

"The sheriff is bound by his lack of imagination. I'm not. I hear you know this swamp better than anyone else around these parts."

"What's the pay?"

"Five hundred a day."

It was a lot of money. More than he'd earned since the market for moonshine had dried up. "I'll think about it."

"Where can I reach you?" Medino asked.

"I'll be in touch with you." Eustace pushed clear of the speedboat and headed downriver toward the bridge. Employment by Robert Medino might be the perfect cover for finding the Mexican.

✝

Dixon waited in her truck outside the courthouse. J.D.'s patrol car wasn't at the sheriff's office; it was parked at his house on Ratliff Street. His Explorer was gone. She'd called his office four times, but Waymon was either dumb as a post or a superb actor. He had no clue where J.D. might be.

The truck's air conditioner began dripping condensation, and Dixon put the truck in gear and slowly drove away. She wanted to talk to J.D. Tommy Hayes had lied—about buying a boom box for Angie Salter and about being in the woods on the day the girls disappeared. She'd verified that he was in Gulfport that afternoon, but it hadn't occurred to her to check on his whereabouts that morning. Hayes, for all his fresh-faced innocent look, was slick.

She knew better than to try and get information from the high-school office, so she sent Tucker to talk to students. He would find out a lot more, and faster than she could. Besides, there was something else Dixon needed to do, something she'd put off.

She picked up the thin phone book and looked up Jones. There were only three dozen names, and she began calling, asking for Willard. She was on the eighteenth name, Olena Jones, when the young woman who answered asked, "What do you want with Willard?"

Dixon noted the address in a small community north of Jexville, close to the river. "I want to be certain that he's guilty of killing my father," she said.

There was a sharp intake of breath. "Willard is my brother. His son, Zander, is here for the summer. He said he was going to see you, but I thought it was just foolishness."

"I'd like to talk with him."

She considered this. "Zander doesn't feel kindly toward you or your family."

"I could say that I had a lot more reason to be angry than Zander. My father has been dead a long time. His is still alive."

"And in prison. Zander hardly knows him." Her voice was gentle, sad. "He thinks he knows his father, based on a few visits and some letters. To be truthful, I don't know Willard well myself, but the little I do know runs counter to his being a murderer."

"My father was a good man." Dixon felt the tears threaten to close her throat. "He didn't deserve to die like that."

"I have no words to comfort you," Olena said. "Zander has ridden his bicycle into town. When he returns, I'll tell him you called."

"It's six miles to town from Vesley."

"I know. He rides it often. He rides by the newspaper and looks at you. I think he's trying to decide if you're the saint who will save his father or the devil who will execute him."

"It's out of my hands."

"Zander doesn't understand that. He's sixteen."

He would have been five when his father was sent to Parchman.

"Would you ask him to call me?"

"I will, but I don't make any promises."

"Thank you—"

"Wait. Would you answer a question for me?"

Dixon knew what she would ask. "I don't know if Willard Jones is guilty or not. I have doubts."

"Who else would profit from your father's death?"

Dixon's hand grew clammy on the phone. "My father pissed a lot of people off. It was part of his job."

"Did you ever think one of those men might have killed your father?"

Dixon had thought of it, more than once. She'd gone back through some of the old issues of her father's newspaper, reading, making lists, taking down names. There were people who were glad Ray Sinclair was dead, but would they have killed him? It was possible.

"I haven't stopped looking," Dixon admitted.

"Look fast, Ms. Sinclair. Willard only has nineteen days left. I'll tell Zander you called."

CHAPTER TWENTY

Heat devils undulated on the hood of the white Explorer. J.D. sat in the broiling interior, waiting. Sweat had saturated his clothes, even running down his legs into his shoes. He sat motionless, left arm out the open window, his gaze on the church. A lone dog, weathered as a cedar fence post, trotted across the dusty street and disappeared behind a vintage truck. The Church of the Immaculate Conception was a modest adobe building as old-looking as the land around it. J.D. had come to an appreciation of age in Zaragoza. Everyone, and almost everything, from the dog in the street to the donkey tied in front of a vendor's stall, seemed ancient. He'd begun to feel the dust of age settling into his bones.

A heavyset woman, a black mantilla covering her face, hurried out of the church. She faltered once, as if she couldn't see well, then disappeared around a corner. J.D. got out of the Explorer and walked into the church. The woman had been the last of the penitents, if he'd calculated correctly. The church was a busy place, frequented mostly by women who came and went, their faces covered by lacy cloth or masked in pain and worry. They didn't stay long, but when they came out, most seemed lighter, relieved.

Religion had never been of much use to J.D., but he understood the value of dropping a heavy burden. If only he believed that responsibility and regret could be dropped, he would be in the church seven days a week. Any church. He thought of the makeshift altar in the woods. Religion, like anything else, could be a dangerous thing. When belief became twisted, it was dangerous. The Spanish Inquisition. The Salem witch trials. The list was endless, and economic gain was usually behind all of it. How would a person gain economically from the murder of Trisha Webster? Or Angie Salter? Of course, a serial killer wouldn't care about money. His gain was more visceral.

The church was dark and cool. J.D.'s perspiration-soaked shirt chilled his back. It took a moment for his vision to adjust. The church lacked the ornate décor of the wealthy American churches. Money. There it was again. He surveyed the stand of candles. Several dozen were burning, and the smell of the hot wax was close. If the priest was present, he was in the confessional booth. J.D. walked forward and hesitated. He tapped the confessional booth's door.

"Father?"

"*Como está?*"

"I don't speak Spanish, Father."

"I speak a little English."

The priest sounded young, more savvy than J.D. had anticipated. He'd expected an old priest, stooped by time and troubles, wearing a black cassock—a stock character.

"I need your help," J.D. said.

The confessional door opened and a thin, very young man stepped out. "I am Father Joseph."

J.D. offered his hand. "I was hoping to talk to the old priest." There had to be an old priest. Father Joseph was still wet behind the ears.

"Father Diego is not here. Perhaps I can be of service."

He saw the earnest desire to help on the young father's face. "It's about a man named Chavez. Francisco Chavez."

The priest's eyes reflected worry. "What has Francisco done now?"

"I'm not certain. He may have murdered a girl and kidnapped another. In Mississippi. One girl may still be alive." He felt the pressure of time in a place where it seemed time had no relevance. "I might still be able to save one."

Father Joseph looked down at the floor. "And what is it you think I can do?"

"Tell me about Chavez. Help me figure him out."

Father Joseph moved through the sanctuary to a partially hidden door. He stepped through it and waved to J.D. to follow. Their footsteps echoed on the stone floor of the narrow hall. The priest pushed open a heavy door and held it for J.D. They entered a small kitchen filled with dark wood and copper pots.

"I will make *café con leche*," Father Joseph said. "You tell me why you think a man from Zaragoza would go all the way to Mississippi to kill two girls."

While the priest made and served the coffee, J.D. told him about the defacing of statues along the I-10 corridor. He concluded with the destruction of Arguillo's statue in Jexville, and finally, the hanging and burning of Trisha Webster.

"You say the body was first buried, then dug up, hung, and burned?" The priest didn't try to hide his distress.

"Yes. Does that mean something to you?"

Father Joseph pushed his coffee cup back from the edge of the table. "This is a terrible story. I know Francisco. He is a little older than I. In all of the years of school, he never hurt anyone, only himself."

"Deputy Sanchez said almost the same thing."

"Francisco was poorly treated by Father Diego. He was often cruel." He shook his head. "I never understood. There are many bastard children born here. Father Diego singled out Francisco for torment and abuse."

"And no one stopped it?"

"The church rules the lives of the people. There is so little to look forward to here. Heaven is the only solace." He frowned. "Like any other dictator, the church can be benevolent or cruel. Father Diego was cruel, at least where Francisco was concerned. He seemed to take pleasure in pointing out that Francisco was a bastard. He whipped him for the most minor offenses. Even worse, he told the boy repeatedly that he was damned."

"That might explain the defacing of church property, but only statues or images of the Virgin Mary have been destroyed."

Father Joseph started to speak, then hesitated. "I often wondered who Francisco's father might be. Maria, his mother, was devout. She was at the church for mass every day, sometimes more than once. Throughout all of my years of school, there were whispers about Francisco's father, speculation. I remember talk that Maria had no living lover, that Francisco was the son of God. One of my parishioners told me that Maria made this claim when she first became pregnant. She boasted of it, which was why her family turned away from her."

"And instead of getting mental help for her they left her to fend for herself and her baby?"

"To my knowledge, Maria never looked at any men. In many ways, she was as much a bride of Christ as the sisters."

"Except for the fact that she had a child. Someone fathered that boy." J.D. thought about Sanchez's words. "I heard Maria Chavez was *una punta*."

Father Joseph looked suprised. "Really? She was here at the church all the time. She scrubbed and cleaned the church and Father Diego's quarters. Her living was minimal, but she managed. She was an attractive woman. There were many men who would have married her even with the bastard child. If she'd sold herself, she would have been very wealthy."

J.D. considered. "Father Diego is Francisco's father, isn't he?"

"It would explain a lot," Father Joseph said.

"Yes, it would."

"I have no proof. Father Diego is in Mexico City. I can give you the address there."

J.D. shook his head. "I can't take the time. I have to get back. If that girl is still alive, I have to find her. If Chavez does have her, and if he is punishing women because of his mother's sins, I have to find her now."

"I can tell you one other thing." Father Joseph loosened his collar with his fingers. "There is a tradition in this land of hanging and burning the effigy of the oppressor. It stems back to the betrayal of Jesus Christ by Judas Iscariot. After Jesus was crucified, Judas, in a fit of remorse, hanged himself. He wasn't found for several days, and the intestines had filled with gas and ruptured."

"This is a version I didn't hear in the Baptist church," J.D. said.

Father Joseph's smile was ironic. "The Catholic church is steeped in blood and suffering, but there is a point to this story. In the old days, the poor citizens made effigies of the rich. They would hang the effigies on a long pole and parade through the streets with them. When the mob of poor arrived in front of the homes of the wealthy, they would gut the effigy and then set fire to it, crying out for justice. These events were called Judas burnings. The people felt betrayed by the rich, just as Jesus was betrayed by Judas Iscariot."

J.D. thought of Trisha Webster, gutted and burned. "Is the Judas burning a Catholic rite?"

"No, but it stems from Catholic beliefs. Francisco was a student of Catholicism. He studied every day after school with Father Diego. I never understood why he came, each day, for such abuse. Now, perhaps I understand a little better. He hoped each day that he might, just once, please his father."

J.D. stood. "Thank you, Father."

The priest rose. "The rich had the final word on the Judas burnings. They began to create the effigies themselves, making them comic and stuffing them with sweets and coins. They would dangle them over their high walls to the angry crowds, who would swat at them with sticks. When the effigy was struck hard enough, it would burst and the money and sweets would fall to the street."

"The *piñata*," J.D. said.

"Exactly. The genesis of the *piñata* is revolt. I would look to the genesis of the abduction of these girls. I can tell you that

Francisco was not a man who would harm even an insect. He may have changed, but I don't think so."

"I don't believe anyone else in Chickasaw County would understand what a Judas burning is."

"Maybe not, but I don't believe Francisco hurt those girls."

"Someone did more than hurt Trisha Webster. A lot more than hurt."

"Will you call me when you find Francisco?"

"Yes."

"I will come as his advocate."

"If he's involved in this, he's going to need one."

J.D. walked across the wooden floor of the old kitchen. A door led out into a garden where ancient bushes bloomed the dying roses of summer. The scent was heady. In the shade of an arbor, he saw a statue. Mary, mother of Jesus. He walked to it and stared at the ancient stone, pitted by the elements of nature. He could see the suffering and the calm the sculptor had captured. She held her hands raised, as if in blessing. J.D. stared at her, wondering what it was about this woman that might incite a young man to murder.

He walked to the garden gate and stepped into the street. The sun was beginning to fall from the afternoon sky. Soon, the relentless heat would let up a little, at least for the night, but there was a sense that in Zaragoza nothing changed much. Tomorrow would be the same as today.

J.D. opened the door of the SUV and climbed behind the wheel. The dog was back in the street, retracing its steps. He watched until it disappeared behind the church and hoped that someone there would have the kindness to feed it. He pulled into the street, images of effigies and fire vivid in his mind.

The Chavez house was half a mile from the church, and he pulled up into a dirt yard that spoke of poverty and neglect. No one answered his knock, but the door was cracked open. The instant he stepped inside, he smelled the illness. Hospital wards, insane asylums, prisons—each had a distinctive odor that lodged in the back of his nasal passages, close to his throat. This was the odor of death.

Maria Chavez was on a sofa, covered with a quilt despite the room's stifling heat. Beside her was an empty glass and a book. She struggled to a sitting position, panting from the exertion. A shaft of sunlight fell across her face, and the sight made him want to weep. Her fine, dark eyes were large and intelligent.

"Francisco," he said softly.

"Gone," she answered in English.

"Can you help me find him?"

"Why?" she asked.

"To save a young girl's life."

She inhaled slowly. "I don't know where he is." She looked down at the empty glass.

J.D. picked it up and went to the kitchen. He filled the glass from a pitcher of water on the table. When he returned, she was watching him.

"I'll take you to the hospital. They have drugs . . ."

She shook her head. "I'm ready to die. I've betrayed my son, and now he is gone." She sipped the water. "I pray for death."

"Ms. Chavez, your son may have kidnapped a teenage girl. I want to find her." He didn't trouble the sick woman with the details of what Francisco might have done to Trisha Webster.

"Francisco did not harm anyone." She spoke softly but with emphasis. "He burns with hatred for the church, but he would not harm any living creature."

"How can you be sure?" J.D. asked.

She drew in a long breath. "When he was a small child, I told him that God was his father. When he finally learned that the man who beat him daily was his father, he realized the full measure of my lies and betrayal." She swallowed and reached for the glass. "He will try to destroy the church, but he will harm no one." She met J.D.'s gaze. "If my son has this girl, then it is because he is trying to help her."

She began to cough, sank back into the sofa, and waved him weakly out of the house. Like the statue in the churchyard, she was a ruin. This was an illness that knew no gentleness. Even so, the shadow of her beauty was haunting.

He got behind the wheel of the SUV. If he drove very fast, he could make the eight o'clock flight back to New Orleans.

✝

The small skiff rocked beneath Eustace's weight. He'd made sure that the other boats were chained to cypress stumps. He could no longer trust Camille to stay off the river, away from the place where the girls had been taken and one killed.

Camille had been acting strangely. Earlier in the day, she'd read the tarot cards, and they'd sent her to bed shivering. Eustace had lifted the cloth that Camille had laid over the cards. The first one he turned over was Justice, a stern woman

186

with an uplifted sword. His heart was pounding, and he could look no further. He'd replaced the card, covered the deck, crawled in beside Camille, and fallen asleep holding her.

In her sleep, she'd moaned and cried. Over and over again she'd begged for someone's life to be spared. When he'd gently shaken her awake, she'd clung to him as if her life depended on it, and she'd wept so bitterly that he felt his heart breaking away in chunks.

So he had come to the river to do what must be done.

He pushed the skiff away from the bank with the paddle and guided it, with a few powerful strokes, into the current. Once away from the cabin, where Camille still slept, he started the motor and turned the boat upstream. Though it had been three days since he'd run his trot lines, he was not going fishing. He was going to Hathaway's Point. Law enforcement officials had combed the area looking for traces of the Mexican. Eustace was going to look for evidence that Camille had been there.

✝

Dixon was walking up the courthouse steps for a final try at finding J.D. when her cell phone rang. Few people had the number; she answered it immediately.

"Ms. Sinclair?" The voice was soft, tentative.

"Zander." There was no point beating around the bush. The young man had been following her for weeks now. Either he would talk or not.

"My auntie said you called."

She kept her voice level. He had no right to expect anything of her. Willard Jones was in prison for murdering her father. "That's right. When can we meet?"

"Why do you want to talk to me?"

"I thought it was you who wanted to talk to me. If you don't want to talk, stop following me and calling me. Stay off my property. If you continue to harass me, I'll have the law pick you—"

"Wait. I have something to say."

"Meet me at the newspaper at eight tomorrow morning."

"Not the paper. I don't want to go there."

"Where then?"

"Can we meet at your house?"

The boy's voice was so soft she wasn't certain he'd spoken. "You want to meet at my house?"

"If that would be okay with you. We could talk without other people hearing us."

Meeting the son of the man convicted of her father's murder, alone, on a secluded lane, wouldn't be the smartest thing she'd ever done. But in her bones, she knew that Willard Jones was innocent. She knew because she bore the guilt for her father's death. She'd been late. She'd been in bed with a married man, Mark Barrett. Now Senator Mark Barrett. Her father had waited at the newspaper for her. If she'd been on time, her father would have been out of the building and safe when the bomb went off.

"Okay," she said. "Seven o'clock. I have to be at work at eight."

"I'll be there."

The line went dead, and Dixon turned the phone off. She sat down on the steps and thought about what she'd agreed to. Zander was a strong boy, almost a man. He spoke softly, but what did that guarantee? He'd already trespassed once on her property, and he'd been following her, stalking her.

She stood up and went into the courthouse. It might not be such a bad idea to tell J.D. a little about her plan, if he ever got back to his office.

The courthouse was closed, but the door to the sheriff's office was always open. She went inside and walked down the short corridor to the metal-and-glass door. She tapped and entered.

Waymon sat at his desk, feet propped up and a magazine covering his face. He dropped his feet to the ground and quickly tucked the magazine into a drawer, but not before she saw the September bunny on the front cover. She liked the fact that Waymon's face turned a bright red.

"Waymon, I like your taste in reading material." Waymon sometimes liked to play it close to the vest, but she had ammunition now.

"The sheriff ain't back," he said.

"Have you heard from him?"

"He's in San Antonio. He says he's got an eight o'clock flight back home. He told me to get the dog handler from up at Parchman back down here to start another hunt."

Dixon felt a rush of anticipation. "Sounds like he found out something." She frowned. "What's in San Antonio?"

"The Alamo, for one thing." Waymon nodded. "I had this thing for Davy Crockett when I was a kid. He died at the Alamo. I know just about every fact you ever would want to know about the Alamo."

Dixon started to point out that the Alamo probably held few clues to the disappearance of two Mississippi girls, but she bit it back. Waymon was trying to be helpful, and there would come a time when she would need his help.

"Maybe we could talk about the Alamo later. If J.D. gets the eight o'clock flight home, he should be in around midnight, right?" She needed to talk to him about Tommy Hayes and Zander Jones.

"More like about two. He has a layover in Dallas. He left his Explorer at the airport, so he doesn't need anyone to get him."

"That's good," Dixon said. She wandered around the office, staring at the coffeepot that looked as if it hadn't been cleaned in the last five years. "Mind if I help myself?"

"I should have offered," Waymon said. He pulled open his desk drawer. "Ruth Ann made some sugar cookies. She brings something good up here all the time." He frowned. "If I didn't know better I'd think she was trying to court me or something." He flushed slightly and busied himself bringing out the cookies and floral napkins. "I put 'em in my drawer because the dispatcher is diabetic and shouldn't eat them. If she sees 'em, she can't resist."

There was a certain charm to Waymon, Dixon conceded as she took her Styrofoam coffee cup and sat down. "No thanks on the cookies, but you could help me with a little background on Tommy Hayes."

Waymon's smile faded. "Why are you interested in Tommy?"

"I think 'interested' is too strong a word. I tried to talk to him several times, and he wouldn't call me back. That intrigues me."

"Maybe he just didn't want to be in the paper. Some folks don't like it. I mean, J.D. hates the medi—" He grimaced. "I didn't mean it like it sounds."

Dixon nodded and smiled. "I understand. And you're probably right about Tommy Hayes. All I wanted to ask him was what kind of student Angie Salter is. You know, if she had expressed any special interests to him." She felt a little bad, pumping Waymon, but not bad enough to stop.

"When we talked to him, he said that Angie had problems. He said he worried something like this would happen to her."

Dixon schooled her face not to show her reaction. "Isn't that tragic. So he was worried that something like getting kidnapped would happen to her?"

"No," Waymon said, rolling his eyes, "something like being at the wrong place at the wrong time."

"I see." She sipped the coffee and thought she might have to spit it out. Not only was it old, it was burned, bitter, and strong. "Do you know Tommy?"

"Some. We both go to the Methodist Church, only I go more regular than he does. He sure seems young to be a teacher, but he was top of his class, from what I heard. He's up at the church a good bit. I think he takes a lot of comfort from Reverend Smart."

Dixon rose and stretched, putting her coffee on the edge of Waymon's desk. "Would you leave J.D. a note and ask him to call me? Doesn't matter what time it is."

"You sure? Could be three or four in the morning before he gets up here."

"That's fine," Dixon said. "I'm often awake then."

CHAPTER TWENTY-ONE

Dixon sat on her front steps with a glass of iced tea and listened to the thrum of the crickets, interspersed with a low bullfrog cadence. It was a sound from childhood. This was the time, on hot summer nights, when her family had gathered for a late supper. She'd loved those evenings, when her mother lit citronella candles on the back porch and they shared a meal as night crept over them. Her father had been there, and she'd felt safe.

The blue hour was passing, and full night was falling in the east. Dixon caught the scent of grape Kool-aid on the breeze. The kudzu, with its blossoms so intensely purple scented with grape, had bloomed early.

Her heart twisted as she remembered childhood evenings when she'd sat in the swing with her father and made wishes on the evening's first star, wishes he'd promised would come true.

". . . wish I may, wish I might, have the wish I wish tonight." She paused. "To find the truth about my father's murder." She spoke the words and stared up at the sky until two other stars blinked into life.

The hoot of an owl drew her focus to the woods. A man stood there, a black silhouette against the darkening sky. She let out her breath when he drew on a cigarette and she realized it was Robert.

"It's a good thing I don't have a gun, or you'd be dead," she said, meaning it. "I don't know how folks act in the big city, but around here they don't creep up on another person's property."

"I parked on the road," he said. "I wasn't going to interrupt if you had company. I thought the sheriff might be here." He walked closer, his cigarette smoke sharp on the soft summer air, and stopped ten feet away. "I heard you wishing."

Dixon rattled the ice in her glass. She wasn't certain what to make of him. He'd hung around town and didn't seem to be pressed by deadlines. Twice he'd stopped by the newspaper, but both times she'd been gone and Linda had not made him feel welcome. Now, here he was in her front yard, eavesdropping on her private wishes. It was annoying.

"The larder isn't any better stocked now than it was the other day."

"I didn't come over to eat. Obviously, you haven't checked your messages. There should be four calls from me. Mrs. Moore at the paper wouldn't tell me where you were, and the blond guy didn't have time to talk with me."

Her employees were protecting her. Linda didn't like the man, and Tucker didn't trust him. Since she hadn't checked her messages, she couldn't blame all of it on Medino.

"I had to go to Mobile and check some things out."

"Would it be a breach of southern manners to ask for a drink?" he asked, putting a foot on the first porch step.

Dixon thought of the Jack. She'd put it under the sink. Out of sight, out of mind.

"Sure," she said. She was going to have to learn to deny herself alcohol while others drank. The whole world wouldn't stop drinking just because she couldn't handle it. "Come on in."

She led the way down the hall and into the kitchen. He took a seat at the old wooden table. The cabinets, with their leaded glass panes, were painted white. The original butcher-block counters had been covered with dark red Corian, and the beaded lumber walls were painted to match. Dixon had added white curtains.

"My great-great-grandmother painted this table," Dixon said as she handed him a drink. She'd replenished her iced tea. "She was a troublemaker, according to the town of Jexville."

"You're pensive tonight," he commented. "What's on your mind?"

She waved a hand around her. "My mother's family has owned this house for better than eighty years. My mother used to come here when she was a little girl and swim in the creek out back." She looked at the amber drink he held in his hand. "My mother always said that I took after JoHanna McVay, the troublemaker. JoHanna wouldn't dance to a man's tune. Mama said that JoHanna liked to wear the pants. That's how she put it."

"And your mother wasn't like that?"

"No, my mother gave up her career to be a wife and mother, but I'm beginning to wonder if she doesn't regret that choice."

"I wouldn't have wanted to be a woman back then." Robert's smile was disarming. "In fact, no matter how men disclaim the rights of being a man, it's true. I wouldn't want to be a woman now. The white male has it made."

"I've never heard another man admit that."

"If they admitted it, they'd have to change the system, wouldn't they? All of this ballyhoo about equality and democracy and no glass ceiling."

"You're willing to say it."

"I'm not part of the system, and I have no economic interest at stake. I'm a fringe dweller. I live in New York, but I'm certainly not a New Yorker. I know more about Spanish culture than American. I like music that no one plays any more, and I can eat any cuisine except McDonald's. I speak four languages, two fluently. I can take the heat or endure the cold. I've perfected the art of cultural chameleon. Since I don't fit anywhere, I understand the status of 'less than.' "

"There's something I want to know about you. Why is this story about the statues and the girls so important to you? You've been in Jexville a while and don't seem to be in a hurry to leave."

"Maybe you should have a drink on this one," he suggested.

She swallowed. "No, I'll take my answer straight."

"This town is in a time warp. Folks here are naïve about evil. They expect to be safe, and it's that trust that makes them a target."

"And you think that's worthy of a story?"

"The Salter/Webster story has broader implications about the way religion has gone askew. I'm looking at how religion has made bombers out of antiabortionists and terrorists out of others. Here we have a guy so obsessed with religion that he's killed two girls in a small town where religion is like a car—everybody has one. That makes it very personal. It'll be a powerful story."

"I can see that." She could also see that with a certain slant, Jexville could look primitive and backwards. "How bad are you going to make us look?"

"I'm a journalist, and a damn good one. I spent six months in Guatemala talking to government officials, shooting the breeze, drinking with them. Ultimately, my goal was to implicate them in the genocide of the native Indian tribes. I did it. Did I feel badly that I had to act friendly to get the story? Hell no. Those guys weren't even human. They deserved everything they got. Were my tactics unfair? I didn't put a gun to their heads to make them brag about the mass executions they'd instituted. Do I feel sorry for them? Not one damn bit. And I refuse to feel sorry for the folks around here who'd close down a day care to exert power."

He finished his drink and got up to make himself another. She watched as he found a second glass and made a drink for her. He handed it to her and then took a breath. "The other reason I'm hanging around town is you."

"Me?" Dixon stared at him over the rim of the glass. Her mouth was watering. She could taste the smoky bite of the Jack, and she wanted it.

"You intrigue me. You gave up a big-time career to come run a weekly. Your dad ran a weekly. He's well known in journalism circles. Some of his stories are taught at universities."

Dixon felt the familiar tug of loss. "He had fire in the belly for a good story."

"And so you've come to prove that you do too."

The glass was sweating in her hand. The ice cubes floated and tinkled against it, a party sound. She took a sip. It was as wonderful as she remembered.

"Yes. That's exactly what I've come to do."

"Because of what happened to your father?"

"You know about that?"

He nodded. His gaze held hers. "It was tragic."

She thought how meaningless those words were. Tragic. Terrible. The word *loss* didn't need a modifier. "Then you probably know that I spent the last year or so pretty drunk."

He didn't say anything.

"This is the first drink I've had in almost six weeks." She sipped it again. "So tell me again why you're here in Jexville."

"I believe in what I do." Though his voice was quiet, there was passion in it.

"For just a moment there, you reminded me of my father." She sipped the bourbon and fought back emotion.

"I take it that's a compliment."

"Your story on Trisha and Angie won't be popular around here. This town takes its religion very seriously."

"If we wrote only what the folks wanted us to write, there'd be no reason for newspapers or magazines."

"My father used to say that, too."

"I couldn't help but hear the wish you made, about your father's murder. I'm sorry, Dixon. That's a terrible thing to live through. My older brother was struck by a hit-and-run driver. My mother never got over it." He reached across the table and touched her hand. "I guess I didn't either. I think about the things he taught me. Gary wanted to be a professional baseball player."

"How old were you?" It was such a relief to talk to someone who understood, someone who had been there. She finished her drink, got up, and made them another round.

"I was fourteen. Gary was my idol."

She didn't say anything. There were no words to help.

"For a long time I was furious. I stopped doing everything I used to do with Gary. By the time I realized that punishing myself wouldn't bring him back, it was too late to return to sports. So I became a writer."

"The professional outsider."

He nodded. "That's right. We become the watchers. It isn't our responsibility to act, just to document."

"There's a man on death row. Willard Jones. He's scheduled to be executed in less than a month." She swallowed. "I'm not certain he's guilty."

Robert stared at her. "If you're not certain . . ."

"I'm meeting with his son tomorrow. Zander wants to talk to me. I don't think he understands there's nothing I can do. Without evidence, the state will carry out the sentence."

"Does he have evidence?" Robert leaned forward and caught her hand. "Is there something I can help with?"

She shook her head. "No, but thank you. I'll speak with Zander, and then I'll make a decision. The evidence against Jones was pretty convincing. My family just wants me to let it all go. They want Jones executed, and then they want to move on with their lives. If only it were that simple."

Killing Willard Jones wasn't the end of the pain. It wouldn't be the end of anything, except a man's life.

"Why do you think Jones might be innocent?" Robert asked.

She hesitated. She'd told the prosecutor, but he'd told her to forget it. Her mother had told her to forget it, and her brother. But she couldn't.

"The night before my father was killed, he called me. He was excited about something he'd discovered, a story. I was to pick him up for lunch the next day so he could tell me all about it." She felt her temples tighten. "I was late picking him up. If I'd been there on time, Dad wouldn't have been there to be killed."

"You were his heir in the profession. It makes sense he'd want to share his story with you. Any idea what it was?"

Robert's face was eager. She'd wanted so much for someone to share this with, someone who would see the importance of it and help her follow through. After Jones was arrested and convicted, no one had wanted to hear any of this. No one.

"It was about dumping waste chemicals in Mississippi. My father believed that it was happening and that some state legislators had taken a payoff to allow the chemical companies to slip into the state and dump the stuff."

"Is it true?"

"Ask the folks around Eula Springs. The incidence of cancer there is six hundred percent higher than anywhere else."

Robert reached into his back pocket and drew out a map. "I have to carry this because I don't know the area. Where is Eula Springs? I've never heard of it."

Dixon put her hand on his. "It's north of Hattiesburg. Look, none of this was ever proven. I looked for signs of a dump site. I hired a private investigator, but he could never find anyone who knew anything about chemical waste. The police arrested Willard Jones on another charge, and when they searched his home they found hundreds of clippings from my father's newspaper. He'd written things on them, saying my father was a racist because of the coverage Dad did on a black politician."

"And when they found that, they also found materials to make the bomb."

"Yes." Dixon could hear her pulse thudding. "You see it, too, don't you?"

"Clearly."

"Willard Jones may have been set up."

"I'd say there's a strong chance."

He picked up her hand and held it. "Dixon, you said you were late picking up your father and that he'd be alive if you'd been on time." He shook his head when she started to speak. "Listen to me. It might just be possible that the bomb was intended to kill both of you."

"No—"

"Folks knew you and your dad were close. If he told anyone, it would be you, right?"

She nodded. "But—"

"Just hear me out. If there was a tap on your father's phone—and there easily could have been, especially if he was poking sticks at the big dogs in the legislature—they would have known he talked to you that night. They would have known he intended to tell you about everything that day at lunch." He tightened his grip on her hand. "The fact that someone made you late may be the thing that saved your life. Do you think you were detained deliberately?"

She knew her face showed the pain she felt. Mark Barrett. The man she'd been in love with. Could he have known about the bomb? Was he protecting her while her father was being killed?

Robert put his arms around her. "What's wrong?"

"Nothing."

The word was barely a whisper. Even with the passing of eleven years, it hurt like a fresh cut. She closed her eyes. "I'd like another drink, please."

He released her and went to the counter to make the drinks. When he put the glass in her hand, he touched her face, stroking her hair. "You're an intriguing woman. Maybe too smart for your own good."

She stood up, the drink in her hand. "Let's go to the bedroom."

✝

The symphony of night had settled around the cabin by the time Eustace returned from upriver. He'd learned too much at Hathaway's Point. He could still hear the buzz of bottle flies swarming the ground where the body had oozed.

His right hand held the tiller, but his left was clenched around something else, a shard of pottery he'd found embedded in the riverbank. The clay, a bluish green, could only be found closer to the coast. He knew, because he'd helped Camille extract it.

He went over the scene again and again, circling his boat in the river until long past his normal time to go home.

When he pulled up to the landing, he was surprised to find the grounds completely lit. He'd installed fairy lights around the trunks of the old oaks and landscape lights around the paths and minnow vats. Camille sat with her legs dangling in the large cement vat. Her pale yellow summer dress was pulled high on her thighs, and her long hair tumbled, unbrushed, down her back. She flinched and giggled softly as darting minnows nibbled at her toes. Eustace stopped and stared. Camille's hair was infused with the twinkling lights, and her soft laughter was as artless as a child's.

He shifted the weight off his bad leg. Camille's enjoyment of the water and the minnows was total. It was a rare moment when her past didn't haunt her, and he chose not to intrude. Camille's remarkable gift of not judging allowed him into her life. She'd asked nothing about his past, told nothing of her own. But Eustace knew he was not so free of judgment.

From her dreams, salted with tears, he had figured out some of her past. She had been badly hurt, emotionally damaged. He'd known it from the beginning but hadn't feared the extent of the damage until now. In her heart, she was a sweet and loving child. Anything else was a result of what had been done to her.

A fast boat passed on the river, and Eustace followed the sound of its motor for a moment. It was a big boat, probably Jimmy Vinter's. Headed to Fitler.

He heard Camille's sharp gasp and had started forward before he realized that she'd slid into the chest-high water. After the initial shock of cold, she cried out with pleasure.

Eustace walked to the vats. He'd urged Camille not to leave the area around the house unless she was going into Jexville. She didn't always obey him, and he wasn't certain that Jexville was safer than the swamps anyway, even with a killer on the loose. He never attempted to stop her visits to her family, though he would have preferred that she avoid Calvin and Vivian. They had nearly destroyed her. They were evil, careless people. They did not deserve even the lingering concern that she held for them. But he knew better than to interfere.

"Eustace!" She held out her arms. "Come in." She jumped and giggled. "The minnows are . . . devilish."

Eustace felt himself smile. Before Camille, there had been days when his expression had never changed. Even now the muscles sometimes reminded him of their long neglect.

"It's wonderful!" Camille insisted. "Perfect. Better than a shower."

Eustace sat on the wall, his feet on the ground. He leaned down to feel the icy water. "I might have a heart attack if I jumped in there," he said.

Camille waded toward him. "Okay, I'll get out."

"I was kidding," he said, starting to unbutton his shirt. She often took him literally. He bent to unlace his shoes.

Camille wiped a drop of water from her eye. "Where have you been? You didn't leave a note. Mama says she's going to sell the houseboat. She asked me to tell you."

He paused with three buttons undone. "Why tell me?"

"She said you'd know someone who wanted to buy it. She's tired of it. She says she only wants ten thousand for it. She just wants to be done with it."

Vivian was spoiled rotten. She'd bought the houseboat three years before at maximum price. Now she was practically giving it away. "What's the rush?"

"She said people were tearing it up when she wasn't there to see about it."

"I'll put the word out," he said, easing into the water.

He watched her, choosing his moment. "The man they're looking for is Francisco Chavez." He waited for her reaction.

Camille leaned against the wall. Her skin was translucent, almost blue. Beneath her sundress, her nipples were hard. "I don't think Francisco did anything wrong. He wouldn't hurt anyone."

Eustace's heart was leaden. She knew him. She called him by his first name. He gently lifted her head and stared into her green eyes.

"Camille, what do you know about this man? You have to tell me."

Her eyes dropped, and she tried to pull her chin to her chest. "I don't like the way you're looking at me."

"I have to know. If you're involved in the disappearance of those girls, it's serious." So serious he was willing to kill a man, even the other girl. "Tell me, Camille."

Camille put her arms around him; her flesh was cold. He held her tightly.

"Let's get out of the water."

"You hate Mother, don't you?"

He sighed. He'd never lied to Camille, and he didn't intend to start.

"Yes," he said. "I do. I hate both of them, for what they've done to you."

"They didn't win."

Oh, but at what cost, he wanted to ask. He closed his eyes against the tears that threatened. He hadn't cried in forty years, but Camille was so fragile.

"You went up there where they found that girl, didn't you?"

"Yes," he said. "Hathaway's Point. When was the last time you were there, Camille?"

"Not so long ago," she answered, turning away and wading to the other end of the vat. "I don't want to talk about it any more."

"There's going to be another hunt tomorrow."

Eustace waited.

"They won't find her." Camille hopped to the ledge, swung her legs over, and stood. She lifted her dress, revealing her nakedness beneath, and squeezed the water from the fabric. "Come on," she said. "I'm hungry."

He climbed out with less grace and followed her. When they were inside, she went to the kitchen. He lingered in the bedroom until he heard her banging pots. Easing out her dresser drawer, he felt for the bracelet. It was gone.

CHAPTER TWENTY-TWO

The leaves of the oak tree hung limp. Already hot and humid with hardly a breath of breeze, the day would only get worse. J.D. sat beneath the tree in his cruiser, his mind far ahead. He rasped a hand across the growth of beard and regretted that he hadn't gone home when he got back to Jexville. Instead he'd begun to put together the evidence. Now, sitting at the end of Dixon's driveway, he wished for a shower, shave, and fresh change of clothes. He also wished that Robert Medino's rental car weren't parked on the road in front of Dixon's house at five-thirty in the morning.

Waymon had left him a note saying Dixon had called repeatedly and been by the office more than once. She had a bee in her bonnet over something, and J.D. wanted to know what it was.

If he were honest with himself, though, he'd have to admit that he wanted to see her for other reasons. His physical reaction to her was perfectly normal; it was his emotional response that worried him. Dixon was a survivor, but she had not come through life unscathed. She was searching for something that would make her whole, and J.D. understood that. Women, or men for that matter, who'd never suffered or lost lived on a different plane. Dixon lived where he lived. He wanted to know more about her.

He almost drove away but instead got out of the cruiser and started down the tree-lined drive. "Fuck it," he said softly as he walked up on the porch and knocked on the front door.

To his surprise, Dixon, dressed in jeans and an unironed shirt, answered immediately. She waved him to silence, disappeared, and returned with two cups of coffee, both black. They walked into the shade of the big oaks.

"Where in the hell have you been?" she asked. There was more weariness than force in her words. "I tried all day yesterday to find you."

"Mexico."

She wore no make-up and her hair was unbrushed. The shadows beneath her eyes showed that she hadn't rested well. Was her sleep disturbed by bad dreams or Robert Medino? J.D. would have liked to ask her.

"Were you tracking Chavez?" she asked.

He nodded.

"I think the killer is right here in Chickasaw County," she told him. "He's right under our noses."

He admired that she didn't beat around the bush. "You got evidence?"

"Yes."

"Let's hear it." He sipped the coffee. It was good, not too strong or old.

J.D. felt the heat of anger as she started telling him about the sales slip. "You should have told me last week." He didn't bother to hide his irritation. He went over where she found the slip several times.

"I am sorry. I only found it yesterday morning. I know you're mad, and I don't blame you. But what do you think?" she asked.

"I think it'll be the last time I ever take a journalist with me."

"I wasn't after a story," she said. "Right after I found it, we found that altar in the trees. I put the slip in my pocket and forgot it until I got dressed. Then I tried to call and you were gone. Ask Waymon."

"Have you taken it upon yourself to talk to Hayes?" he asked.

"He won't talk to me."

At least she hadn't trampled all over that. "He won't have that luxury with me." He handed her the coffee cup. "I'm going on a hunt later today. You want to come with me?"

"And Hayes?" she asked.

He hesitated. "I'll send Waymon to pick him up."

There was something in her face, something he didn't understand.

"You don't believe Hayes did it," she said.

"No, I don't. Not because he lives here, but because I know him, and I don't think he's capable of killing anyone."

"Not even a girl who's going to ruin his career?"

"Not even her." J.D. saw someone pull the curtain aside and look out. Medino. He was surprised when anger seared him.

"I'm going to step out of line here and tell you to watch out for Medino. He's a slippery guy with a quick tongue. Ruth Ann has told everyone in town that he's the best thing since sliced bread."

"That would be Ruth Ann's problem, not mine."

He saw defiance in her eyes, unwillingness to back down. He admired that about her. "If you get rid of your playmate and want to go with me, I'll be leaving at noon. If you come, come alone." He turned and started back down the driveway.

"J.D.?"

He couldn't remember if she'd ever called him by his name. He turned and saw the sun coming up over the tops of the trees in the east. "What?"

"What does it take to stay an execution?"

Her hair was blowing around her face, but it didn't hide the hurt. He walked back to her. He sensed Medino at the window, eavesdropping.

"It would take some extraordinary evidence and a call from the governor."

He could see she anticipated his question.

"I don't have any evidence, yet."

"You think Jones is innocent?"

She took a breath. "I don't know. But one thing for certain, I don't want an innocent man to die."

He tipped his hat toward the sun. "You call me if I can help," he said.

He felt her gaze on his back as he walked down to the road. He felt someone else watching, too. Someone who made his back muscles twitch and his hand climb up his hip until it rested on the butt of his gun.

✝

Dixon was dressed and ready for work when she saw the bicycle flashing through the trees. She walked out on the porch and stood. It had taken some work to get Robert to leave before Zander arrived, but she'd managed it. She warmed thinking about Robert's insistence on staying. He'd been worried for her, afraid that the young man would get angry. She hadn't had someone to worry about her like that since her father died.

The bicycle came into clear view. It had no fenders, the handlebars were rusted, and the seat was gnawed. Zander rode it up to the porch and stopped.

"Can you help my daddy?"

Dixon looked at him. He was tall and strong, a born athlete. His posture was good, his clothes neat and clean.

"I don't know if I can," she said. "I also don't know if I should."

"He didn't kill your daddy." It was a bald statement.

"Come inside and we'll talk. Have you had some breakfast?"

"Aunt Olena made me some grits. I'm not hungry."

She heard him clumping after her and realized he hadn't yet obtained his full growth. He looked like his father, but with a softer edge. The cheeks were full, only touched with stubble. His eyes, too, were softer.

She motioned to the kitchen chair where Robert had sat only an hour before and took the chair opposite him.

"Why do you think I can help Willard?"

"You're a reporter. You can get the facts."

"Don't you think if I knew facts, I would have come up with them a long time ago?"

He thought about it. "Daddy didn't kill no one."

Zander's face reflected his need to believe in his father's innocence.

"You hardly know your father. He's been in prison most of your life. Why do you believe he's innocent?"

The boy reached into the back pocket of his pants and brought out a bundle of letters. "He says so. He writes me every week. Since I was five. I saved all the letters, but these are the ones where he talks about being innocent."

The stack wasn't large. For a man who'd written close to six hundred letters, he hadn't spent a lot of time trying to convince his son he was innocent.

Her hand trembled as she took the letters he held out. To read them would be to know much more than she wanted to know. Willard Jones was almost dead. Would probably die no matter what she believed or did. She didn't want the grief, but she opened the first one and read the flowing script that talked of a spring day when he had an eleven o'clock meeting with a newspaper publisher named Ray Sinclair.

Dixon looked up from the letter. "He had an appointment to meet my father?"

Zander nodded. "He had things to tell him."

"What things?" Dixon felt as if the world had tipped on its side.

Zander shook his head. "He would never say. He never told Mama, and he wouldn't tell no one. He said it was what got him in the mess he was in, and he wasn't going to put us in danger."

Very convenient, Dixon thought. She leaned back in her chair. "Do you have any idea what it was about?"

"You'll have to ask him. Make him say." There was desperation in Zander's voice, and Dixon realized that though he was sixteen, he was still very much a child. "My mama is sick. She's in New Orleans with her sister where she can get the treatments every day. If they kill Daddy, she won't even try to keep living."

It was one thing to feel sorry for a young man pleading for his father. But she simply couldn't accept all he said at face value. Jones had had an attorney. Not a public defender, but a respected lawyer. None of this had come out at the trial.

"Did your father ever write that he met with Ray Sinclair?"

Zander thought for a minute. "He said Mr. Sinclair was interested in doing a story. Then he wouldn't say any more."

Dixon realized that pressing Zander would yield nothing further. The man she had to see, if she pursued this, was Willard Jones. A witness had seen him around the newspaper office. The prosecutor said he'd taken that opportunity to set the bomb. Ray's appointment book and all of his records had been destroyed in the blast, so there was no way to verify Zander's story.

"Will you help him?" Zander asked.

Dixon returned the letters. She didn't want to read more. She didn't want to know what a father who counted the years away behind bars said to his child.

"I'll look into it." She would have to, for her sake as well as Zander's.

"Can you help him?"

She shook her head. "I don't know."

"But you'll try?"

He had such hope.

"I'll look into it, but I probably can't do anything."

Zander stood up. He reached across the table and offered his hand. "In one of the letters, my father said that he suffered during the trial because Mr. Sinclair's family thought he was guilty. He said that was worse than going to jail."

"Zander, I've been to see your father. Why didn't he say something about this before now?"

The boy shrugged. "Maybe he thought Mama and me would be better off if he just stayed quiet. Now, though, Mama . . ." He blinked hard.

"I'll look into it. No promises."

But she only had to look into the boy's face to see that nothing short of a miracle would save him from despair.

✝

School was about to start when J.D. parked the cruiser and walked down the hallway to the biology room where Tommy Hayes taught. J.D. hadn't bothered to check in with the front office. He saw the principal scurrying toward him and held up a hand.

"Official police business. Stay out of it."

He opened the door and stepped into the classroom, where thirty freshmen turned toward him with excitement and worry.

"Sheriff?" Hayes looked pale and frightened.

"Tommy, we have a problem." He pulled the sales slip out of his pocket. "We should take this outside."

They left the classroom amid rising whispers and catcalls. The hallway was dim and quiet. J.D. turned to the teacher and handed him the sales slip.

"We know you bought the CD player for Angie. Now, I want you to tell me the truth."

It looked as if Hayes were melting, but J.D. had no sympathy. "Start talking."

"I did buy her the boom box. She said if I didn't, she'd tell everyone I'd made a pass at her. At first I told her I wouldn't get sucked into her blackmail scheme. I never made any kind of advance toward her. I'm just not . . . interested."

"But you did buy the boom box."

He nodded. "She started in on something else. Something about another man." He stared down at the floor. "She said she'd start rumors all over the school. I need this teaching job. If I get fired for being gay . . ."

J.D. might have pitied Hayes if he hadn't lied. "Tommy, you've just given yourself a motive for murder."

"I went down to the coast and talked to a lawyer about what to do about Angie. I went the day she and Trisha disappeared. I wasn't even around here when it happened."

"The sales slip?"

His pale skin flushed. "I don't know. I guess it was taped to the box. I just gave her the whole thing. Angie loved presents. She was always showing off something new someone had given her. She thought the expensive gifts made her special. She was wearing a bracelet that had to cost at least five grand."

"Where'd she get the bracelet?" J.D. felt a prickle of hope. He'd reluctantly bought into the theory of a Mexican's destroying church property and then moving on to killing girls; it had been the only bone he had to gnaw. This, though—expensive gifts and a girl who liked blackmail as a tool of her ambition—this was more in line with murder as J.D. knew it.

"She never said. She hinted. She said something one day that stuck with me."

"What was that?"

"She said the older a man got the easier he was to manage. She said a little flattery worked every time."

J.D. snapped, "You could have told me all of this earlier, Tommy. It could have saved a lot of time."

"I'm sorry. I really am. I was scared. I knew if it came out that Angie was blackmailing me, it would give me a reason to kill her."

J.D. sighed. "You didn't see those girls that day?"

"I swear to you, I never went near them."

"And I should believe you now, after you've already lied to me?"

"It's the truth."

"Maybe you can help me in another area."

Hayes nodded. "Sure."

"Where would a girl like Trisha get hold of crystal meth?"

"Trisha?" He frowned. "Doesn't seem likely. Now, Angie would do it."

"Where would Angie buy it?"

"Meth is all over the schools. It's not hard to get or expensive. Angie always had money. Plenty of it."

They could hear the din of the students rampaging in the classroom. J.D. also heard footsteps coming down the hall. He looked up to see Big Jim Welford and Calvin Holbert.

"Where did she get the money?" J.D. asked quickly.

"From whoever was giving her the jewelry, I'd say. She never said any names. At least not to me. The students haven't said anything either. They'd be buzzing about it if they knew."

Holbert and Welford drew abreast of J.D. and Hayes.

"What on God's green earth do you think you're doing?" Welford spat. "This is a school."

"I'm questioning a witness in a murder investigation." J.D. was tired, and he had a long day in front of him. He wasn't in the mood for Welford's blustering or Holbert's threats.

"If this is an example of how you do your job, it's no wonder Angie Salter hasn't been found." Holbert's face was red. "The man who took those girls is right down there at Fitler. Eustace Mills. He's probably got that poor girl somewhere in the swamp, using her for his sick desires. And you won't do a thing about it."

J.D. stopped himself from swinging, from smashing his fist into Calvin's smug face. "What makes you so certain Eustace is involved?" he managed to ask calmly.

"Vivian says he's all the time running up and down the river in his boat ogling the young girls. She says he's a pervert. She says he watches her when she's water skiing. He comes all the way down the river to Plum Bluff so he can do his nasty things without my daughter knowing." His face had gone even redder. "He's a vile man, a deviant. I know what he's doing to her and someone should stop him!" he shouted.

J.D.'s mouth was dry. "Calvin, I've known Eustace for most of my life. He isn't a pervert, and he isn't interested in young girls. He loves Camille. That's something you can't understand."

"Calvin! This isn't the place for this scene." Welford was looking up and down the hall. "What kind of example are you setting for the students?"

Hayes had stepped back against the wall. He looked pleadingly at J.D., who nodded, releasing him.

"I'm done here," J.D. said. "Calvin, if I hear one more word about Eustace . . ."

CHAPTER TWENTY-THREE

The bay of a hunting dog wafted through the swamp like the sounds of a far-distant party. Or better yet, a wake. Eustace knew that J.D. would not give up, but this wasn't the lawman with tracking hounds. More likely it was Boday McKay illegally hunting a young deer.

He knew that J.D. had called off the dog searches, opening a window of opportunity for Eustace to move after Chavez. The problem was that Chavez had become damn good at hiding. He knew Eustace was stalking him, and he'd become doubly cautious. He'd stopped coming to the camp to steal things, but Eustace felt certain Camille was still meeting him in the woods, giving him food and supplies.

Camille. She had no idea of the repercussions. She'd hidden the dead girl's bracelet where he couldn't find it, and a shard of her pottery told him she'd been at the scene where the body had been discovered.

He put the ammunition in the bottom of the boat along with the high-powered rifle and covered them with an old tarp. His plan was to wrap the Mexican's body with weights. That would hold Chavez underwater for so long that even if he did eventually float, there wouldn't be much of him left. First, though, he had to get Chavez.

He'd just finished stowing the gear when he heard Camille calling him. She was wearing the fedora she'd taken a shine to. Her hair was tucked up inside it, and her knees showed through her old jeans. He smiled. Not even those clothes could detract from her loveliness.

"I'm going into town for a while," she said. "I need some more glaze for the clay."

"Be careful."

"I'll probably eat lunch at the Hickory Pit. Do you want me to bring something back?"

"Fried chicken, fried okra, English pea salad, yams, and cornbread." He didn't really want the food, but it was one more assurance that Camille intended to come back to him. He sometimes wondered if, one day, she simply wouldn't return. She was a talented artist, and Vivian and Calvin were always holding that out to her, offering her opportunities he could never give her. He accepted that one day she might choose the world her parents offered. And then they would destroy her.

"You look sad," she said, walking up to him and touching his lips with her finger. "You don't sleep well anymore, Eustace. What's wrong?"

He felt the weight of his worries crushing him. "I'm fine. My leg hurts sometimes."

"That doctor did a piss-poor job of fixing you. If you would go to Mobile, one of the orthopedists there might be able to make it better. At least fix it where it didn't hurt all the time."

"I'll think about it." She was so tender. When she'd first come to the camp, she cried when he killed the fish. She still ate little meat, and she avoided the skinning shed when he was working there.

"Eustace, you don't like me to say this, but I have money. I could pay for the doctor. You don't have insurance, but we could cover it."

He hated it when he felt less than able to provide in her eyes. He turned away abruptly. "I said I'll think about it."

Her hand grazed along his shoulder and down his arm. "Okay. I'll be going then."

He turned back to watch her walk away, and cold fear gripped him. He'd spoken harshly to her, something she couldn't take. She hadn't reacted, though. She'd simply walked off. Did it mean she wasn't coming back? He stopped himself from going after her. He had to hold on to the fact that he loved Camille. Whatever was best for her was what he wanted. If she chose to leave, he would not lift a finger to stop her. That was the one thing he could offer her that no one else ever had—a choice.

As soon as her car had disappeared from sight he got in the boat. He'd been searching for Chavez for the past three days and had seen no sign of him. Eustace expected the woods to erupt any day with national guard, state troopers, and volunteers. He had to find Chavez, and he had to find him fast. He headed upriver, away from the mournful baying of the hound.

J.D. hadn't stopped by lately, either. That wasn't a good sign. J.D. was smart, and he would eventually put it all together. It was Eustace's job to see that whatever facts J.D. had gathered, none of them pointed to Camille.

Eustace had tracked Chavez to Dupree's Hideout, where the outlaw Pascal Dupree was supposed to have buried a treasure. The land was more marsh than solid ground, and a careless man could find himself sinking beneath the fetid muck. Eustace hoped to help Chavez become fatally careless.

He opened the throttle of the boat, kicking up a large wake, and let the boat fly. An hour later, he turned into the right bank of the Leaf River. A small creek emptied into the river, and he navigated beneath the high banks and into the interior. When he'd traveled as far as he could, he cut the motor. Drifting to a tree, he tied off the boat and got out, his rifle in his hand, listening to the chatter of blue jays.

The ground felt firm, but he knew to use caution. Little sunlight penetrated the thick canopy, and the ground was damp with rotting leaves and humidity. Mosquitoes droned around his head, but he ignored them. More dangerous were the snakes. A thick brown body eased off the bank and into the water, spiraling away. Moccasins gave no warning, unlike rattlesnakes, and their bite was just as deadly.

Pushing tree limbs out of his way, Eustace began the trek into the swamps. Half a mile in, he came upon a maze of fresh springs, hillocks, and cypress trees. The Mexican had hidden the boat, and Eustace hadn't tracked it down yet. He'd hoped to find it in the small canal, but it wasn't there.

A limb snapped. Eustace swung toward the sound, aiming the rifle as he turned. Chavez was a dim shape among the trees. Eustace didn't bother to sight. He didn't have time. He pulled the trigger and saw the man flinch and go down to one knee when the deer slug hit him. Then he was up and running, too fast for Eustace to give chase.

Eustace sat down on a cypress knee. He was trembling, and he had to catch his breath. He'd hit the man; he knew that much. He'd wounded him. Now Chavez was running through the woods, bleeding. Eustace heard the splash of water, the crackle of dead limbs underfoot. The man was moving fast. He was getting away.

A good hunter would follow the blood trail and bring an end to his quarry's misery. In his younger days, Eustace would have done exactly that. He'd followed his share of deer and cut their throats to end their suffering.

He closed his eyes. The deer slug should have brought the man down. Even a hit in the shoulder ought to have felled him. But it hadn't. Chavez had been little more than a shadow, half real and half imagined. Ghostly. Eustace's trembling increased. He was starting to see the man as not real, not human. As something more.

It was his responsibility to go after him. He couldn't have gotten far. Using his rifle as a crutch for his bad leg, he stood and listened. The swamp was silent. Not even a bird fluttered through the trees. He moved to where Chavez had been when he was shot. He found no trace of the man. In the trunk of an old sweet gum he found his bullet. If he'd hit him, the bullet had gone clean through. If he'd hit him. The man had fallen to his knees. Eustace searched the ground and found no evidence either way.

He made his way back to the river. For the first time in his life he didn't notice anything on the river as he sped toward home.

✝

J.D. watched the sweat darken the back of Dixon's shirt as she moved through the thick underbrush, retracing her steps in an effort to find the spot where she'd picked up the sales slip.

"Damn it all to hell. Everywhere looks like everywhere else," she said.

The day was murderously hot, the humidity as high as it could get without liquefying the air. They'd been at it for two hours, and Dixon was determined to find the place. He had to give her that; she was tenacious.

"Right in here," she said, sweeping her hand around an area. "It had to be right in here."

J.D. looked at the ground. He'd had to look, just on the off chance there was a print or some other physical evidence. In all likelihood, the wind had carried the sales slip into the woods until it had hung on the underbrush.

"Thanks, Dixon," he said.

"It didn't help, did it?"

He shook his head. "I don't know what will help now." He felt as if Angie Salter stood just out of sight, waiting for him to find her, to save her. It was an oppressive feeling.

"Chavez has to be here, in these swamps," Dixon said. She pushed her hair off her hot forehead. "He has to be here."

J.D. agreed. Francisco Chavez could not have left the area. He'd had men checking every vehicle that came and went from Fitler. Every boat. Chavez had to be there, but no one had seen him. The man had to eat, and without a gun or fishing gear, he couldn't sustain himself.

Unless someone was helping him.

The thought came unbidden and fully developed. He pulled out his cell phone and dialed the sheriff's office. When Waymon answered, he asked, "Camille Holbert. Have the roadblocks been checking her car?"

The pause told him. He wanted to curse but didn't.

222

"Waymon, find out when she's come and gone. Don't upset the volunteers, but get the times and get them exact. I'll find out where she went."

"They were afraid of Calvin," Waymon admitted. "They were afraid if they stopped her and she complained, Mr. Holbert would call up the loans they owe."

J.D. leaned against a tree and closed his eyes. He felt sick. Angie Salter was probably dead and buried in the woods and would never be found. The man responsible had very likely hitched a ride in the roomy trunk of a Mercedes with a crazy woman who didn't realize what she was doing.

"Just find out what you can." He hung up and began his descent down the river bank.

"What's wrong?" Dixon asked.

"There's a chance he caught a ride out of here." Eustace's camp was blocked from view by the trees, but J.D. knew exactly where it was.

For most of J.D.'s life, he had turned to Eustace in times of need. But not now. If Camille had helped Chavez escape, she was an accessory to kidnapping and murder. It would prove what Calvin and Vivian had been saying—that Camille was incapable of making sane decisions. He didn't have to look far down that road to see what would happen. Vivian would have her institutionalized. Anything to get her away from Eustace.

"Who would give him a ride?" Dixon asked, sliding down the steep bank beside him.

He didn't answer.

She stopped. "Camille Holbert?"

The way she said it, he could tell she didn't want to believe it.

"It's a possibility. Just that, a possibility," he said.

He started down the river to the west toward a trail that would take them back up the bank and to his SUV. He'd wanted Dixon's company. He'd wanted her not to be with Medino. Now, he needed to get rid of her before he confronted Camille and Eustace.

"Why would Camille do such a thing?" Dixon asked.

He thought about his answer. "She's tender-hearted. She might have thought Chavez was in a bad way and had no one else to turn to."

Dixon kept pace with him. "I don't think she did it."

He turned to look at her. "You don't?"

She shook her head. "Your friend watches her like a hawk. I doubt he leaves the camp if she's there alone. He would have known, wouldn't he?"

"I hope you're right."

They made their way to the Explorer. J.D. turned the air conditioner on high. The SUV lumbered across the bridge, dodging potholes. J.D. stopped and looked out the window at the river. It was only against the bridge abutments that he could tell how swift the current really was. Was Angie Salter beneath the water? He didn't believe so. She hadn't drowned. Dead or alive, someone had her.

He chanced a glance at Dixon. She rode with her eyes closed, the air blowing so hard on her face that it lifted her hair off her forehead. Her eyelashes were dark against her cheeks, which showed the faintest trace of freckles.

"Why are you staring at me?" She opened her eyes.

"You're a beautiful woman."

He liked that she didn't deny it.

She looked past him to the river. "Will they really replace this bridge?"

He shrugged. "Probably. In ten or twenty years."

"Good. I like it this way. If the bridge were easy to cross, folks would start building across the river."

He knew what she meant, and he was unreasonably pleased. "One of the reasons I came home to Chickasaw County was because of the woods and the isolation. I spent some time working in the Atlanta police department. Too many people. Too many cars." He laughed. "Just too much of everything. I wanted to be somewhere with lots of trees and dirt roads and country people."

She faced him as he drove slowly off the bridge. "I came here because I had to prove something to myself. And I was becoming an alcoholic."

He didn't protest. "How's it coming?" he asked.

"Better than I thought in some ways, not so good in others."

He turned down the drive to Eustace's camp. The Mercedes wasn't there. "You sure put a kink in Big Jim's tail."

"He needs to have it snatched out."

J.D. laughed. "I couldn't agree with you more."

"You do?"

"He's a pompous ass who runs the county with an iron fist. As long as he has Calvin Holbert at his side, he has power. Calvin controls the bank, which controls the loans. And right now Big Jim controls Calvin. It's an ugly combination."

"Thanks for telling me that."

"As if you didn't know." He smiled at her as he parked the Explorer. "You're smart, Dixon Sinclair. I'm going to treat you like I understand that."

"You're not the average lawman," she said.

"God, I hope not." He got out and went around to open her door.

She stepped into the shade of a big oak and looked around. "I don't think they're home."

"Eustace keeps beer cold in the minnow vats. We could pop a top and take a dip in the artesian water. I need to wait until he or Camille comes back, and we might as well make ourselves comfortable."

He could see the idea appealed to her.

"I didn't bring a swim suit," she said.

"Good. Neither did I," he said. "We can swim in our clothes."

CHAPTER TWENTY-FOUR

Tormented, Eustace kicked the throttle of the boat wide open as he drew close to home. Finding Angie Salter wouldn't conclude the investigation. J.D. was like a snapping turtle that had caught hold of a hand. He'd hang on until he gnawed through the flesh, or until someone bashed him in the head. He would not stop until Chavez and Angie had been found. Killing Chavez—if indeed he had—had only delayed the inevitable.

Once he got back home, he'd talk to Camille. For the last few days, he'd felt as if she were slipping away from him. He would take her somewhere. Whatever she'd done, he wouldn't let anyone hurt her. He'd take her some place where he could watch over her.

He didn't know what Camille's involvement with Chavez was. Camille was tender. She wasn't cruel. But she drew a line between creatures and humans, and her compassion often didn't extend to her fellow man. She sometimes seemed trapped between dreams and reality. In a dream state she could do almost anything, especially if she were being led by someone she viewed as a spiritual leader, a man who communed with the natural world.

It wasn't right for her to hurt someone. Eustace understood that. He could never allow her to do it again. And he would watch her. He would be vigilant. It would be okay.

He tried to convince himself that, somehow, he could make it all work out right as he sped toward home. Nearing the camp, he slowed the boat and listened. Silence. He coasted into the landing and saw the sheriff sitting at a picnic table. The reporter was in the minnow vat, her hair slicked back with water. Eustace swore. He needed time to convince Camille to let him lead her.

Eustace tied the boat and walked up the steep bank to J.D. The reporter jumped to the side of the vat and pulled herself out, water sluicing off her. He noted that she was wearing her clothes, and he couldn't help but think that J.D. was slipping. Four empty beer bottles sat on the table.

"What brings you here?" Eustace asked. It wasn't a friendly greeting.

"I came to ask a question." J.D. squinted against the sun.

"I remember the days when you'd come here to visit, not to ask questions."

J.D. slowly stood up. "And I remember when I used to feel welcome."

"Ask what you came to ask." Eustace felt the sun on his back. His feet were slightly apart. He'd deliberately left the rifle in the boat, but now he wished for it. The reporter, still by the vat, wrung out her shirt. She was watching the scene unfold.

"Is it possible Camille took Chavez out of here?"

Eustace considered it, trying not to show the terror that momentarily overtook him. Camille had not helped Chavez escape, but if J.D. could not produce the man, then Camille might get the blame for that. He decided on a simple answer. "No."

"Look, Eustace, I know Camille's had so many labels applied to her that she might not give credence to what folks are saying about Chavez. If she helped him, it would be without full knowledge. If he's gone from here, I need to know it."

Eustace's voice rose. "She hasn't done anything. Why would she? Why would she help a stranger?" His heart was thumping. He tried unsuccessfully to calm himself.

"Where is Camille?" J.D. asked.

"She's gone in to town. She sees her folks a good bit. I don't know why they want to act like I keep her prisoner down here. She's free to go anywhere, anytime."

"Eustace, there's a girl missing who could still be alive. God knows what she might have been through, but if she's alive, we have to find her."

"Angie Salter isn't alive."

"You know this?"

"I haven't seen the body, but she's dead. I'd be willing to bet she died when the other one did."

J. D. exploded. "I'm not willing to *bet* one way or the other. This is a girl's life we're talking about."

"No, it isn't. She's dead, J.D., and you might as well give up the hope that you're gonna find her alive. She's dead and you won't ever find that Mexican."

"How are you so certain she's dead?"

It wasn't a question but an accusation. Eustace had to divert J.D.'s suspicions away from Camille. It would be better if J.D. suspected him.

"I lied to you about the girls. I saw them the day they disappeared. The Salter girl was just a slut. She was carrying on with her tits uncovered. Whatever happened to her, she brought it on herself."

J.D. was very still. "And what did happen?"

229

Eustace cast a sidelong glance at the reporter. "Someone came up or down the river and decided to do the world a favor."

"We've been friends a long time, Eustace. Most of my life. I thought I knew you, but I was wrong."

"We all have two sides, J.D. Even you. You've done things that creep out of the darkness and sit on your heart. We all have."

"You're wrong there, Eustace. We all haven't."

Eustace turned at the sound of a car. The Mercedes pulled down the long drive, dodging the mud holes. He wanted to rush out, to wave Camille away. She couldn't protect herself. But he didn't move. The car stopped beside the house, and Camille got out. Her smile faded as she took in the scene.

"What's wrong?" she asked, walking toward them. "Eustace?" She still wore her hair tucked up in her hat and lifted her arm to secure it on her head.

He saw the bracelet as it slid up her bare arm almost to her elbow. The sun caught the braided gold and shimmered. Eustace felt his face freeze. He glanced at J.D.; the sheriff's attention was focused on the bracelet. Eustace thought about his skinning bat in the shed.

"Camille, go in the house," Eustace said, his voice sharp.

She looked up, hurt.

"Go on inside." He tried to modify his tone but failed.

She was past hurt and ready to fight. "I don't take orders from you or anyone else."

He regretted his tone, but he had to get her away from J.D. "Go inside. Now."

"Fuck you." She lifted her chin and her hat tipped off her head. Her red curls cascaded down her shoulders and back.

"Camille, go inside." He knew the panic in his voice cut her like a razor.

"You forget who you are, Eustace Mills. I used to have to take it when my father spoke to me like that. I won't take it from you. Do it one more time and I'm out of here."

Eustace saw J.D. watching. He was going to let them hang themselves.

Eustace let out a cry that tore his throat as he lunged at his friend.

"Eustace!"

He heard Camille and the reporter call his name just before he brought his shoulder into J.D.'s solar plexus. He heard the *oof* of air expelled from J.D.'s lungs, then felt the blow that knocked him to the ground where blackness swirled.

✝

Dixon drove through the small community of Vesley, wondering where Olena Jones might live. It was rural, with a general store-post office that made her feel as if she'd fallen back fifty years in time. The dirt roads and dilapidated houses reflected tight financial times. The three-car-garage, five-bedroom, four-bath developments mushrooming in nearby Mobile hadn't crept into Vesley. Modest brick homes were the benchmark of prosperity here. Asbestos shingle and clapboard two-bedrooms were the norm.

She kept her eyes open for a teenage boy on a bicycle, but her mind was on the scene she'd witnessed at Eustace Mills's camp.

J.D. had not arrested Eustace. He'd carried him to the skinning shed, laid him out on the table, then brought him around with a scoop of ice-cold artesian water. Camille had gone into the house. The two men had a terse, whispered conversation, then J.D. had driven Dixon back to town. He'd said little, and she hadn't pressed the matter. She knew what it felt like to be betrayed.

When he'd dropped her off, he'd asked her out for dinner on Saturday night. She'd accepted, wondering now what she'd agreed to, exactly. What did Horton want from her? She was curious to know.

The road curved around a pecan orchard, and she slowed. A boy on a bicycle was coming her way through the orchard. As he drew closer, she recognized Zander.

He rode toward her, his face hesitant and hopeful, and stopped next to the truck.

"I'm going to talk to your father," she told him. "I'll do that much. I can't make any promises, though. I want to talk to your aunt first."

He nodded. "Follow me home."

She nodded.

Zander straddled the bike and pushed off down the road. He made good time on the sandy path that turned and twisted until Dixon lost all sense of direction. When he jumped off in front of a small wooden house, she parked. She didn't know if Olena Jones would welcome her, but Dixon wanted to see this family for herself.

"Aunt Olena isn't here." Zander looked around the yard as if his aunt had disappeared from right in front of him. "She was cookin' supper when I went for a ride." He frowned. "I'll be back."

He dashed up the steps and into the house, and in a moment he reappeared at the door. "Come on in. I'll fix you some ice tea."

Dixon went inside. There was a sprawl of baby toys on the floor and the smell of cornbread coming from the kitchen. She sat down at the kitchen table while Zander emptied an ice tray and fixed her drink. He was nervous.

"Sit down, Zander," she said softly. "I just want to talk to your aunt for a minute or two."

They heard her car in the yard, and Zander went to tell his aunt about their visitor.

Dixon rose, but she remained in the kitchen. It was only right to give Zander a chance to explain things to his aunt. Five minutes later, Olena Jones came into the room, her eyes darting from corner to corner until they settled on Dixon.

"Ms. Sinclair," she said softly. "Why are you here?" She was breathing fast.

"I wondered if you had any documents or anything from your brother, something where he says he's innocent."

Olena patted her hair into place. She was a striking woman with a red hue to her skin and light eyes. She'd regained her composure and took Dixon's glass and refilled it with tea. "Zander has his letters. I have a few myself."

"Could I have them?"

Olena took her measure. "You'll keep them safe." It was a statement.

"Of course. In fact, if you want to copy them, I'll be glad to take the copies."

She nodded, then brushed her hands down her thighs. She turned to the oven and opened the door to check the cornbread.

Dixon rose. "I have to get to work. Bring those letters by the newspaper, the sooner the better."

"I will," she said. She glanced past Dixon, and her face changed expressions. She looked fearful.

Dixon turned, but the doorway was empty. "Are you okay?"

Olena nodded. "Just a little frazzled. My baby has been sick, and I got to get to Minnie's house for some help." She shrugged. "I don't have insurance. Minnie's 'bout as good as any doctor around anyway."

"I'll head home then." She started toward the front door.

"Ms. Sinclair, don't raise Zander's hopes."

She turned back. "I won't. I told him I would talk to his father. I'm going to do that. Then I'll talk to the district attorney who prosecuted the case, if I have anything to tell him." She hesitated. "You asked me an important question, Olena. You asked me who would gain from my father's death. I've been thinking about that a lot."

"And have you figured it out?"

"I'm not sure, but at least I have a lead to pursue."

She walked through the house but didn't see any sign of the sick baby. Outside on the porch a red stain had soaked into the thirsty wood. Its odd shape resembled hands clasped in prayer.

Dixon got in her truck, maneuvered around the old Ford, and headed back to the newspaper and a long night's work.

CHAPTER TWENTY-FIVE

J.D. had suprised himself in asking Dixon to dinner. Thinking about it, he lost his temper twice, regained it, and was on the verge of losing it again as he turned in to the rutted camp road for the second time that day. Camille's car was still there; he realized then that he'd been afraid she would run.

He'd concealed the significance of the bracelet from Dixon because he had to ascertain for himself exactly what it meant before he talked about it with anyone else.

He walked up the camp's twenty-three steps and knocked at the stained-glass door. Eustace opened it and turned away.

Camille, pale, sat at the kitchen bar. A tarot spread was laid out in front of her. She pointed to a card when he drew near. "The Tower," she said. "A collapse." A tear drifted down her cheek. "Eustace says I have to tell you about the bracelet."

J.D. had done many hard things in his life, but looking into Camille's face then was one of the worst.

"Tell me," he said, taking the seat across the bar from her. Eustace stood at the door.

She brought the bracelet out of her pocket. It shifted in her hand like something alive. For a long moment she stared at it. "Here," she said, putting it in his hand.

"Where did you get it?" J.D. asked.

Camille looked up at Eustace. J.D. could read the lie beginning to form on her face. "Eustace wants me to tell you I found it on the sandbar. But I didn't—"

"Camille!" Her name was a howl.

J.D. lifted his hand. "Hush up, Eustace. Let her tell me the truth."

"I told Eustace it was just a mistake. Mama gave me this bracelet." She poked it with her finger. "It was one she didn't want anymore. That's what she told me."

J.D.'s stomach lurched. Vivian Holbert wasn't the kind of woman to give away an expensive bracelet, not even to her daughter. Especially not while her daughter was living with Eustace.

"When did she give it to you?" J.D. asked softly.

"A week or so ago." Camille's face registered recognition. "It was the day the girls disappeared."

"She didn't have it then," Eustace said. "She didn't, J.D."

"Yes, I did," Camille said. "I hid it from you because I knew it would make you angry."

She looked at J.D. "Eustace gets mad when they give me expensive things, because he feels he should be able to get them for me." She shook her head. "I don't care about gold bracelets. In fact, you take it if it'll help you."

J.D. got up and walked to the stove, where he picked up a dishcloth. "Would you mind if I took this too?"

"Why?" she asked.

"To protect the bracelet."

"Sure, have it." She stood up. "I'm going to make fish in *court bouillon* for dinner. Can you stay?"

"No, thank you, Camille. I have to get back to town." He picked up the bracelet with the cloth and put them both in his pocket. On the way out, he asked Eustace to follow him.

They stood on the landing, the cicadas whirring below them. "Why didn't you tell me?"

"How would I know?"

J.D. pulled the bracelet from his pocket. "You saw the girls on the sandbar. Is this the bracelet Angie Salter was wearing?"

Eustace stared at it. At last he met his friend's gaze. "I don't know. I was too far away. It could be. Then again, it might not be. Look, I tried to get Camille to lie. She was determined to tell the truth—Vivian gave her the bracelet. Why can't that be true?"

J.D. put the bracelet back in his pocket. "It can be true. In fact, I'd give a whole lot to make it true."

"But you can't take it at face value." Eustace was angry.

J.D.'s hand shot out and grasped Eustace's shirt. "There's a young girl out there. I have to find her. Do you get it? I have to find her, and I have to believe she's still alive."

Eustace twisted free. "Angie Salter is dead. You might as well accept it. There's nothing you can do to save her." He turned and walked into the house, closing the door and locking it behind him.

✝

Dixon rubbed the back of her neck and got up to make a fresh pot of coffee. She was laying out ads for the next edition. Layout had never been her strong suit, and now it seemed the space she'd allocated for a florist's advertisement was completely unmanageable. She threw her ruler down and walked to the front of the office.

Main Street, silent and dark, stretched out in front of her. It was a weeknight, and not even the high-school kids were out riding around. The town looked as if the sandman had come, sprinkling the entire area except for her. If only she could sleep without dreams or anxiety.

She was turning to go back to work when she saw the sheriff's SUV glide down the street. He waved at her, and she waved back. He was a strange man. Intensely focused on his work, wounded somehow. She hadn't figured it out. It was unfair that he was able to dig out her background but she couldn't find much more on him than idle gossip. The badge made the difference.

A sudden movement outside the window made her heart lurch. Robert Medino, smiling like a Cheshire cat, tapped on the glass. He held up a brown paper sack and made eating motions.

She unlocked the door.

He held out the sack. "Fried catfish, cole slaw, baked beans, hushpuppies, and iced tea." He carried the sack to a desk and removed two Styrofoam containers. The delicious smell of fried fish wafted through the room.

"I have four dozen ads to make up," she said.

Her stomach growled loud enough that Robert grinned.

"How's about you eat, then I'll help you with the ads?"

"Can you make up ads?" she asked doubtfully

He handed her a container of food and put a hand dramatically on his chest. "She doubts me. Now, that wounds my heart. Of course I can make up ads. I worked for a weekly once. I learned to do everything. It's just that I was better at investigative reporting than I was at making up ads. But I can help."

She took the food; she was starving. And she was glad Robert had shown up.

They sat across from each other. Dixon ate as much as she could hold. She groaned and closed her container. "Now all I want to do is go to bed."

"And I didn't even have to seduce you," he said.

She laughed. "Not what I had in mind." She rose. "Besides, I am the slave of a weekly newspaper."

"I heard you went off with the good sheriff," Robert said, picking up the remnants of their meal and putting them in the watebasket. "Did you find anything?"

She shook her head. "It would seem Angie Salter has disappeared into thin air. What did you do today?"

"I rode upriver this morning with a character named Eustace Mills. He gave me a tour of the Leaf and Chickasawhay. An unusual guy."

She nodded. "I've met him."

"In the line of duty?"

"Not exactly. His place is close to the sandbar where the girls disappeared."

"So he said." He followed her to the back and moved to the lighted layout tables. When she pointed to the Beckham's Florist material, he picked up the various elements of the ad. "What size?"

"Two columns, six inches."

He nodded and began to arrange the ad. "What about your father's murder?" he asked.

Her reply was terse. "What about it?"

"Hey, don't get upset. I was just wondering if you'd had a chance to think about it any more. If there's something I can do, I'd like to help."

"I'm sorry." She walked up beside him and watched as he dropped the copy into the box he'd made with black tape. He was good at arranging the elements of the ad. A lot better than she was.

"Are there any copies of your father's newspapers left?"

"Why?"

"Because if he was on to something involving the state politicians, maybe there are some leads in the stories he wrote before his death."

She sat down on a stool, her knees rubbery. "The newspaper was totally destroyed, but the library kept copies." She stared at her shoes.

"He was your father, Dixon. This isn't just some case. It's hard to investigate and protect yourself at the same time." He put his arms around her and pulled her to him. She could smell Old Spice, a choice of cologne as eccentric as he was. It was comforting, though.

"Thank you, Robert."

"It's my pleasure. I'll tell you what, since you're tied up here getting the paper out, I'll go up to Jackson and see if there are any bound copies of the newspaper in the library there. If there are, I'll go through them and make copies of whatever I think would be useful."

She'd been alone in this for so long, she was eager to grasp the offered help, the support. Robert could act as a buffer from the pain of what she'd have to see once she started looking.

"Let's get those ads finished, then we'll head to your house, have a drink to unwind, and I'll give you a massage."

Dixon kissed his cheek, then his lips.

✝

Tommy Hayes stared at the bracelet in J.D.'s hand. In the back yard, two dogs were barking frantically.

"Well?" J.D. asked.

Hayes nodded. "It looks like the same bracelet that Angie wore to school."

"This is a valuable piece of jewelry. Do you know where Angie got it?"

He shook his head. "I didn't ask because I didn't want to know. Angie was like tar baby. If you brushed against her, you were stuck." He wiped perspiration off his upper lip.

J.D. watched the young man. He'd always liked Hayes. Had felt for him, knowing the difficulties of his sexual preference in a town like Jexville. "Is there something else you want to tell me?" J.D. asked.

"No." Hayes spoke quickly. "Look, I have papers to grade."

J.D. walked back to his Explorer and drove to the other side of town.

He sat outside the Holbert home and watched the lights go on and off around the house. Calvin's car wasn't in the driveway. If the last few days were any indicator, Calvin didn't spend a lot of time at home. J.D. waited another fifteen minutes and drove slowly away, heading to the bank.

It was nearly eight o'clock. If Calvin didn't go home, where did he go? J.D. circled the bank and found no sign of Calvin's Jaguar. He drove down Main Street. The Hickory Pit was filled to the rafters, but Calvin wasn't there. He continued past the funeral home, took a right, and headed to a part of town where a lonely guy could sometimes buy a little company. J.D. had seen too much to label the activity morally good or bad. Commerce was the word to describe it, a business transaction. He felt no need to try regulating it. He drove past the two double-wides where Monica and Jasmine conducted their business. If Calvin was there, he hadn't left his car.

J.D. turned back toward the school board offices, where he found the Jaguar parked in back. For half an hour, he sat in the dark, watching. From his secluded parking place, he could hear the occasional shush of car tires on pavement, the bark of a dog, the sound of a stereo in a passing vehicle. Once he caught the strains of an old Eagles song, and he thought about the passage of time and how he'd come to be where he was.

The big question for the town gossips was why he'd come back. The marines had given him a taste of the world. No one understood why he'd wanted to come back to a small town in a poor county. Had he been married with children, they'd have understood. Jexville offered a sense of safety to young families. Church was the extracurricular activity that ruled the town and county in every aspect from political to social. Now, a perversion of that religious fervor had shown up in his county, carved into the thigh of a fifteen-year-old girl.

There was such a twisted logic in a religious fanatic—a man so obsessed with his mother's sins and virginity and holiness that he defaced statues of Mary—that he might see two young girls with a wild streak as evil. Might. But what didn't add up was how this religious vigilante had transported Trisha's body across the river to a spit of land and how Camille had ended up with the bracelet Hayes had identified as the one Angie had worn to school that day. Camille said her mother gave it to her. J.D. didn't believe in the tooth fairy, and he didn't believe Vivian was running around handing out five grand in gold.

If Camille were lying, she did it with the heart of a child, and there were several possible explanations for it. Eustace had killed the girls and given the bracelet to Camille. Chavez had killed them and given Camille the bracelet in repayment for . . . what? Use of a boat?

But the most likely explanation had J.D. here, looking for Calvin. The bracelet was worth at least five thousand dollars. It wasn't a gift a lot of men could afford. If it had come from Vivian, then only one man could have given it to Angie. Calvin.

The humid night lay on J.D.'s skin like a damp cloth. He left his SUV, approached the building, and stepped onto the scaling porch. Dead paint crunched beneath his shoe. He paused and listened. He could hear the faint sound of words over the drone of the air conditioner. Holbert and Welford. It was possible that Big Jim was involved in this, too.

He eased closer to the door.

"I don't want to go over this again. I told you the shit was going to hit the fan," Welford said. "I'm not in this. I wash my hands of you and everything involved."

"It's not that easy," Holbert said angrily.

"You should resign as school board president. That's my final say."

"That would be mighty convenient. Maybe you'd want to put Vivian in my place."

The silence dragged on too long.

Holbert said, "That was a joke. Surely you wouldn't consider—"

"Wait, it has merit. You could resign and say you're too busy. Vivian would be perfect. She'd do exactly as you told her."

"What planet do you live on? Vivian would do everything in her power to spite me. And you. She has no love for you, either, Jim."

The voices dropped lower, and J.D. knocked. He could hear scrambling. Whatever they had or hadn't done, they certainly acted guilty.

"Who is it?" Welford called out.

"It's the sheriff."

Welford swung the door open and walked back to his desk. "I would have thought you'd be out hunting that missing girl," he said testily.

"Oh, I am," J.D. said. "I was hoping maybe you two could give me some help."

"Us? How?" Holbert asked, his eyes wide.

"I've been thinking about the talk. Angie had an older, wealthy lover." Calvin's cheek twitched. "I was wondering if you could ask the faculty and students if they had any ideas who she might have been seeing. Maybe she let it slip."

Holbert had recovered. "That's nonsense. You can't take the word of a bunch of high school kids."

"I'm a little short on leads here, Calvin. I'll take what I can get." He took a chair. "And I'm curious about something else, too. Tommy Hayes. I thought y'all voted to fire him, and yet he's right up there at the high school big as life."

"The board changed its mind." Welford squared some folders. "I'm ready to call it a night, Calvin. How about you?"

"Sure am." Holbert stood.

"Now, my understanding is that you all had some evidence that Tommy Hayes had done something improper with Angie. It would sure help me out if I knew what he'd done and how you found out about it, since there were no charges filed."

"Strictly confidential." Welford frowned. "Personnel matters are private."

"Not in a murder investigation," J.D. said. He settled back in his chair and looked up at Holbert. "Have a seat, Calvin. I'm not finished here."

"My wife is waiting for me." Holbert started toward the door.

"Okay, I'll send a deputy over to the bank tomorrow to drive you to the sheriff's office to answer the questions. Six of one, half a dozen of the other to me."

"What are you implying?" Welford demanded.

"Only that both of you had knowledge that may have contributed to two deaths. You can try to hide it, but it won't do any good. I'm going to find Angie, and I'm going to find whoever killed Trisha. If either of you are involved in it, God help you."

He stood up and arched his back. The bracelet would wait until he had the opportunity to interview each man separately.

"These twenty-four-hour days tend to make me a little fractious. I'd keep that in mind."

He walked out, his footsteps hard on the porch. Behind him was silence. As he reached the Explorer, the radio crackled to life.

Waymon's voice was brittle. "J.D., call the station. J.D. hurry up and call. They've found the Salter girl. J.D., it's real bad."

Chapter Twenty-six

Five dark-haired men sit rigidly as the van careens along the dirt road. Dixon is in the van, but she doesn't recognize anyone. She can't remember why they have taken her, what she may have done.

The men stare straight ahead, their expressions blank as the sun flashes in and out of the tree branches throwing them into shadow and light.

She looks at the fat man in the back of the van. Beside him is a three-foot tall person. Not a midget; a chimpanzee-man. His long, wiry arms are covered in thick blond hair. Ape arms. He is the only blond in the vehicle, and his eyes are a startling blue. He watches her and smiles, and she feels as if ice water has dripped down her back. He is dangerous and means to hurt her, but she doesn't know why.

The road is sandy, and the van slues back and forth, taking both lanes. She can smell water and remembers that it has rained. Rained hard. For many days. She turns to the driver, who doesn't look to left or right but pilots the van at a dangerous clip. She knows where she is, a place from the safety of her childhood, but she isn't safe now.

"There's a bridge up ahead," she warns him.

He ignores her and keeps up a pace that has the van sliding left, then right. No one moves. The little man in the back laughs.

"There's a sharp curve and a narrow bridge," she calls out. She remembers the name. White's Creek. She swam there as a child, and the curve is treacherous, the bridge one-lane and wooden. Once a man and his three children drowned there.

"There's a narrow bridge!" she says again.

The driver ignores her. They are upon the curve. He turns the wheel, and suddenly there is no road, only raging amber water. The creek has overrun the bridge. At the edge is a man and three children. They drip water into the sand as they watch the van with sad eyes.

"Go right! Go right!" she screams at the driver. She knows where the bridge is beneath the flood.

The right front wheel hits the bridge, but the left goes into the water. The van lumbers slowly onto its side, then the flood waters catch it and begin to spin it downstream. Water gushes through the windows. Dixon realizes that she is chained to her seat.

"Hey! There's someone at the front door." Robert, standing by the bed, held her shoulders. "Wake up, Dixon. There's someone at the front door."

Dixon looked up, the shadow waters of her dream still in her eyes. The bedside lamp was on, and Robert's dark eyebrows were drawn together.

"Are you okay?"

Her voice was still paralyzed by the dream; she nodded and rose. She tasted ashes, and someone was pounding on the front door. Her foot hit the ashtray on the floor, and she connected the taste and her sudden fall from the nonsmoking wagon. On top of that, her head was pounding from the bourbon. She took three steps and tripped over the empty bottle. Oh, it had been a night. She had a vague memory of straddling Robert as she drained the bottle.

She found her robe and pulled it on as she walked down the hall to the front door.

Her robe hung off one shoulder and she shrugged it up as she cracked the door. Waymon stood frowning at her. The look on his face wiped away the night.

Dixon opened the door all the way, looking outside for J.D.

"What's wrong?" she asked, ignoring Waymon's pointed look toward the rental car parked under the oaks. It looked furtive in the light of day.

"They found the Salter girl."

For once, Waymon seemed more interested in gathering information than dispensing it. He looked past her into the living room. Behind her, Dixon heard Robert in the kitchen. "Is she alive?"

"Hanged and burned, just like the other one."

Dixon closed her eyes and gripped the door frame. Trisha Webster and Angie Salter had not lived long enough to make many choices in their short lives. Their first big mistake had been their last. They'd let a killer into their lives, and now they were dead, before they'd ever lived. It was over now.

"J.D. wants you to come down. He said if you could photograph the body, like the other one, it would help him."

"I'm not exactly eager to do those photographs," she said. The idea repelled her. Her dreams were already infused with tragedy and horror. And Trisha Webster visited her now, a ghostly after-image of torment in photographic sequence.

She heard Robert in the kitchen and thought of his body, so tender and so fierce. For a moment she wanted to stay there, with him, to hide against him from the past and the present.

But she knew she'd go. She felt a growing loyalty to J.D. and, even more, to the job she'd chosen to do.

"Let me get dressed."

"This one's a real mess," Waymon said. He craned to see over the top of her head. From the kitchen they heard glass breaking and "Fuck!"

"Where is J.D.?"

"He's down at Eustace's. That's where the body is."

Dixon looked up. "At Eustace Mills's?"

"Yep. She was hanging in that big oak right in his yard. It's a mystery how she got there without waking Eustace or Camille. Some folks are saying that J.D.'s hunting the wrong man."

"Some folks like Vivian and Calvin Holbert?"

"Them two for sure, but there's others."

"I'll get dressed and drive out there." She wanted her own vehicle.

"J.D. told me to bring you," Waymon said, his lips a thin line of determination.

From the kitchen Robert called out, "Coffee's made. You want a cup?"

Dixon stepped out on the porch and closed the door behind her. "I'll meet you at the river."

"You could bring me out a cup of coffee, and I'll be glad to wait."

"I'll meet you at the river in thirty minutes." Dxion went inside, closed the door firmly, and padded through the living and dining rooms into the kitchen. Robert was heating milk on the stove, and the aroma of fresh coffee filled the room.

"They found Angie Salter hanging in a tree," she told him as she began pulling clean shirts out of the clothes dryer.

"Was she burned?"

250

"Apparently. It sounds like the same type of scene."

She dug deeper for clean socks. In her haste she left clothes on the floor and dangling from the dryer.

"Are you going out to the scene?"

"No." He held a cup of coffee out to her.

"Why? Aren't you interested in covering this?"

He gave a casual shrug and looked at the hot milk. "I don't have the stomach for it."

Dixon considered for a moment, took her black coffee, and turned toward the bathroom and a shower. "Want to take a quick shower?"

He shook his head. "You go on. I'll clean up after you're gone, if that's okay."

"Sure."

Robert was a strange breed of journalist.

✝

J.D. stood back from the ruin of a body, waiting for Dixon to arrive. There was nothing in the grotesque lump that recalled the girl who had been Angie Salter.

He'd had little faith from the beginning that the girls would be found alive, but the systematic debasement of their bodies was hard for him to take. He had seen debasement before, certainly. He'd seen too many things—half-dead soldiers dragged behind trucks and fellow prisoners forced to urinate on them, decapitated heads on wooden pikes at the outskirts of an encampment, scalps left dangling, necklaces of ears, pregnant women gutted and left alive.

He'd seen worse than Angie Salter, but in all of those instances there had been an enemy. The ritual of debasement had served a specific purpose—to frighten and demoralize the enemy.

He looked at the corpse turning slowly in the breeze. The day had dawned cool, with the first promise of autumn on the fluttering leaves. Angie Salter and Trisha Webster should be sitting in class, anticipating the next football game. Twelve days ago they had been laughing on the sandbar. Eustace had seen them. He looked to be the last person to have seen them alive.

J.D. glanced up at the camp. He saw a flurry of movement at the window and Camille's bright hair as she stepped back. Eustace was sitting at the fish vats, staring into the water as the fish whirled from one corner of the vat to another.

He heard a commotion from the end of the drive and knew that Vivian Holbert was lighting into Waymon again. Vivian wanted to see her daughter, but J.D. had no intention of allowing her anywhere near the crime scene. Waymon was suffering the brunt of her attack and, for all his shortcomings, was holding his own.

The deputy hadn't brought Dixon back with him, but J.D. did not fault him. She was not a woman who could easily be pressed easily. She had said she would come, and she would. But the coroner, watching him and the corpse with the sharp eyes of a rattler, wanted to collect the body, deliver it to the morgue, and get on with his job as a used car salesman.

J.D. looked down the road again, hoping to see Dixon. Instead, Beatrice Smart rounded the curve. He felt a profound sense of relief. He had not thought to call her, but she might be able to reach Camille. He mentally gave Waymon a gold star for having the sense to let her through.

He stepped away from the body, hoping to avert Beatrice's attention, but he was too late. She halted and then staggered. Through Beatrice's eyes he saw anew the horror, the decaying body, the burned flesh, the fluttering of the once white sheet. Camille had told him that she'd seen the body on fire, had awakened Eustace, who had rushed out of the house and doused the flames with water. In places the sheet still clung to the body.

He strode across the distance and caught the minister's arm, holding her steady as he blocked her view.

"Reverend," he said, supporting her. "Bea?"

"I thought I was prepared."

"Nothing can prepare you for this. Nothing." Man's brutality against his own kind was beyond comprehension.

"Calvin asked me to speak to Camille," she said, her gaze directed at J.D.'s shirt.

"I'm glad you came. Camille is in the house." He led her past the body.

"How is she?"

In her voice, he could hear Beatrice reaching for control.

"Not good. She's withdrawn. She's been sitting in a chair in the den, but a moment ago I saw her at the window, so at least she's moving around." J.D. was concerned that Camille could slip into a catatonic state, a mental limbo land from which she might never emerge. Her voice, when she'd called him at six A.M., had been dead.

"And Eustace?" Beatrice asked.

"He's pretty shaken up."

"Will he talk with me?"

"I don't know," J.D. answered softly. "I hope so."

J.D. heard Vivian's voice again. He heard Beth Salter, too, breathing fire and threatening lawsuits against everyone in sight.

J.D. glanced up at the camp's large window. "You want me to go in with you?" he asked.

"No, I think it would be better if I went alone. Besides, it sounds like you're about to have a riot on your hands with Vivian stirring everyone up."

He let her arm go. She took a breath, nodded, and walked toward the camp.

The commotion at the head of the drive increased. Waymon was holding back angry men and women who were worried that a violent killer was free. Everyone felt vulnerable, even those who normally buffered themselves with money and power. J.D. knew he should get up there before things got out of hand, but he couldn't leave the body until Dixon had photographed it.

He saw her headed down the drive and crossed the clearing, moving upwind of the body. Her gaze met his and slid away. He wondered why. Dixon had never failed to bore directly into him. It was one of the things he liked about her.

"I made it as fast as I could." She spoke to her cameras and there was a challenge in her voice. Her hands shook, and she dropped a lens. Cursing, she picked it up and bent to snap it onto the camera body.

J.D. noted her red eyes and thought she'd been drinking.

"Thanks for coming." He reached out to touch her shoulder and stopped himself, suddenly self-conscious.

Dixon lifted the camera and went to work. She repeated the sequence of photos she'd done on Trisha Webster, and when

J.D. lifted the sheet to show the carving in Angie's thigh, he saw that Dixon's face was covered in sweat. Her hands trembled as she clicked the camera, but she didn't complain, and she worked with quick efficiency, shooting both color and black-and-white.

She was finished in fifteen minutes. J.D. waved to the coroner, who'd remained in the shade of an oak, drinking orange sodas, one after another. J.D. touched Dixon's back and guided her away. She flinched at the zip of the body bag and the rattle of the stretcher wheels against the rocks.

The macabre humor that sometimes accompanied body collection was missing. The only sound was the rough intake of air as they struggled against the odor and the growing volume of discontent at the road.

"My God," Dixon said as the coroner rolled the body toward an old ambulance. "Who found her?"

"Camille."

Dixon looked at him. "Is she okay?"

"Beatrice Smart is with her," J.D. answered.

Her expression changed, and he knew she'd noticed Eustace. She watched him for a long moment.

"What are you going to do about the crowd?" She tilted her head toward the road, where the mob was growing louder and angrier.

"Send Beth Salter home with an escort and wait for the others to disband."

"What about Chavez?" Dixon asked.

"Two national guard units are on the way. The roads are blocked, and men are posted at every timber trail and path that comes out of the swamps. We'll bring him in."

"Dead or alive?" Dixon asked.

He nodded. "Dead or alive."

"I heard the men at the roadblock. They intend to kill him in the swamps," she said.

He knew that the men who'd volunteered to help him might attempt to take justice into their own hands. "Not if I can help it," he said.

"What does Eustace say?" she asked.

J.D. looked over at his friend. "Nothing."

CHAPTER TWENTY-SEVEN

Eustace waited until J.D. left. He watched the lawman stop on the driveway, pull out his cell phone, and begin to talk. The reporter kept going. She walked as if she were in a daze. Eustace just wanted all of them gone—everyone off his property so that he could talk to Camille. The preacher woman was in the camp now, but he knew that Beatrice Smart had no words that could reach Camille. He'd seen Camille's face as she'd watched the body burn, twisting at the end of the rope. A rope from the boat Chavez had stolen, now floating gently among the others.

Chavez had returned the boat and the body, as if he were fulfilling a pact, a connection he'd made with Camille. But Eustace realized that he'd been wrong in what he thought about Camille's involvement. He'd been wrong about a lot.

He looked up and caught a brief glimpse of Vivian, rabble-rousing and demanding blood. His blood. He almost wished that one of the deputies would shoot him and put him out of his misery. He'd believed that Camille was capable of terrible things. But in the end, he was the one who'd done them. He'd shot the Mexican. He'd been willing to let Angie Salter die in the woods. He'd lost all trace of humanity because he could not live without Camille.

There were things he should have told J.D. but hadn't. Someone had picked up Chavez after he'd brought the body to the camp. Someone was helping him, but it wasn't Camille.

Eustace knew the man's route away from the camp because he'd erased the trail to the road, where it had ended. The man had bled into the sand. The compulsion to hang and burn Angie Salter must have outweighed even the pain of his gunshot wound.

Eustace looked down at the fish. All of his life he'd viewed them as a means to an end. He harvested them for survival. He'd never considered it from their side. Now, though, he understood something of what they must feel as they rushed from one end of the vat to the other. The cement wall blocked them. They were trapped, waiting for fate to net them and pull them into death.

If he managed to survive with Camille still at his side, he was going to free the fish. All of them. He would never kill another living creature.

He got up and walked to the house. The steps seemed insurmountable. Camille was up there, waiting for him. Maybe needing him. He started up, his bad leg dragging. When he entered the house, Camille was in a rocker, holding a mug of tea. The minister sat across from her, leaning forward. "Sometimes we can't understand the workings of God," she told Camille.

Camille stared at her. "What kind of god is that then?"

The minister slowly shook her head. "Faith is the ability to believe, even when there's no rational explanation, Camille."

"I believe," Camille answered. "I believe in the trees and the animals. I believe in the wind and the river, and that love can heal."

"Even the animals commit acts of violence."

Camille shook her head. "Not like this. Not so . . . sick." The last word was a whisper.

Eustace went to her. He took the mug of tea and put it on the table, then pulled her into his arms. At first she resisted, but then she fell against him. He felt her shaking. When the sobs came, they sounded as if her throat were being torn out.

The minister picked up the mugs and went to the kitchen. Eustace could hear her running water and putting things away while he patted Camille's back and made soothing sounds.

Camille gradually stopped crying, then pushed back from him and wiped her face with her shirt sleeve.

"He was my friend," she said. "He was my friend, and he did this terrible thing again. Even after he promised he wouldn't."

Eustace froze. He stared into the minister's eyes across the kitchen counter. She looked as horrified as he felt. He wanted to beg her not to say anything. But that would only give more weight to Camille's words. He had to minimize the damage.

"Camille, why don't you lie down and rest," he said, angling her toward the bedroom. He looked over his shoulder. "Reverend, could you put on a pot of coffee? I think J.D. could use a cup. Everything is right there on the counter." He closed the bedroom door behind him and helped Camille to the bed.

"Just rest," he said. "Once all these folks are gone, we'll drive over to the kiln site. I think we should start on it right away. This afternoon."

"This afternoon?" Her eyes questioned him.

He didn't meet her gaze. "I was thinking that after this mess with those girls, it would be good to create your pottery in the woods. I'm no expert on nature or the spirits, but it seems to me that would please them."

"Eustace," she said, kissing his cheek. "You surprise me sometimes. And all along I thought that you thought I was crazy."

His chest ached. "No, Camille. I never thought that. Not ever."

He covered her with a light spread and turned the air conditioner on high. The drone blocked the noise from outside. When the blinds were adjusted to darken the room he left her, closing the door behind him.

He walked toward the minister, waiting in the kitchen.

"Camille is resting. She's been under such pressure."

"She said she was friends with that man, Chavez."

He shook his head. "Reverend Smart, I have to be honest with you. This business with those girls has troubled Camille greatly. It's been on her mind, waking and sleeping. She's . . . absorbed it, for want of a better word, and in her own mind she's woven herself into the story. See what I mean?"

"Are you saying she's hallucinated herself into the murders?"

"That's taking it a little too far. She wanted to help. She wanted to save Angie. In her mind, she believes she talked to Chavez. That doesn't mean it happened in reality."

The coffeepot hissed and sputtered. Eustace went to the cabinet and got a large Styrofoam cup. He poured it full. "I'll take this to J.D."

"Is it possible Camille actually talked to Chavez?" the minister asked.

He waited, not wanting to seem to rush into an answer. "Anything is possible, Reverend, but I don't see how she could have. I've locked up the boats. The only way she could talk to him would be on the road to Jexville or here at the camp."

The minister leaned against the counter. "Yes, and we know that Chavez knows how to find his way here."

Eustace looked down to hide his anger. She was aptly named. Nothing much got past the Reverend Smart.

"Vivian has spoken to me about having Camille committed. She feels her daughter isn't capable of making decisions about her own safety. I have to say, Mr. Mills, if Camille is running around with a man who may be a double murderer, Vivian has a point."

Eustace felt as if he were balanced on a narrow ledge far above pavement. "If Vivian and Calvin had been as interested in raising a healthy daughter as they are in controlling Camille, we wouldn't be having this discussion."

To his surprise, the minister smiled. "Well put."

"Vivian doesn't care whether Camille is happy or not. She only cares that she has the ultimate say-so. I love Camille. I would do anything for her, even let her go."

The minister walked up to him and held out her hand for the coffee. "Your love for Camille has never been in question. I'll take that to J.D. I need to talk to him anyway."

✝

Dixon walked up the long, twisting drive toward the main road. The sun had come on strong, bouncing through the oak limbs to create lacy patterns of shadow on the white sandy path. She could hear shouting. J.D. had a volatile situation, and Vivian Holbert was doing everything she could to push the spectators into a mob.

Dixon pictured Angie Salter, an overly made-up girl with naked ambition in her blue eyes. She'd dreamt of becoming a model, but she died instead. And she'd taken Trisha Webster with her. Orie Webster had set up a college fund for her daughter. Trisha had wanted to be an elementary teacher. She had followed Angie to the river for a day of mischief and had paid with her life.

But something about the disappearance and murders didn't ring true as two innocent girls' simply being in the wrong place at the wrong time. Angie was not an innocent. At her instigation, serious charges had been brought against a teacher. Conveniently, on the day that official action was taken, Angie had disappeared. How could Francisco Chavez have shown up at exactly the right time to abduct Angie and Trisha? The timing troubled her.

That and Tommy Hayes. Angie had been blackmailing him. Dixon didn't have evidence, but she knew it. The biology teacher had delivered a bribe in the form of a boom box, and he could have been on the river when the girls were taken. Angie's web had caught not only herself and Trisha but a number of others too.

Why had the killer brought Angie's body to Eustace Mills's yard for the final ritual? She could see that it troubled J.D., too. She wanted to talk with him, but several things held her back, not the least of which was Robert Medino. The animosity between the sheriff and Medino was deeper than a professional or personality aversion. Looking at it too closely would require her to examine her own thoughts, and she wasn't ready for that.

In fact, if she could have anything in the world right now, it would be a shady spot, a cold beer, and a cigarette. At least she had cigarettes in her truck.

The mob, held back by Waymon and two volunteer deputies, was growing in number and intensity. Another injustice would become fact if J.D. didn't get them under control. If he could. As she drew closer, she felt revulsion. They'd breakfasted on blood lust and fear, and they wanted their pound of flesh. God help anyone who got in their way. Dixon spotted Vivian's bright red suit at the front of the mob.

"Those girls cry out for justice," Vivian was yelling into the crowd. "Their murderer will go free unless you do something about it. Sheriff Horton won't do anything because Eustace Mills is his friend. Well, I'm going to do something." She ducked under the tape, her high heels sinking in the sandy roadbed.

"Hey! Hey! Mrs. Holbert!" Waymon's voice rose. He maneuvered in front of her. "I'm sorry, ma'am, but you can't go down there."

"I want my daughter, and I'm going to get her." She brushed past him and continued walking.

Waymon put a hand on her shoulder.

"Take your hands off me or you and your department will be sued." Her threat was echoed by Beth Salter, who took a swing at Waymon.

J.D. stepped out from the shadow of an oak. "Escort Mrs. Holbert back behind the tape and turn her loose. Then escort Mrs. Salter home." Ignoring Vivian, he pointed across the river, giving directions to a group of fifteen men, all armed with rifles. He ignored the media, who photographed him with telephoto lenses and a certain wariness.

The men climbed into pickup trucks. With a blast of white exhaust, they took off. They bucked over the potholes in the road and spun gravel as they headed for the bridge and the west side of the river. Dixon felt queasy. If they saw Chavez, they'd kill him on the spot. Trisha and Angie were dead. There was no reason not to kill Chavez. He was an outsider who'd come into their county and violated two young girls. He would pay a severe price.

She was almost at her truck when she saw Zander pumping his bicycle hard as he churned through the sand of the road.

"Zander!" she called out, but he didn't slow.

She opened the door of her truck and saw the bundle of Willard's letters, tied with a dirty white string. She looked up again at the man-child. He'd stopped and turned back to look over his shoulder.

She held the letters up and started to call out his name again. Before she could say anything, he turned and disappeared around a curve.

Dixon stood holding the letters. For someone who wanted her help, he certainly acted peculiar.

✝

Vivian was raising holy hell, but it wasn't anything less than J.D. expected. He wanted to slap her into next Sunday but had restrained himself. He needed to ask her something important.

He watched as she made another run at Waymon. The deputy caught her around the waist, picked her up, and carried her back outside the crime scene tape. Vivian was spluttering threats.

Sighing, J.D. stepped forward. When the mob saw him, they roared, swelling into the crime scene tape Waymon had hurriedly strung. J.D. held up a hand.

"There's nothing else to be done here. Go on home."

"Those girls are dead!" a woman shouted. "Are you gonna catch the killer?"

J.D. stared at her until she closed her mouth and stepped back. "Angie and Trisha are dead. There's nothing we can do for them. The worst thing that can happen is for you people to rush to take justice into your own hands."

"The killer is sitting up there!" Vivian screamed.

J.D. ignored her. "We'll find the person who killed these girls. He, or she, will be punished according to the law. Now you people go home and tend to your own children."

"Eustace Mills killed those girls!" Vivian lunged at J.D., but Waymon deflected her.

"If I believed Eustace killed those girls, I'd arrest him," J.D. said, addressing the crowd. "No man is above the law."

Vivian was beside herself. "Liar! You goddamn liar!"

J.D. turned to Waymon and spoke softly. "Put her in the back of the patrol car. Lock it up. Then get Beth Salter out of here."

"Yes, sir," Waymon said. Waymon lifted a thrashing and writhing Vivian up and walked her to the patrol car.

"Go home," J.D. told the crowd, his patience wearing thin. "Go home or I swear I'll have you all arrested and put in jail where you can wait for me to bring in the killer."

"Let's go," one of the men said. "We'll meet up at the Stop-N-Shop."

J.D. didn't care for the sound of that, but he couldn't stop them. With any luck they'd gather at the store, drink a few beers, talk big, and go home to grumble away the afternoon. With any luck.

He went to the patrol car. If he thought it would do any good, he would lock Vivian up. But Calvin would post her bail. Arrest would only serve to further incense her.

He got in the back with her. Vivian looked like a cornered cat. Her eyes were large, her lips drawn back.

"I'll have your fucking head," she hissed.

"Maybe, maybe not. I need your help, Vivian."

That stopped her cold.

"Why should I help you?"

"Why not? What do you have to lose?" He would counter question for question. Vivian never listened to answers anyway.

"I wouldn't spit on you if you were on fire."

"But you want me to catch the killer, right?"

"And what do you think I can do to help?" she asked.

"You and Calvin have been very generous with Camille, haven't you?"

The switch in conversation seemed to confuse her. She didn't answer right away.

"We've been more than generous. She's had every opportunity. The best doctors, the best medical care. Therapists!" She threw up her hands. "To what end? So she can waste her youth with that swamp creature you insist on defending."

"Camille is a lovely young woman with a lot of artistic talent. You've encouraged that, haven't you?"

Vivian was wary. "Why are you so interested in Camille?"

"You've given her expensive things. The car, her clothes, jewelry."

Vivian bit her bottom lip. "What of it?"

"Could you put a monetary figure on the luxuries you've given her?"

"Don't be an ass. A mother doesn't put monetary amounts on the things she gives her daughter."

"Really, Vivian." J.D. looked at her. "Of course they do. Look, the car had to be an easy forty grand."

"So what?"

"And her medical care, what? Sixty thousand?" He paused. "And another twenty for those clothes she wears around the swamps like she bought them off a Goodwill rack." He had her attention. "And the jewelry?"

"What are you getting at?"

J.D. pulled the bracelet from his pocket. It came out curling and clinking around his hand and fingers. Vivian drew back, as if it might bite her.

"Did you give this to Camille?" he asked.

Vivian stared at the bracelet. "I've never seen that piece of jewelry before in my life."

CHAPTER TWENTY-EIGHT

J.D. stepped out of the patrol car and walked into the principal's office at Chickasaw County High School. He had a warrant in his hand for the arrest of Tommy Hayes. If Hayes got a good lawyer, the charges wouldn't stick, but J.D. didn't intend for them to. He wanted to make a point with the school teacher, who'd lied to him.

With the principal huffing behind him, J.D. went to Hayes's classroom and called the teacher out to the hall.

"What's up, J.D.?" Hayes asked. He glanced back into the classroom, where his students were unnaturally well behaved.

"You're under arrest, Tommy," J.D. said.

"For what?"

"We should talk outside."

"Well, I want to know," the principal said.

J.D. ignored him and led Hayes outside. There was no need to cuff him. There wasn't any fight in him. He put Hayes in the back of the patrol car and drove toward the courthouse.

"What's going on?" Hayes asked from the back seat. He sounded as if he were about to cry.

"You've lied to me," J.D. said. "More than once."

There was a miserable silence for two blocks. They were headed up Providence Street when Hayes spoke again.

"I did lie. I bought Angie a boom box, and I took it to her at the river. I saw both girls that morning."

J.D. slowed the car. "Why did you lie?"

"Because it makes me look guilty of murder. I was there. She was blackmailing me. I had a motive to kill her, and I was at the place where she disappeared. But I didn't kill her, J.D. I didn't. I gave her the boom box, and I left."

"What time was this?" J.D. pulled over and turned to look at Hayes through the grill.

"It was close to ten. I'd bought the boom box the day before, and I had it for her. She was supposed to come by the house and get it. That's why I wasn't at school. Then Angie called me on her cell phone and told me I'd better deliver the boom box to the river right away or she was going to call the superintendent and tell him about my relationship with Craig. I did what she said, and then I drove to Biloxi to hire a lawyer."

"Your relationship with Craig Baggett is homosexual."

"That's right. I wanted to protect Craig. His father will—" Hayes's voice was little more than a whisper. "We'll both probably be stoned to death. You know how it is here. Everything is a sin. Being gay—Jesus, people will think I'm in league with Satan."

J.D. looked past Hayes to a pickup truck driving by. Hayes was in danger of losing his job and a whole lot more. Jexville wasn't a community that tolerated those outside traditional relationship and family patterns. He had a right to be afraid. Getting fired might be the least that happened.

"What time did you leave the river?"

"I didn't stay more than five minutes."

"Did you talk to Angie?"

Hayes wiped his right eye. "I begged her not to tell anyone." His voice was strained. "Trisha promised she wouldn't say anything, and she tried to get Angie to promise. But Angie wouldn't. She said she never gave up a weapon."

He hesitated, and J.D. pushed. "You were angry with Angie."

"She was a stupid bitch who didn't care who she ruined. Poor Trisha. She didn't want to go to the river with Angie. She only went because no one else would. Angie didn't have a single friend in the world, so Trisha went along to disguise the fact that Angie was all alone."

"Tommy, did you see anyone else on the river when you were there?"

"Just the two girls."

J.D. drove to the courthouse. He exited the car and opened the back door. "Tommy, I'm not going to kid you; you're in a lot of trouble."

"I know."

"I want you to go to the sheriff's office and wait for me at my desk. I'm not going to charge you or put anything on the books unless you leave. Once this goes down in the docket, it's on your record for good. Do you understand what I'm saying?"

Hayes gave a feeble smile. "I'll be right there when you come back."

J.D. watched as the teacher disappeared into the courthouse. Hayes had lied to protect his secret, but J.D. didn't believe he'd killed anyone, least of all the two girls.

He pulled the bracelet out. He'd dusted it for prints and found only Camille's. Camille had said her mother gave it to her, but Vivian had denied it.

He put the car in gear and headed toward Main Street. If the bracelet had been purchased at Easterling's Jewelry, it would simplify things. And if it hadn't, Clive Easterling could probably tell J.D. where to begin looking for the store that had sold it—and to whom.

He passed the Magnolia B&B and saw Robert Medino reclined on the porch swing, his bare feet extended toward Main Street. J.D. didn't like him, but he knew that soon enough the writer would pack up and move on. He didn't have what it took to put down roots and stay in a place.

†

Dixon sat on the edge of the bed with the packet of letters beside her. She held one page of lined, three-holed notebook paper and read the words written in pencil. The date was November 18, 1995.

My son, I want you to know my days here are not terrible. I eat and sleep and mark off the hours, knowing that you are growing strong in your mother's care.

Winter is coming to the Delta, and soon the cotton fields will be empty. Today I watched a thunderstorm move across the fields. The clouds reminded me of dragons, and I thought of that book I used to read to you. Ask your mama to read it for me tonight.

Your mother's family comes from Kentucky, and when you are old enough, you must ask her to tell you the stories. She has a proud heritage, and I want you to always remember that. No matter what is said about me, remember that you have many things to be proud of. Ask your mama.

I love you, son.

Daddy.

Dixon picked up the second letter, written the following week, on Thanksgiving Day. It went into great detail about the prison holiday meal. Dixon could read between the lines. Jones did not want to leave a legacy of grief to his only child.

She read several more letters, then put them aside to think about her visit with Willard Jones. She'd gone to Parchman after a three-day drunk. She hadn't shown up for work or even called in. She'd driven from Memphis across the flat landscape of the Delta, thinking about the sheer physical labor that had been required to remove all the trees for those vast stretches of farmland. Topsoil eight feet deep. But not since the river had been controlled by the levee.

When she'd arrived at the prison, only her credentials as a reporter had gotten her onto death row to see Jones. Even then, an assistant warden had stayed at her side. He'd probably thought she was going to try and assassinate the prisoner. Hardly.

She'd talked to Jones in a small room, the one used by lawyers and priests. Prison had aged him. The years behind bars had turned him gray, both hair and skin. He'd said nothing about the smell of bourbon on her.

"Did you kill my father?" she'd asked. She could remember her rage.

"Go home, Miss Sinclair."

It was the only thing he'd said to her. He'd refused to say another word, and she had left the prison angrier than before. It had been a lovely excuse to turn into the first bar she came to on the outskirts of Memphis and drink until she'd passed out. She'd come to in a clinic where some of her coworkers had taken her.

And from there, she'd gone on to drink harder, just to show them she could. But Jones had remained in her thoughts. Present every day. Now she heard his voice, and she understood why his son wanted so desperately to save him.

The air conditioner fluttered the pages of the letter. She stood up and went outside, taking the letters to the front porch swing. She began to read again. A year in prison had passed before Jones mentioned the murder.

My son, I am well, if not happy. Today I thought I would tell you a few truths. I did not kill Ray Sinclair. A jury convicted me, but they made a mistake. Let me tell you what happened, so you will always know the truth.

Mr. Sinclair was a newspaper man who wrote hard facts about powerful people. He had written several articles about Bo Duelly, a man with power in the black community. Bo Duelly and I were enemies. He is a man you should never trust.

As I've told you about your mother's people, I also come from a proud family. The Jones family has lived in Jones County, Mississippi, since long before the Civil War.

During the Civil War, Jones County refused to join in the secession from the Union. It declared itself a Free State. There was an outlaw during this time who rode the county taking what he wanted from the wealthy families, and one of the things he took was your great-great-grandmother. He bought her freedom, eventually, and she had his child. She carried the name of Jones, which was from the family she was stolen from.

Your great-great-grandmother never married. She kept the Jones name, and she eventually acquired nearly three hundred acres in Jones County. This land was considered worthless because there were old caves on it, salt domes. But the land was in our family for a long time, until it was stolen.

On the morning of the newspaper bombing, I had a ten o'clock appointment with Mr. Sinclair. He'd been asking questions about that land in Jones County, and I had information to tell him. So we met and talked, and I left the newspaper.

Two hours later, he was dead, and a few hours after that I was charged with his murder. Alexander, I never made a bomb, and I don't know where the newspaper clippings they found in our home came from. That's the truth. Now just hold this in your heart. Don't go asking questions. By the time you understand this, I will probably be dead, so there won't be any point in digging all of this up. But I want you to know the truth. Your daddy is an innocent man. And you should hold yourself with pride and dignity. Love, Daddy.

Dixon put the letters aside. She didn't have to read any further. She had the answer, and now she needed the proof. She needed to go to Jackson and research her father's newspaper articles. But, she couldn't. She had a paper to put together, and she'd shoved far too much responsibility on Linda and Tucker in the past few days. She was grateful to Robert for volunteering to go for her.

She dialed the Magnolia and asked to speak to Robert.

"Darlin', he's out on the front porch in the swing. Is it important enough that I disturb him?"

"Ruth Ann, if you don't put him on the phone right now, I'm going to drive over there and snatch you bald-headed."

"Well, there's no call to talk to me thataway."

Dixon didn't respond. She heard Ruth Ann's tread and the screech of the screened door. Then, "You have a call from a very rude person."

Robert's voice was warm and easy. "What's happening, Dixon?"

She was amused. "You knew the rude person was me."

He laughed. "It had to be a woman, and since you're the only woman in town who would telephone me, it was easy to figure out."

It had been such a long time since she'd trusted anyone. Especially with something this important. "Could you go to Jackson and look up those newspaper articles right away?"

She heard his feet hit the floor and realized he'd been reclining in the swing.

"I can leave in the next ten minutes."

"Thank you, Robert."

"No thanks necessary. Did you find out something?"

"I'll tell you all about it when you get back. Look in particular for stories about the Mississippi salt domes."

✝

Easterling Jewelry was a narrow store between Main Street Drugs and a cheap furniture store. J.D. had known the owner since first grade. Clive had been a thin child with a too-big head and glasses with thick black frames. He'd collected stamps and coins and knew the pantheon of Greek gods by heart. Even the teachers were afraid of him.

J.D. was thinking about Clive's first-grade show-and-tell as he entered the jewelry store. Clive came out of the back with a jeweler's magnification device on his head.

"I kept telling everyone you'd get a girlfriend," Clive said. "At last you're here to buy her a gift. Gold or silver?"

J.D. shook his head. "Wishful thinking. No girl, yet."

"Then what brings you to the store?" Clive asked.

"Is anyone else here?"

Clive shook his head. "Lydia went down to the Hickory Pit to pick up some lunches. She just left."

J.D. probably had half an hour. He reached into his pocket and brought out the bracelet. Clive's eyes brightened.

"That's some beautiful work."

"Not yours then?"

Clive picked up the gold and let it ripple through his fingers. "No. I wish it were. This is exquisite. Gold is malleable, but the person working this knew the exact limit. See how the interlocking links make it look alive as it bends?" Clive examined the bracelet in silence. "So who does it belong to?"

"A dead girl."

Clive examined the gold more closely. "And you want to know where she got it?"

"You're as smart as ever."

Clive picked up the bracelet. "I've seen work like this." He hesitated. "Most retail jewelers don't design any longer. They carry national or international designers. A piece of this quality shouldn't be hard to trace. If you can give me a few hours, I'll photograph it, get on the Internet, and I'll bet I can find the jeweler who sold it."

"Thanks, Clive."

"You could do this yourself, but I probably know where to start quicker than you."

"Could you put a monetary value on the piece?"

276

Clive thought about it. "I'd say that if the buyer paid full price, it had to be around seven thousand dollars."

It was a very expensive gift for a fifteen-year-old girl.

Clive sighed. "I heard they found the Salter girl. There was talk in the Hickory Pit this morning. Folks are riled."

"I know."

"I heard more than one man say folks should get their rifles and go hunting in the swamps for the man who killed those girls." Clive frowned. "Folks seem to believe it's a Mexican man."

J.D. nodded. "I'm looking for a man who defaced some property at the Catholic church. There's reason to believe he might be involved in the disappearance of the girls."

"You think he kidnapped them and killed them?"

That was the crux of it. J.D. wasn't sure what he believed. The idea of a man coming to destroy a statue and ending up killing two girls was hard to swallow.

"J.D.?" Clive touched his shoulder. "You look haunted, man. Can I get you come coffee?"

J.D. nodded. "That would be good."

Clive went to the back and returned with a paper cup of black coffee. "I know this business with those girls is tearing you up. Most folks don't know how hard this is for you."

J.D. sipped the coffee. It was hot and bitter.

"You joined the service after Karen was killed in the accident. Right after the funeral. You never wanted folks to see you hurt."

"Most folks don't care to show their pain in public."

"It's more than that with you. You left everything. Your folks, the farm. You just let it all go. I never thought you'd come back here."

J.D. shrugged. It wasn't that he didn't have regrets; he'd just accepted that the past couldn't be undone. He'd run away from the pain of his sister's death. It had cost him everything, but he hadn't known what else to do. Going into the marines had given him a focus away from the loss that had destroyed his parents.

"How long have you been sheriff now?" Clive asked.

"Five years," J.D. said. "I'm into my second term."

"Amazing." Clive smiled. "Maybe if you run again, I'll vote for you."

"Maybe it won't be too long before I'm back to buy a present for a . . . woman."

"You'll get a twenty-percent discount on anything in the store," Clive said.

"Thanks. I'll stop by again before you close."

"How about I give you a call the minute I find something?" Clive asked.

"That's even better."

CHAPTER TWENTY-NINE

Dixon spent the afternoon at a meeting of the board of aldermen, who were discussing renovation of the town's sewage system. A handful of citizens protested the location of the new sewage treatment plant, and one person complained about garbage pickup. Not exactly a meeting of global significance, but Dixon felt good about covering local governing bodies. Once the stories appeared in the paper, more citizens might get involved. Ray Sinclair had been a big advocate of such coverage.

Her father was much on her mind as she walked from city hall back to the newspaper. Willard Jones's letters to his son had brought back memories. Jones and her father had been leading diverse lives that had collided one day in May, a day that changed both families forever.

She checked her cell phone for messages. It was hard waiting to hear from Robert, but she had to stay in Jexville. There were stories to write and photos to print—for her newspaper. The *Independent* was her chance to prove herself to her father. It was also an excuse to hide from a past she didn't want to confront. She was lucky to have Robert, a man who cared enough—and had the skills—to help her.

Tucker was waiting for her at the newspaper office.

"What about the preliminaries for the Junior Miss pageant?" he asked. "Will we cover the pageant? It's tonight."

"Why don't you do it? I should think the least you get out of it would be a date."

"Right. Those girls are underage," he said.

"My grandmother used to tell me that looking and getting are two different things." She patted his shoulder.

"I'll cover the talent competition," Tucker said, pretending to be miffed. "What about Angie Salter's funeral? It's tomorrow afternoon."

Dixon considered. "You can cover it for the paper, but I think we should both go. For Linda's sake." The typesetter had gone home, too upset to work.

"Right. We should do that." He hesitated. "Dixon, there were men up at the Hickory Pit at lunchtime. They were talking, saying they were going to hunt down the guy who killed Angie and shoot him in the woods."

Dixon had hoped the mob mentality would wane once the shock of finding the second body had passed. "It was probably just big talk."

"I don't think so. They're gathering tomorrow morning. Some of the men are taking off work. They're going to search the woods with four-wheelers and boats. If that Mexican is in there, they say they're going to kill him."

Dixon slumped in her chair.

"I want to catch the guy who did this, but those men aren't planning on bringing him back alive," Tucker continued

Dixon stood up. "I'm going to set this story into type, and then I'm going to find J.D. and tell him what you heard. Did you recognize any of the men?"

"Mack Prentiss and Edward Smith. The others I didn't know."

Dixon took her copy to the typesetting machine. In another year, she'd have computers so the stories could be typeset in column inches. Now, though, they just had to limp along as best they could. She'd finished when the telephone rang. Tucker answered, then came to get her.

"It's some kid. I could hardly understand him." He handed her the portable.

"Dixon Sinclair."

"Daddy tried to hang himself." The voice was lost in sorrow. "His friend called me and told me. Said they took Daddy to the hospital and no one knows what happened."

"Zander?" She stood up. "Where are you?"

"Even if he lives, they're gone put him in the gas chamber anyway." He sobbed. "He's going to die and he didn't do anything."

"I'm coming out to your house. Stay there. I want to talk to you." She listened to his crying. "Stay right there, Zander. I mean it. I'm on the way."

She hung up the phone. "Tucker, you're going to have to talk to J.D. about those men. I've got an emergency."

"Who was that?" he asked.

She considered how much to tell him. "Zander Jones. His father is going to be executed soon for the murder of my father." She grabbed her purse as she talked. "I've got to get out to his place. Something bad has happened."

"I'll take care of things," Tucker said.

She took a breath. "Whether we can afford it or not, you get a raise."

She stepped into the late afternoon heat and headed to her truck. Things were getting out of control.

✝

Light slanted through the bedroom window, falling directly on the open suitcase on the bed. Eustace put a second pair of jeans into the suitcase, along with his socks and four pair of underwear. From his dresser drawer he got four pullover shirts. That would be enough.

He shut the suitcase and carried it to the living room, where Camille sat motionless in a rocker. Light filtered through the stained glass window onto her face. Eustace stopped beside her. "I'll be okay," he said.

"Don't leave me." She whispered the words.

"I have to." He swallowed something hard and painful in his throat. "I have to, Camille. If I go, they'll look for me. They'll leave you alone."

"I didn't do anything."

He set the suitcase down and knelt beside her. "Where did you get that bracelet, Camille?" It wouldn't be long before J.D. came back, asking that very question. Camille's answer, whatever it might be, would be less important if Eustace were gone. With Vivian's encouragement, the finger of guilt would point to him and the chase would be on.

"I told you, and I told J.D. Mama gave me the bracelet."

Eustace touched her hair, running his fingers lightly down the fine, reddish gold tresses. "I wish that were true, Camille. That bracelet belongs to a dead girl." Eustace could still see the sparkle of it on Angie Salter's wrist as she'd held up the beer.

"You're mistaken. Daddy gave it to Mama. Mama got tired of it and gave it to me."

"When?" Eustace asked.

"Last week. It was the day the girls disappeared. She was up here in the ski boat. She came to the landing."

Eustace held himself very still. "Vivian was here?"

Camille hesitated. "Only for a while. She didn't come to the house, just the landing. She was upset. Something had happened. She had the bracelet, and when I told her it was pretty, she gave it to me."

"Where was it?"

"On the seat of the ski boat."

"Did she say anything else?"

"She told me to keep it hidden, somewhere safe."

The tide of rage was so strong it left Eustace light-headed. Camille's eyes narrowed. She could sense his emotions, and he knew he had to be careful.

"It's okay that Vivian was here," he said calmly, watching to see if she believed him.

"She told me not to tell you."

"Camille, you can tell me anything."

"Can I?"

His heart was pounding. "Yes, you can. Why was Vivian upset?"

"She didn't say."

"You're smart. Why do you think she was upset?"

"Why do you care?" she countered.

"Because I care about you. If Vivian is in trouble, it's going to make you unhappy."

"Mama's not in trouble."

"The day she came to the landing, was that the same day she told you she wanted to sell the houseboat?" He rocked back on his heels.

"Are you leaving?"

He considered. He only wanted to protect Camille. Now he had to determine the best way to do it.

"I'm not sure. I don't want to go."

"Okay, I'll tell you. It wasn't the day she told me she wanted to sell the houseboat. It was before that. She'd been skiing on the river, and something had gone wrong. That's why she was upset."

Eustace thought about it. "If she was skiing, who was driving the boat?"

Camille was puzzled. "She didn't say."

Eustace shrugged, playing it cool. "Doesn't really matter. Did she say why she was upset?"

"Her shirt was torn. She was dirty." Camille frowned. "Mama's never dirty."

"Was her hair wet?"

"Sure. She'd been skiing."

"Camille, I'm going to ask you something, and I need for you to tell me the truth." He touched her hair. "Do you know what happened to those girls?"

She shook her head. "I saw them on the sandbar. I was afraid to tell."

"It's okay. You can tell me now."

"I went up river to Hathaway's Point. That's when I saw the man. He was in the woods, and he was hiding."

Eustace took her head. "Did he have the girls?"

"No, they were on the sandbar."

"This was before or after your mother stopped by?"

"Before. I came home. I wanted to be home before you came back from running the trotlines. I was drawing down by the dock when Mama came by."

Eustace pieced the time together. "I never saw her on the river."

"She went back downriver to Cumbest Bluff."

"Camille, did you look in her boat?"

"Why are you asking that?"

"Please, just answer me."

"From the dock. I walked down to meet her, and I waited at the landing. I saw the bracelet on the seat of the boat." She smiled. "It was sparkling in the sun, like the water."

He stroked her hand. "Could you see into the bottom of her boat?"

"You think she had those girls." She pulled her hand away. "You hate her enough to think she took those girls."

Eustace couldn't deny it. "Someone took them."

†

J.D. drove to the back of the jewelry store. He hadn't been expecting the call from Clive so soon. When he drove past the newspaper, Tucker was at the front desk. There was no sign of Dixon or her truck.

He knocked on the back door and felt the metal give as Clive pulled the door open.

"The bracelet was sold at Zimball's Jewelry on Hillcrest Road in Mobile," Clive said.

"You're certain?"

"Better than that. I know who bought it."

J.D. grinned. "Damn, Clive, I should put you on the payroll."

"Big Jim Welford."

J.D. blinked. "Welford?"

"Who did you think it would be?" Clive asked. "A bracelet like that, had to be someone with money."

"True enough," J.D. said. "They were positive?"

"Without a doubt." Clive tilted his head to examine J.D. "They had Welford's Visa card account number. He made the purchase about four weeks ago. Had his correct address."

J.D. nodded. "Does Welford purchase a lot of jewelry?"

"Not from me. His wife wears a diamond engagement ring and a diamond ring guard." His lip twitched up. "Showy but not really expensive. Last thing he bought in here was a pair of hoop earrings for Attie for Christmas. About fifty dollars. Big Jim feels jewelry is too flashy for his wife." He nodded. "So who was the bracelet for?"

"Thank you, Clive." J.D. turned toward the back door.

"Do you want to see the e-mail confirmation I got?"

"Right now, what I have to do is find Welford."

"That could be tricky. I heard at the Rotary meeting that he was headed up to Montana for a week of vacation. I think he wants to avoid that reporter woman. She sure tanned his hide in the newspaper."

"She sure did," J.D. said, but he was thinking about Welford and his sudden vacation plans.

✝

The Jones house was dark against the twilight sky, and Dixon sat in her truck. Something held her back from walking up on the porch and knocking on the door. The house was isolated, tucked back on a dirt driveway off a poorly maintained dirt road. It looked as if the paper companies owned the land behind the house. It had been clear-cut at one point but now had a ten-year growth of too-thick pines. The trees were black against the fading light, surrounding the house with darkness.

She thought back to Zander's call. He'd been upset, but surely not enough to harm himself. She didn't want to walk into a scene where a kid had given in to despair over his father's suicide attempt. Still, she couldn't sit outside the house all night. She had work to do at the newspaper, and if Zander needed help, she had to find him now. The truck door creaked as she opened it and got out. She went to the steps, listening for anyone inside the dark house.

"Zander," she called. "Come out and talk with me." Her cell phone was in the truck. She could call J.D., but the sheriff had his hands full with a mob on the verge of going berserk. She could handle this on her own. Chances were the boy was just upset and needed someone to talk to.

"Zander?"

She went up the steps and onto the porch. The stain she'd noticed before was still there, though faded. A fly buzzed and settled on it.

She knocked hard on the door and called out, "Zander!"

She turned the doorknob and the door opened. Where were Olena and her baby? Her car was gone. She could be anywhere.

"Zander?"

She stepped inside. The lingering smells of food hung heavy in the air. This was ridiculous. She had no right to be in the house, even if she was trying to help Zander.

She was turning around to leave when she heard a noise in one of the back rooms. The hair on her arms stood on end. The sound was unidentifiable. It could have been someone dragging across the floor or moving something heavy. She was going to call J.D.

It was darker now, and she heard the sound again, definitely something being dragged. Her mouth was dry with fear. If Zander or Olena were sick or injured and she left . . .

She took a step backward and felt something under her foot. She flailed her arms in a vain attempt to keep her balance. Her hand snatched at a small table that came over on top of her as she fell. She hit hard enough to knock the wind out of her lungs, and as she lay huffing on the floor, she heard steps. In the dim light she saw a silhouette.

"Be still," he whispered, his accent Spanish.

Dixon stopped all movement. "Francisco," she said.

"*Si*," he answered. "Do not move."

CHAPTER THIRTY

Big Jim Welford. Hollywood Hog. Mr. Religion. All were popular nicknames for the Chickasaw County superintendent of education.

J.D. drove the twelve miles to the Welfords' place on Lolly Road at ninety-five miles an hour. He'd never thought about Welford's being involved in the girls' disappearance. He should have, though. If Welford were sexually involved with Angie, he would have a lot to lose.

J.D. berated himself as he made a ninety-degree curve, his right wheels sliding off the shoulder as he pressed the gas harder to correct the car. Calvin had been the suspect. J.D.'s absolute dislike of Vivian had affected his logic. He'd sympathized with Calvin, married to such a paranoid bitch. Calvin's taking up with a mistress would be understandable. Angie had been far advanced for her age. She was the kind of girl who would set her cap for someone like Calvin, a man who could buy her things and pave her way. A man with power and influence.

But Big Jim? The man was a deacon in the Baptist church. He was a pillar of the community, the man who set the moral tone for the school system. If Welford was screwing and murdering girls, the entire county would be in a crisis of faith.

And what of Chavez? Robert Medino, with his theories and suppositions, had planted a seed that had grown into a fearsome briar. J.D. felt as if he'd been played.

He turned down the drive, lined with balsa cedars, and sped up to the house. He was gratified to see lights in the cedar-shake house. It must have cost at least half a million. Welford's political connections had served him well. J.D. had heard that Calvin financed Welford's hundred-acre spread and six-thousand-square-foot home at an interest rate of 3 percent. That had never been J.D.'s business—before.

Lydia Welford answered his knock. She was a petite blonde who normally hid her curvaceous figure in jumpers and sack dresses. This evening she wore Capri pants and a halter top that revealed plenty.

"What are you doing here, J.D.? We're just about to walk out the door."

"Montana," he said.

"Right. We're—"

"Where's Big Jim?"

She frowned at his rudeness. "Packing. As I was saying, we're running late for our flight."

"I need to talk to him." J.D. moved past her into the house.

She put her hands on her hips. "Can't this wait?"

"No. Where is he?" He didn't wait for an answer but stepped onto the expensive Persian carpet and headed for the interior of the house. Lydia was following at his heels, yipping like a Chihuahua.

"You can't come barging in here like this. We don't have time for—"

He moved through a study and down a hallway to a ground-floor bedroom. Without knocking, he opened the door and stepped into the room. Welford was folding a sweater into his suitcase. He looked up, confused.

"What are you doing here, J.D.?"

The sheriff brought the bracelet out of his pocket. He saw a flash of recognition.

"What's that?" Welford asked

"You should recognize it since you paid for it," J.D. said.

"What?" Lydia made a grab for the bracelet, but J.D. moved it out of her reach.

"He bought that? For whom?" She was almost hopping in her high heels, trying to grab the bracelet.

"Shut up, Lydia," Welford snapped. "J.D. has made a serious mistake."

"No, I haven't," J.D. said. "I have a copy of the credit card transaction from Zimball's Jewelry in Mobile."

Welford pointed at his wife. "Go put some coffee on."

"I'm not leaving here until I find out where that bracelet came from and why you bought it. You told me I couldn't have expensive jewelry. You said the people in Chickasaw County would resent us if I wore things like that." Her words were becoming more heated.

"Lydia, go put on a pot of coffee. Then you're going to wait in the kitchen until I come in there."

"What about our flight?"

"Fuck our flight!" Big Jim thundered.

Lydia turned on her heel and left the room. Welford closed the door behind her.

"I did buy the bracelet."

J.D. waited.

"I picked it up at Zimball's a few weeks ago. For Calvin. He wanted a present for someone he was seeing, and he didn't want it to come back on his credit card because of Vivian."

J.D. couldn't be sure, but he thought Welford was telling the truth. "So you were an accessory to Calvin's extramarital affair?"

Welford waved his hand in the air. "Could you imagine being married to Vivian? She had Calvin's balls in a vice so tight he was almost emasculated. When he told me he was seeing someone on the side, I thought 'good for him.' "

"Except who he was seeing was a fifteen-year-old girl who is now dead."

Welford didn't fake surprise. "I know. He told me just after Angie disappeared that he'd been seeing her. He'd arranged with a photographer in Mobile to do some pictures of her for a modeling portfolio. He was terrified."

"And you didn't come to me."

"Calvin didn't kill that girl. He didn't. He begged me not to tell anyone because he knew how it would look."

"You're an accessory to his crimes, whatever they are, Big Jim. I just want you to understand that right now. If he killed those girls, you're an accessory to kidnapping and murder."

"Don't be ridiculous. I never—"

"You've got to cancel your vacation."

"Lydia will be fit to be tied."

"That's actually the least of your problems. Don't leave Chickasaw County. And don't make me lock you up."

Welford thrust out his chin. "You're kidding me. You wouldn't put me in jail."

"Try me. Where's Calvin?"

"How should I know?"

"Don't call him. If you do, I swear to you I'll make sure you spend the rest of your life behind bars."

J.D. walked out of the bedroom and through the expensively appointed house. When he got out into the night, he took a deep breath.

✝

Once the storm of emotion had passed and Camille had fallen asleep on the sofa, Eustace thought about calling J.D.

From the tidbits Camille had told him, Eustace had put together a disturbing picture, with Vivian Holbert squarely in the middle of it. Vivian had been on the river when the girls disappeared. She'd lured the girls into her boat, killed them, and carried the bodies downriver to her houseboat, where she'd stored them until she could bury them. He hadn't figured out how she'd managed to haul the two bodies out of her boat. Maybe they'd only been unconscious.

Certainly there were holes in his theory, but he was convinced that Angie Salter and Trisha Webster had died at the hands of Vivian Holbert, not Francisco Chavez.

Placing his hand on Camille's cheek, Eustace noticed that her skin was cool. He got a blanket and covered her. If he were right about Vivian, then Camille might soon be free of her mother forever. On the other hand, such a trauma could push her over the edge.

He was torn. He'd given her a mild sleeping pill, crushed in the orange juice he'd insisted she drink. He had to take action, and he needed to know she was out of danger.

He tried to call J.D., but there was no dial tone. He depressed the switch rapidly several times. Still no dial tone. The phone sometimes went out during storms if a tree fell on the line somewhere down the road, but there had been no storms. He tried again.

Night had fallen dark and quiet, and he stepped out on the landing to listen. The air conditioner made it impossible to hear inside the house. Even when he was standing outside, it hindered his hearing. He went back in, cut it off, and stepped outside again. The sound of low voices drifted through the darkness. He tensed. Someone was at the boat landing.

He moved silently down the stairs, taking care not to let his bad leg drag. Even with his disability, he could move quickly. He used the pilings of the house for cover as he moved toward the men's voices. When he was at the skinning shed, he could see them. There were two of them, and they stood on the bluff by the landing, smoking cigarettes and talking. He picked up the baseball bat that he used to kill the fish and began to move stealthily down the slope.

He was almost there when he felt something cold and hard press into his back.

"Where you goin' old man?"

He heard the cock of the rifle.

"Who are you?" Eustace asked.

"We're folks who want some justice for those two dead girls."

"So what are you doing here?" Eustace started to turn around, but the barrel of the rifle poked harder into his back.

"Don't move, old man. I don't need a reason to blow your spine all over the river."

"What do you want?" Eustace asked.

"I hear you were involved in what happened to those two girls," the man said, jabbing the barrel hard. "I want to see you suffer."

"I didn't hurt those girls," Eustace said calmly.

"That's not the way I hear it." The man pushed his shoulder. "Get down to the river."

Eustace knew that if he got in a boat with the men, he would be killed. He stumbled deliberately, falling to the ground. If they got him, they were going to have to carry him.

"Get up," the man said.

Eustace could see him in the light of the skinning shed. A young man, probably no older than twenty. He didn't recognize him.

"I'm not going anywhere with you," Eustace said. "Vivian Holbert's daughter, Camille, is asleep in the house. I'm not leaving her."

The man kicked him hard in the ribs. "You're gonna do what you're told." He kicked him again.

Eustace didn't try to fight back. He could only hope that Camille would not hear what was happening and that she would sleep, safely, until everything was finished.

CHAPTER THIRTY-ONE

Dixon thought her heart was going to stop. The man who had abducted and murdered two girls stood not five feet from her. She was alone in a strange house with him, far removed from any help.

When he staggered, she realized something was wrong. He took a step toward her but fell back against the wall. He was seriously injured. Scrambling to her feet, she backed to the door. Chavez did not try to follow her. Instead, he sank to his knees.

"What's wrong with you?"

"I was shot." His voice was feverish.

Dixon hesitated. She could run to her truck and drive away. In his condition, she doubted he could follow her.

"Where are Olena and Zander?"

"She went for medicine. The boy left on his bicycle. He was crying." Chavez spoke excellent English. He sounded well educated.

"Why did you take those girls?" she asked.

He didn't answer for a long moment. "To save them," he said. "Sanctify the flesh."

"They were just girls. You didn't have to kill them."

"I did not kill them."

"If you didn't, who did?"

"The woman with the red hair."

"Camille Holbert?" Dixon didn't try to hide her incredulity.

"Not the girl. The woman."

Dixon stepped forward. "Vivian?"

"I do not know her name."

"Why would Vivian Holbert kill two teenage girls?"

Chavez shook his head, and she saw sweat on his forehead. "I don't know," he answered. "She had them in her boat."

"Who shot you?" Dixon asked.

"The old man who lives on the river." He began to slide down the wall. "He is afraid."

Dixon heard a car pull into the yard. She glanced out the door and recognized Olena's old clunker. She heard a baby crying as Olena hurried up the steps, the infant in her arms.

"Francisco!" Olena called.

"He's in here," Dixon said, pushing the door open. "Could we have some lights?"

Olena hit the switch and looked around. "Francisco! Where's Zander?"

"That's what I came to find out. He called me and said his father had attempted suicide."

Olena thrust the baby into Dixon's arms. "Hold him. I need to see to Francisco." She went to the wounded man, who struggled to his feet and then collapsed against her. Holding him up, she got him to a chair and sat him down. In a moment she had his shirt pulled open to reveal the bullet hole in his shoulder. It was an ugly mass of savaged muscle.

"Can you help me?" Olena asked Dixon.

"He needs to go to the hospital."

"Don't be a fool. If he goes to the hospital for treatment, someone will turn him in to the sheriff. Or worse."

Dixon jostled the baby on her hip to keep him quiet. "I have to call J.D. You can't keep Chavez here. He's wanted for two murders."

Olena swung around on her. "And he didn't do either of them. He's innocent. If you take him to that jail, there's a good chance the rednecks around here will kill him before he has a trial."

"What if he isn't innocent? What if he hurt those girls?"

"Like my brother killed your father?"

Dixon had no answer. "J.D. won't let anything happen to him."

"The sheriff is one man. Don't you think a mob would run over him to get to Francisco?"

"How did Chavez get here?"

"I gave him a ride. He was hitchhiking on the highway, and I picked him up. He didn't seem to have a destination, so I brought him here and fed him, then took him down to Fitler. He's been in the swamps since then. When he got hurt, he made it back here. I guess I was the only person he had to turn to."

"Olena, you have to call the sheriff. You can't harbor a wanted criminal."

"Girl, that's where you're wrong. I'm not in the business of seeing another innocent man get punished for a crime he didn't commit. I can do what I damn well please as long as I believe it's the right thing." She stood up. "Now, I need some hot water. Are you going to help me or not?"

✝

Vivian Holbert opened the door to J.D.'s knock. She tilted her head and smiled. "You're beginning to make a habit of stopping by when I'm home all alone. Is that deliberate, Sheriff?"

"Where's Calvin?"

"The bank, maybe. Or he's holed up with Big Jim, drinking." She frowned and looked up, feigning deep concentration. "Or, maybe he's fucking his mistress." She smiled. "You didn't think I knew? That bitch."

"Who are you talking about?" J.D. asked.

"Oh, play innocent, that's okay. I know she's a friend of yours."

For the life of him, he couldn't begin to imagine who Vivian was referring to. "Dixon?"

She laughed again, this time the sound was brittle. "Don't play me for a fool, J.D. You know Beatrice Smart and Calvin are having an affair."

"I know no such thing," J.D. said. "I need to see Calvin. Now."

"Check at the parsonage. I think it's rather kinky, don't you? Having sex in the church."

"I can't speak for Calvin, but Beatrice is happily married. I can't believe she'd cheat on her husband."

"You are such a pussy, J.D. You are. Get out of here." She slammed the door hard.

J.D. stood for a moment, wondering if the entire scene had been a ploy to protect Calvin. No. Vivian was far too self-centered to expend that much energy on saving anyone except herself.

He went down the walk to the patrol car. He would try the bank and the school board office.

✝

Eustace came to and felt a sharp pain in his side. He knew his ribs were broken. His hands were bound behind his back, and he was seated against the base of one of the oaks in his yard.

Three men wearing camouflage were milling about, drinking beer, laughing, and joking. They intended to take justice into their own hands.

The most important thing was to avoid waking Camille. He could endure anything they did to him as long as Camille was safe. If she stayed in the camp, he didn't believe they would bother her. These men were Vivian's agents. But Vivian didn't understand that no one governed a mob. If Camille came outside and the men were drunk enough and aroused enough, they would punish her, too.

"He's awake," one of them said. They started toward him.

He looked down at the ground, forcing his body into total relaxation.

"Are we gonna hang him first or burn him?" one of the men asked.

"We'll do it at the same time, like he did those girls."

"I don't know what Vivian told you, but I didn't hurt those girls. If you do anything to me, J.D. will see to it that you spend the rest of your lives in jail. Vivian can't protect you from that."

"Old man, the sheriff won't touch us."

Eustace kept his gaze on the ground. He didn't want to provoke the men. "Boys, you don't want to sacrifice the rest of your lives. I didn't hurt those girls."

"Let's do it," one said.

"You can kill me, but you'll pay a terrible price."

"He's just trying to bluff you." The man who'd been talking stepped forward. He put his boot on Eustace's shin. "I could snap that crippled leg of his."

In the light from the shed Eustace could see the man's tucked-in camouflaged pants and his combat boots. He wasn't a soldier; he was a hunter, a man who was used to killing things that couldn't fight back. More than anything, Eustace wanted to hit him. If he were going to die, he wanted to do it while he was trying to kill his opponent. To make that attempt might endanger Camille, though, so he would sit in the dirt like a tied dog.

"What's the matter, old man? You afraid."

"Yeah," Eustace said.

The man pressed harder on his leg. Eustace wanted to scream, but he didn't. He'd failed to turn the air conditioner back on in the camp. It would be getting hot in there. Camille didn't sleep well in the heat. The least noise might awaken her.

"I didn't hurt those girls," he repeated.

"Stop saying that." The man with his boot on Eustace's leg pressed harder. "If you say that one more time I'm going to snap this bone."

Eustace sat silent.

"Get the rope and the gasoline," the man said.

Eustace could hear the river. It had been his life for a long time. Things were changing. Pollution from the Leaf had begun to affect the harvest of fish. Folks were moving onto the banks, pouring sewage and filth into it. Boats were churning back and forth, filled with drunken teenagers who had more money than sense. Maybe it wasn't a bad time to leave. His only regret was Camille. God, he didn't want to leave her. And he wanted to see Vivian punished. She'd hurt those girls. He didn't know why, and he didn't care. But he knew she'd done it. And now she'd set him up so that he would die for what she'd done. He had to hand it to her. It was a masterful plan.

The man returned with a can of gasoline. Eustace felt the rope jerked around his neck, and he closed his eyes in preparation for the gas.

"What do you men think you're doing?" Camille's question came from the edge of the darkness.

Eustace opened his eyes to see her not fifty feet away, in a long white nightgown that billowed around her thin frame.

"Grab her!" one of the men ordered.

CHAPTER THIRTY-TWO

J.D. had scouted all of Holbert's usual haunts. No luck. The bank president didn't seem to be anywhere in town. J.D. wondered if Big Jim Welford had telephoned him and warned him off. If so, Big Jim would pay for it.

On the off-chance that Holbert had been injured, J.D. swung by the hospital. Nothing. Back in the patrol car, he drove to Main Street and turned toward the newspaper. In his several passes, he hadn't seen Dixon Sinclair's truck, either.

When he pulled past the newspaper, he saw Tucker sitting at one of the front desks. Pulling into a parking space, he got out and walked to the front door. It was locked, but when he tapped on the glass, Tucker rose and let him in.

"Where's Dixon?" J.D. asked.

"She got a call. That black kid, Zander, called to say his father had tried to commit suicide. Dixon took off about two hours ago, and I haven't heard from her."

"She has a cell phone?"

"I've called. Four times. No answer."

J.D. slowly inhaled. He remembered her asking him about a stay of execution. "She really believes Jones is innocent?"

"She doesn't confide in me, but I'd have to say she's got serious doubts."

"I'm going to check on her." J.D. started toward the door. He felt Tucker's hand on his arm and turned around.

"I'm going, too."

"The hell you are."

"I am. I can either ride with you and entertain you, or I'll follow in my own car. If something's going on, I'm going to be there. Dixon is not only my boss, she's my friend."

J.D. had no doubt the reporter would follow him. He'd best keep the young man under his thumb. "Come on." He stepped out the door so Tucker could lock it. "Have you seen Calvin this evening?"

"I saw him downtown about an hour ago."

That stopped J.D. "Where?"

"He was in the Hickory Pit. With Beatrice Smart."

The dots connected in J.D.'s brain. "I've got to go." He bolted toward his patrol car, Tucker right behind him. As J.D. got behind the wheel, Tucker hurled himself into the passenger seat.

"Get out. This could be dangerous."

"All the more reason I'm not going to budge."

J.D. put the car in drive. "When this is over, I'm going to charge you with something."

Tucker's grin was self-assured. "I always wanted to be one of those journalists who gave their all for a good story."

"This isn't a joke." J.D. coasted past the Hickory Pit. Only two tables were filled, neither by Holbert or Beatrice. He took a right and floored it, doing seventy down Providence Street toward the Smart residence.

"Is it Beatrice or Calvin you're worried about?" Tucker asked.

"Both of them."

"And Dixon?"

"I have a lot more faith that Dixon can take care of herself."

When he stopped the car at Beatrice's home, J.D. grasped Tucker's shoulder. "Stay in the car. If you don't, I'll pick you up and throw you in the back. Then you won't have a choice."

Tucker leaned against the seat. "I'll stay here. You have my word."

J.D. got out and walked around the house, skirting the front porch, where a light burned. He checked the garage and saw John Smart's vehicle, but there was no sign of Beatrice's. Slipping past the hedge that surrounded the old clapboard house, he peered through the back window into the kitchen. John Smart was pouring a glass of red wine. His shoulders sagged and he checked his watch twice while J.D. watched.

J.D. knocked at the back door.

"Sheriff," John said as he opened the door. "Is something wrong?"

"Where's Beatrice?"

"She got a call from a member of the congregation. An emergency. She was supposed to be home an hour ago."

"Where'd she go?"

"She wouldn't say." John's worry was obvious. "I tried her cell phone, but there wasn't an answer."

J.D. thought about Dixon and hoped that his assessment of her was correct. "You don't know who called?"

John shook his head. "Beatrice has this confidentiality thing. If the person requests secrecy, she obliges. Even from me. It used to be one of the things I admired about her."

"Do you have caller I.D.?"

John stepped back to let J.D. enter. "I'm such a fool. That never occurred to me. I guess I'm not much of a detective."

"No, you're just an honest man," J.D. said as he walked past him to Beatrice's office. He picked up the telephone and checked the caller I.D. log. The call had come from the bank just after six o'clock. Holbert, or someone at the bank, had called. But Vivian could as easily have been at the bank.

"Did Beatrice say anything at all before she left?"

John considered. "Only that the caller had dropped a real bombshell."

Which could mean anything, J.D. thought. Maybe Holbert had called to confess his relationship with Angie Salter. Or the murders. If that were the case, Beatrice could be in real danger. If Calvin did confess and Bea didn't offer the absolution he sought, then Calvin could kill her. The person who had killed the girls was twisted enough for anything.

"What's wrong?" John asked.

"If you hear from Bea, call me immediately," he said. "It's possible she's with Calvin. If she is, tell her to get away from him as quickly as possible."

"What's going on?" His voice cracked with worry.

J.D. shook his head. "There's nothing I can tell you that will help. Just call me on my cell phone if you hear from Beatrice. Find out where she is, who she's with. If it's Calvin or Vivian, make her get away from them."

John nodded. "Is she in danger?"

"I can't say for certain."

✝

Eustace struggled against the bonds that held him to the tree. "Camille, get out of here."

She stood motionless. The men, too, were frozen. They stared at her as if she were an apparition.

"Get her," the man beside Eustace barked again, though he made no move toward her. Her lineage was her shield. No one wanted to lay a hand on Calvin Holbert's daughter.

"Goddamn it, if I have to kick some ass—"

Two of the men started forward slowly, as if they were uncertain what to do.

"Run, Camille! Run!" Eustace yelled. The man beside him lifted his boot and kicked Eustace in the side of the head. He thought his neck would snap, but he didn't lose consciousness. Through a haze of pain he saw Camille reach into the folds of her gown. The long barrel of the Winchester shotgun rose from her side. She brought it to her shoulder in one smooth motion and didn't hesitate when she pulled the trigger.

Eustace felt the blowback of the man's brain and blood as the tight scatter pattern of the shot hit him full in the face. He fell backward, missing Eustace.

One of the men started forward. Camille fired another shot. He reeled back, his chest blossoming red in the light from the skinning shed. He was dead before he hit the ground.

"Get away from Eustace," Camille ordered as she pumped another shell into the gun. "You," she pointed at the remaining man. "Untie him and then move back. If you don't do exactly what I say, I'm going to kill you."

The man knelt beside Eustace. His hands were shaking as he cut the ropes with a hunting knife, which he dropped into the dirt as he backed away.

"Don't kill me," he pleaded.

"Why not?" she asked. "Why shouldn't I?"

"Please," Eustace said as he rubbed circulation back into his hands. To his shame, he wasn't able to stand. "Camille, please stop."

"They were going to kill you."

"He killed those two girls," the young man said, his voice unsteady with fear. "He killed those girls. We were just going to even the score."

"Eustace didn't kill anyone," Camille said.

He inched forward on his knees. "Your mama said he did. It was your mama who sent us down here. She said to do what we did. She paid us three thousand dollars each."

The gun faltered, but as soon as the man moved forward, Camille raised it again. When she pulled the trigger, the ground in front of the man jumped in tiny clods. "What else did my mama say?"

"She said the old man was a pervert. She said he had you down here and wouldn't let you go, and that he'd killed those girls and would likely kill you."

The gun shook in her hands. "Let me tell you about my mother," Camille said in a voice Eustace didn't recognize. "She forced me to take care of my father's needs." The gun waved dangerously. "She said she'd sacrificed everything for her marriage, and I could sacrifice a little to keep Daddy happy."

Eustace got his feet under him, stunned at Camille's revelation of the ugly things he'd only dared guess at. The circulation was back in his limbs, but his mind was numb. He shifted his weight. His leg hurt terribly, but he could walk. He had to take care of Camille.

"Please put down the gun, Camille." As soon as this was over, he was going to drive into town and kill Vivian first, and then Calvin. Vivian's betrayal was the greater. She'd forced her daughter into incest to protect her vested lifestyle. If Eustace spent the rest of his life in prison, it would be worth it.

The young man started to rise from his knees.

"Come on," Camille said. "Give me a reason." The gun didn't waver any longer. It was pointed straight at his chest.

Eustace moved to Camille's side. "It's okay," he said, afraid to touch her, afraid that it would set her off. "Can I have the gun, Camille? You could go in and call the sheriff."

"Are you afraid to leave me alone with him?" she asked.

"No," he said. "I don't care if you kill him. I'll swear it was self-defense." He stepped back. "Do what you have to do."

"Please!" the man groveled. "Don't kill me. Please don't kill me."

Camille handed Eustace the gun. "You watch them, and I'll call J.D."

CHAPTER THIRTY-THREE

Dixon held the basin of hot water as Olena cleaned Chavez's wounded shoulder. The baby had fallen asleep in his playpen, and there was only the sound of the crickets drifting in through the open window and the baby's gentle snores. There still was no sign of Zander, and both the women were worried, though neither spoke of it. Olena had called the prison, but the officials wouldn't release any information to her about Willard Jones. Stalled on that front, Olena had worked on Francisco Chavez as if she could save her brother by saving the Mexican.

For the most part Dixon had watched quietly, holding the hot water, handing Olena clean gauze and unfamiliar powders. Olena was almost done, and Dixon could hold back her questions no longer.

"Chavez, did you destroy the statue at the Catholic church?"

He nodded, trying not to wince as Olena poured what looked and smelled like turpentine into his ragged flesh. It was some concoction the local healer had given Olena, and it obviously burned fiercely.

"Why did you do that?"

His face hardened in the overhead light from the kitchen. "Religion is a lie. A deliberate construction of lies."

Dixon studied him. He was a handsome man, his dark hair long and his skin bronzed by the sun. There was a gentleness about him, until he spoke of religion.

"What kind of lies?"

"The Church does not forgive. It judges. The image of Mary, Mother of Jesus, woman among women, is a fraud."

He was getting worked up, and Dixon hesitated for a moment. "You feel very strongly," she offered, and she felt the angry look Olena gave her. It was clear Olena wanted the conversation to end.

"It is my mission to destroy images of Mary where she is portrayed as benevolent and loving. The Blessed Virgin." His last words were almost a sneer. "The Church has many stories to excuse the conduct of the chosen. Everyone else is judged and sentenced to hell and damnation. Mary had a child that was not her husband's. Instead of a bastard, she had a god."

"Tell me about the girls on the river."

Chavez shifted his position on the kitchen stool so that Olena could work on the exit wound at the back of his shoulder. "They were young. The blonde was loud; the other afraid. Then the woman came and took them."

"Did you see Vivian kill the girls?" Dixon asked.

"The red-haired woman with the big boat got the girls to ride with her. They were laughing when they got in the boat. She took them up the river. When she came back, the blonde was hanging over the side vomiting. She was very sick. I couldn't see the other girl. I think she was already dead in the bottom of the boat."

It could have happened as Francisco Chavez said. But it still didn't explain what had been done to the bodies. "You said you wanted to sanctify the flesh. How do you mean?"

For the first time, Chavez looked at the wound in his shoulder. It looked as if he were trying to determine if he'd been injured too badly to keep on running.

"The body is sacred, a temple for all emotions. Catholicism denies sexuality to women. Mary represents this repression. Mary, who had an immaculate conception, which is intercourse without sex." He stared at Dixon. "I honored the idea of woman with a Judas burning."

Olena had stopped working on him. "A what?"

"It is an old tradition, far older than any of the doctrines taught by the Church. The girls symbolized the female ideal, and they were hung in effigy and burned. This is what the Church does to women."

"Where did you keep the bodies?"

"The red-haired woman first took them to her houseboat and kept them for a few days. Then she moved them with help from the man. They buried them down by an old cemetery about ten miles down the river. Then I dug them up and brought them back here."

Dixon pushed aside the macabre vision of Chavez's actions. "Who was the man with Vivian?"

He shook his head. "I don't know."

"Could you identify him if you saw him again?"

"*Sí.*"

Dixon put the pan of bloody water she'd been holding on the floor. "I have to call J.D.," she said.

Olena rose slowly. "No, you don't. I can't let you. Not until Francisco is safely on his way out of town."

"We have to," Dixon insisted. "He can prove who killed those girls. Vivian Holbert has to be put behind bars."

"And you can guarantee me that Vivian will pay instead of Francisco?"

"We have to call J.D.," Dixon said. "Then we have to go looking for Zander."

"I haven't forgotten my nephew."

"Good, because I'm worried about him. He's been gone for too long. We don't even know which direction he went."

Olena taped the bandage into place on Chavez's shoulder and handed him his shirt. It had a hole where the bullet had torn through, but it was freshly washed. "Zander's in the state he's in because of your family."

"That's not even worthy of a comment," Dixon said, refusing to get angry. "I'm the one person who's trying to help Willard. You know that's the truth."

Olena looked down at the floor. "I don't trust the law."

"And I don't blame you, but there's a woman out there who killed two girls. She could kill again. We need to clear Francisco's name, and we need to see that Vivian is captured."

"You trust the sheriff?"

"I do," she said. "J.D. Horton is a fair man. I trust him."

"Then use the telephone," Olena said. "By the sofa."

Dixon left the kitchen and walked into the darkness of the living room. She found the phone and dialed the sheriff's office.

Waymon answered. "Boy, the sheriff has been looking for you!"

"I need him to come out to Olena Jones's home." Dixon gave the address.

"He's a mite busy."

Dixon swallowed her exasperation. "This is important, Waymon. Just tell him."

"He's out looking for Calvin Holbert and Beatrice Smart. They've disappeared without a trace. Oops, could you hold on? I got another call. Man, it's like Grand Central Station around here tonight."

He switched lines, and Dixon tapped her fingers on the receiver as she waited. The news about Calvin and Beatrice was unexpected. And disturbing, based on what she now knew about Vivian.

"Miss Sinclair, I got to go. Eustace is holding off a bunch of vigilantes who tried to kill him, and J.D. won't answer the radio."

"When did you hear from J.D. last?"

"He'd just headed back to the Holbert home."

She hung up and went back to the kitchen.

"J.D. is already looking for Vivian. Listen, Olena, I want you both to stay here. If Zander comes back in, all of you come to the sheriff's department. You'll be safer there than anywhere else. I have to go." She wasn't sure if she should go to Fitler or into town and hunt for J.D.

"What about Zander?" Olena asked. "Will you look for him?"

"Do you think he might ride his bicycle toward town or toward the river?"

"Probably town," Olena said. "He might have been looking for you."

"I'll hunt for him," Dixon said as she hurried out the door to her truck. She checked her cell phone for messages. There were several from the newspaper, two from J.D., and one from Robert Medino.

She listened to her voice mail as she gunned the truck down the winding dirt drive.

Tucker and J.D. were looking for her.

Robert had news. She could hear the excitement crackling in his voice. "Your father had done a series of stories on the salt domes around Richton. They'd once been used by the federal government to dispose of nuclear waste, but that had been stopped in the seventies. What's interesting is that your father had linked several state senators with representatives from chemical waste companies. Dixon, I think your father may have stumbled onto a sweetheart deal between some politicians and Chemco. I'm headed home to talk to you about this."

The voice mail beeped. Robert had run out of time. If he had more to say, she'd have to wait to hear it in person.

✝

J.D. parked three blocks from the Holberts' house. He glanced at Tucker. There was really no one else he could count on. Waymon was on the radio, working dispatch, and he needed him there.

J.D. answered his cell phone on the first ring. "Horton."

"Vivian Holbert killed those two girls."

J.D. was relieved to hear Dixon's voice. "Where are you?"

"I'm fine," Dixon said. "Francisco Chavez has been shot. He's okay. Olena Jones is taking care of him because he won't go to the hospital. Eustace shot him. Waymon says there are some vigilantes out at Eustace's."

J.D. didn't say anything.

"Where are you?" Dixon asked.

"Vivian's house. Tucker is with me. Calvin and Beatrice are missing. I'm afraid they may be inside."

"I'm only about five minutes from town now. You haven't seen Zander Jones, have you?"

"Not tonight. Dixon, stay away from here. I have no idea what Vivian is capable of doing, and the more people who are around, the more likely it is she'll do something rash."

"What's Tucker doing there?"

"He wants to be in on the action. I gotta go." J.D. clicked off the phone. Reaching around Tucker he got a nine-millimeter Glock from the glove compartment.

"Do you know how to shoot?" he asked.

"I'm a fast study."

J.D. checked the clip and handed the gun to Tucker. "The safety's on. Click it off. Point and pull the trigger. Aim for the chest; it's easier to hit than the head."

Tucker got the balance of the gun in his hand. "Do you really think we're going to have to shoot her?"

"I'd rather you shoot her than the other way around."

Tucker grinned. "Put that way, I guess I agree with you."

"By the way, I'm deputizing you."

"If I weren't so afraid, I'd think this was really cool."

"Stay afraid," J.D. said. "It might keep you alive. Now let's go."

✝

Eustace finished the last knot on the ropes that held the lone surviving vigilante. In the last few minutes, Camille's demeanor had changed drastically. At first she'd been animated, but now her eyes were glazing over and her breathing was becoming shallow. Standing up, he lightly grasped her shoulders. "You ready?"

"Sure," she said, and her teeth were chattering.

Eustace considered a gag for the man but decided he didn't have time. He'd already confiscated cell phones and weapons. Now he was headed into town to deal with Vivian himself.

He took her hand and led her to the Mercedes. Once she was in the passenger seat, he got behind the wheel.

"What about me taking you over to visit that minister woman?" he asked.

"What are you going to do to Mother and Father?"

Eustace was beyond lying, even to protect Camille. She needed to know from the outset. "I'm going to kill them."

Camille didn't say anything. She stared into the darkness, her hands gripping each other.

"If I kill them, you'll be free of them forever."

Camille turned to him. Her hand floated over to touch his thigh. "But I am free of them. Don't you understand? After tonight I'm free of them. For the rest of my life."

Eustace looked out the side mirror at the camp, illuminated against the black sky and the canopy of tree limbs. He loved his home and the river and Camille. Those things were the price he'd have to pay if he leveled justice against Vivian and Calvin. He could pay it. He could live in an eight-by-eight cell. But Camille would be left alone, and he didn't think she could endure that.

"Let's head into town," Eustace said. "We'll find J.D. and tell him what's happened." He stepped on the gas and pulled out onto the dirt road that would take them to Jexville.

CHAPTER THIRTY-FOUR

Before heading into town, Dixon swung by her house on the off chance that Zander had gone there looking for her. She saw his bicycle leaned against a tree before she saw him hunkered down against the wall in a corner of the front porch. The depth of relief that she felt was unexpected. She thought about her mother, and how often Marilyn had suffered anxiety at Dixon's hands.

In the beginning it had been daredevil kid stuff. Diving off bridges into the river, climbing water towers to spray-paint initials, driving too fast, drinking. All normal teenage pranks; all anxiety-provoking incidents for parents. When Dixon had gone into journalism, Marilyn had been unreasonably angry. At last, Dixon understood why. Sitting back on the sidelines was the worst job in the world, especially for the parent of a child who seemed determined to self-destruct.

"Zander." She called to him as she walked up to the front steps. She'd left the headlights of the truck on so she could see.

"I've been waiting for you," he said, with a hint of accusation in his voice.

"I know. I went to your aunt's house looking for you."

"Is my father dead?"

Dixon didn't have an answer. "We can call the prison. We can ask." She unlocked the door and flipped on the lights. She didn't wait for him to follow but went to the telephone. She dialed, and as she was explaining who she was and why she'd called, she heard Zander coming down the hall. He stopped in the kitchen doorway, uncertain what to do.

After a two-minute conversation she hung up. She wasn't going to get any information, but she knew someone who could.

"We'll get the sheriff to call," she said, picking up her keys from the table. "They'll tell J.D. what they won't tell us."

✝

On the way to the sheriff's office, Eustace saw the J.D.'s cruiser parked three blocks from the Holberts' house. It looked as if J.D. were a step ahead of him. He wondered, though, if J.D. knew what he was dealing with. Beside him, Camille seemed to have slipped beneath the weight of her own thoughts.

"I want you to stay here," he told her as he pulled behind the patrol car.

Camille stared out the window, and he wondered if she saw the man's face disintegrating from the blast of the shotgun. Violence was like a leech, hooking into the brain and sucking out everything else.

"Camille." He touched her thigh.

She didn't respond, and he felt a desperate need to put the car in drive and rush out of town. To just keep driving until he found a place with warm sun and a gentle breeze and moving water. The past couldn't be undone, though. And J.D. was in danger because of Eustace's lies. He had to get to Vivian before she got to J.D.

"I'll be back soon," he said and leaned over to kiss her cool cheek. He got out and walked around to her side, holding the sight of her deep in his mind. He opened the trunk of the Mercedes and took out the shotgun. He'd also brought a hunting rifle, two .38-caliber pistols, and the weapons he'd taken from the vigilantes. More firepower than he'd ever need, but he hadn't wanted to leave the guns at the camp. They were evidence.

He closed the trunk, hefted the shotgun, and began walking. Tonight it would be finished, one way or the other.

✝

Dixon ran up the courthouse steps, trusting that Zander would follow. Her footsteps echoed hollowly. When she burst into the sheriff's office, Waymon looked up and frowned.

"Is J.D. still at the Holberts'?" she asked.

Waymon nodded, and looked past Dixon as Zander entered. He was worried and didn't care who knew it. "I can't raise him on the radio, and he's turned his cell phone off."

"Waymon, I need you to do something for me," Dixon said. "This is Zander Jones. His father is an inmate in Parchman. There was an accident this evening. Could you call and check on Willard Jones for me?"

"I'm a little busy."

Dixon reached across the desk and touched his hand. "This is a personal favor for me. J.D. would want you to do it. Like I did the photographs at the crime scene for him," she said. "One phone call. It won't take long."

Waymon got a pencil from the desk drawer. "Okay, tell me the name again."

Thirty seconds later Dixon was out the door and headed for her truck and the Holberts' house. Zander had remained behind with Waymon.

Her throat constricted when she saw J.D.'s cruiser and Camille's Mercedes. She pulled behind them and got out. The Mercedes was unlocked and empty. If Camille were visiting her parents, she could become a hostage. Had she come here after she and Eustace were attacked?

Dixon hesitated. She had to find Tucker without putting herself in a position where she might have to be rescued.

She started down the sidewalk at a run. As she drew closer to the house, she slowed. She didn't want to draw attention to herself or in anyway thwart J.D.'s plans. She stopped at the next-door-neighbor's driveway. The Holberts' house was dark.

She stepped off the walk and behind a thick oak. She felt an arm circle her throat and tried to scream, but a hand was clamped over her mouth.

"Hush!" J.D. whispered fiercely into her ear.

She nodded, and he released her. It took her a moment to get her heart rate down.

"Where's Tucker?" She kept her voice to a soft whisper.

"Watching the back." He tapped her shoulder softly. "Vivian is inside. We don't know if she has hostages or not, so we're trying not to spook her."

"What are you going to do?"

J.D. shifted slightly. "I want you to get out of here and call Waymon. Tell him to call Cooney, Ray, Mark, Graham, and Justin. No one else. Tell them to come and park down the street. Bring weapons and move in quietly. Can you do that?"

"Sure," Dixon said.

"If Calvin or Beatrice is in there injured, I can't wait much longer. I was hoping Vivian would come out on her own."

"As soon as I get out of hearing, I'll call." Dixon said. She had begun to back out of the foliage when she felt J.D.'s fingers grip her arm. She froze and looked toward the house. Eustace Mills was coming around from the far side of the house toward the front porch, a shotgun in his hand.

"Shit!" J.D. said as he drew his own weapon.

✝

Eustace didn't bother with the doorbell. He pounded on the door with his fist. "Open up, Vivian."

He knew J.D. was somewhere close and would try to intervene. Eustace had to do what he was going to do fast. When no one answered the door, he used his good foot to kick it. The wood splintered around the lock, and the door flew back, slamming the wall so hard it almost bounced shut. He caught it with his free hand and flung it wide.

"Vivian! You can come out, or I'm coming to get you. I know you killed those girls."

He sensed movement behind him. It would be J.D. or one of his deputies. Eustace didn't bother to look. "Vivian, I'm coming in to get you. This is what you always wanted. Kill me if you can."

"Eustace."

Eustace ignored J.D.'s voice. He stepped into the darkened house. Vivian wasn't making a sound. He took two steps and stopped to listen. He heard something scraping or tapping against the hardwood floor, but he didn't know where it was coming from. He'd never been in the Holbert home. Had never been invited and wouldn't have gone if he had been. He'd always suspected the worst of Vivian and Calvin, and now he knew it was true. They'd used their own child, their own flesh and blood, in ways that were incomprehensible.

He pushed a door open with the gun barrel. His eyes had adjusted to the dark, but even so, he couldn't see into some of the corners. Vivian might be standing fifteen feet away and he wouldn't know it.

The scraping sound came again and he took another few steps into the room, trying to locate where it was coming from and what was.

"Vivian?"

He never saw her or the knife. The blade arced through the air and struck his arm with so much force it penetrated to the bone. Wrenching away, he swung at her with the barrel of the gun and struck only air. The force of his swing threw him off balance, and he stumbled. She was on him then. She leapt on his back and brought the knife down toward his chest, but the angle of the blow deflected the blade. Using all of his strength, he threw himself backwards. He and Vivian struck the wall together.

The air went out of her lungs in one big *whoof*, and she fell to the floor. Eustace swung the gun like a club. When it made contact with her body, it shuddered in his hand, and he had the satisfaction of hearing what he hoped was a bone snap.

He took a minute to catch his breath. J.D.'s voice calling his name drifted to him, muted by the closed windows. With any luck at all, Vivian was dead. When he reached down to touch her, there was nothing there but bare floor. It was impossible. He'd hit her hard. Really hard. Where had she gone?

A sound like material ripping came from his right. He didn't even recognize it as a sound that could be made by a human, but it was Vivian. He shifted just enough to miss the full force of her attack and was able to spin away from her, pushing her against a sofa. She was completely insane. She had the strength of ten women, and she meant to kill him.

Eustace made for the hall. He'd almost reached the front door when he heard her. She was running after him, breathing so harshly she sounded like a freight train. When she was almost on him, he fell to the front porch, half in the house and half out.

✝

J.D. was on the front walk, his attention focused on the house. He held his gun at the ready. Dixon realized he didn't know that Camille had come up behind him. She wore a long, white nightgown, and her red hair hung in loose waves down her back. She looked as much a child as a woman, and she was in a state of shock. Dixon started toward her. She didn't want to startle Camille or give Vivian warning that her daughter was in the yard.

"Camille," Dixon said gently. "Camille."

If J.D. heard, he ignored it. He was fully focused on the house. Dixon took a step closer to Camille.

"Come over here with me," Dixon said in a voice she might have used on a stray dog. "It's okay. Just come with me." She had almost reached Camille when Eustace burst through the open front door and fell to the porch.

Vivian followed and stood over Eustace. She had a butcher knife, and her face was a mask of hatred. A guttural noise came from her throat, and she raised the knife.

"Vivian!" J.D. pointed his gun at her. "Vivian!"

The shot was so loud that Dixon had no idea where it came from. She looked at J.D., who still held his gun pointed. Vivian looked at him, too, surprise on her face. Red began to seep across her blouse. She sank to her knees and dropped the knife. She fell, face forward, across Eustace.

Dixon saw J.D. turn, his gun still at the ready. The barrel swung past Dixon and pointed at Camille, who held a pistol. Slowly she lowered it and let it fall to the sidewalk. Ignoring everyone, she ran up the porch steps. She pushed her mother's body aside and knelt beside Eustace.

Eustace pushed himself up to a sitting position. One side of his shirt was soaked in blood. He put his arm around Camille and held her, rocking as he whispered into her ear.

J.D. walked forward, and Dixon galvanized herself to stay beside him. He stepped around Eustace and Camille and entered the house, snapping on lights as he went.

Dixon heard thumping, and she followed J.D. into the back, where he kicked open a locked door and found Beatrice Smart in the laundry room, tied hand and foot and gagged.

J.D. removed the gag. "Are you hurt?"

"No."

J.D. cut her bonds to release her hands and then her legs. She looked toward the doorway. "Where's Vivian?"

"She's dead," J.D. said. "Where's Calvin?"

"In the bathroom. She killed him. She thought we were having an affair. She said she was going to kill me, too."

"Dixon, can you give her a hand?" J.D. stepped out of the room and called Waymon.

"Are you sure you're okay?" Dixon helped Beatrice to her feet.

"I'm okay. Vivian wouldn't listen to reason. She said she'd sacrificed everything to have this marriage with Calvin, and she wasn't going to let me or any slutty teenager take it away from her. Calvin was having an affair with Angie Salter." Beatrice swallowed. "I've counseled Vivian for the past year. She was always accusing Calvin of philandering, but I never believed her. I never believed her."

"She killed Angie and Trisha," Dixon said. "Then Camille killed her."

Beatrice started out of the room. "Is Camille hurt?"

Dixon restrained her. "She's outside with Eustace. I think we should leave them alone."

Dixon could hear an ambulance in the distance. She watched Beatrice walk down the hall and into the night, then she turned to follow J.D.

Calvin had been stabbed in the neck. Blood, already turning dark, covered the black and white tiles where he lay beside the bathtub.

"Damn it all to hell," J.D. said tiredly.

"At least she didn't kill Beatrice," Dixon said.

"If I'd listened to you about Tommy Hayes—"

"Nothing would have changed. It would have ended like this."

"If I'd put more heat on Hayes, he would have folded. He was involved from the moment those girls disappeared. Someone had to help Vivian bury those girls, and my money is on him. Whatever his reasons."

"Knowing that wouldn't have changed anything," Eustace said from the doorway. He held a towel to his shoulder. "Vivian and Calvin would still be dead. I intended to kill both of them." He came into the room and closed the door. "They both deserved to die for what they did to Camille. When you hear it, you'll agree."

CHAPTER THIRTY-FIVE

Dixon lingered in the sheriff's office, writing down the events of the night as she sat at Waymon's desk. Waymon had been unable to get any information from the prison, but J.D. was calling. Across the room Olena and Zander sat on plastic chairs and watched the minute hand notch down the face of the big clock.

"What will they do with Francisco?" Olena asked.

"Once he's released from the hospital, he'll be taken to a mental institution. Someone from Mexico, a priest, is coming to take charge of him."

"A priest?" Olena hadn't missed the irony.

"A friend."

Dixon shifted on her chair and called Tucker at the newspaper. He was writing the story, and she was more than glad to let him. It would probably catapult him out of Jexville. Some big newspaper would offer him five times what she could pay, and she would lose her only reporter. Nevertheless, she couldn't stand in his way.

"Will you get a quote from J.D. for me?" Tucker asked.

Tucker had it bad. He was a newshound, and he would never go back to the safe life of academia. "I'll have him call you."

"Thanks, Dixon." He hesitated. "Are you sure you don't want to write this story?"

"Go for it, Tucker."

Voices came from J.D.'s office. Waymon was huddled in the back with him.

"Will the prison call Sheriff Horton back?" Zander asked her.

"I think so. It just takes time for things to happen in institutions. If J.D. didn't think they'd call back, he'd send all of us home."

The telephone rang.

J.D. answered, and Waymon closed the door to his office. Olena had begun to cry, her hands wringing a tissue. Zander put his arm around her.

The door opened, and J.D. stepped out of his office. He nodded at Dixon and spoke to Olena and Zander. "It was touch-and-go for a few hours, but Mr. Jones is going to make a full recovery."

Zander's head dropped to his chest, and he covered his eyes to hide his tears.

Olena stood up and held out her hand to the sheriff. "Thank you."

"Someone from the prison will call you tomorrow and explain the details to you." J.D. put his hand on Zander's shoulder. "I'll drop by tomorrow and see if there's anything I can do. I feel certain we can arrange a visit."

"Thank you," Zander said. He put his arm around Olena as they left.

For a long moment, Dixon didn't say anything. She blinked back tears. "I don't think he killed my father."

"Are you hanging out here because you're a masochist, or are you afraid of the dark?" J.D. took her elbow and maneuvered her out the door of the sheriff's office.

"I refuse to answer on the grounds that I might incriminate myself. Listen, I'm pretty done in. Would you care for a drink? I promise not to salt my booze with tears."

He gave her a sidelong look. "You've been through hell tonight. Are you sure it's a wise thing to drink?"

"I've never been accused of being wise. Look, I'm going to drink with or without your company, and I'd like your company. And I might need your help."

"Then I accept your offer."

"We can go to the house. Why don't you follow me?"

"You've got it," J.D. said, and he squeezed her arm lightly before he took a right to get his SUV.

Dixon eased the truck toward Peterson Lane. J.D. fell in behind her, his lights reflecting in her rearview mirror.

It was midnight in Jexville, and the streets were empty. On the surface it appeared to be a picture book town, all snuggled down for the night, children in bed with their prayers said, parents sleeping side by side. Dixon knew better but decided she didn't want to try to reason her way through the events of the last six hours.

She stopped short in her driveway. Robert Medino's rental car was parked under the oak trees.

J.D. pulled up behind her and rolled down his window. "You're home safely, Dixon. Call me if you need me."

"Thanks, J.D." She walked up to the porch, where Robert was sitting on the swing.

"You're mighty late," he said.

"It's been a long, bloody night. Calvin and Vivian are dead. Vivian is the one who killed Angie and Trisha."

Robert frowned. "What about the hangings and burnings?"

"That was Chavez. It was some sort of protest or ritual. I didn't understand everything he said." She started to walk past him.

"I found some interesting stuff in Jackson."

As tired as she was, Dixon felt her heart beat faster. "Something solid?"

"Solid enough to reopen the case. Willard Jones is telling the truth."

CHAPTER THIRTY-SIX

Eustace watched the sun climb over the oaks in the courthouse yard. He hadn't slept all night. J.D. had been out of the office, but he was on his way back now.

J.D. pulled into the yard. He helped Tommy Hayes, handcuffed, out of the cruiser. Eustace rose and followed them. At the door to the jail, Eustace touched J.D.'s arm. "I have to tell you something. It's about Chavez. About his wound."

J.D. led Hayes to a cell in the back. He locked him in and turned to face Eustace.

"J.D., I have to tell you the truth. I stopped by the room where you put Chavez. He's going to be okay, isn't he? What's going to happen to him?"

J.D. led the way to his office. He closed the door. "You look like hell."

"I shot him. I meant to kill him, but I didn't get a clean shot."

J.D. poured two cups of black coffee and handed one to Eustace. "Frank Pierce is the surviving vigilante who came to your house. He confessed that he and the other two men had been paid by Vivian to kill you. Camille's actions were self-defense."

"I'm trying to tell you that I tried to kill Chavez."

J.D. sipped his coffee. "Is that so? It's an odd thing, but Chavez said it was Vivian Holbert who shot him. He said he saw her clearly."

"Are you making this up?"

"You know me better than that. When I talked to Chavez at the hospital, he told me Vivian shot him. He signed a statement to that effect. Want to see it?"

Eustace shook his head.

J.D. put his hand on Eustace's shoulder and moved him through the office and into the hall. "I don't have a clue what's going on here, but take my advice and leave. Take this gift and go."

Eustace looked at his old friend. "Come see me and Camille. Come have dinner with us."

"You bet."

✝

Dixon woke up with a pounding headache. The sun was full up and glaring through the window. She moaned and covered her eyes. The night before, she'd had several drinks in rapid succession without eating. Now she was paying for it. Beside her, Robert slept on his back.

She slipped from the bed and made coffee, leaning against the counter as she waited for it to drip. When she had a cup in her hand she went in the bathroom, found the aspirin bottle, and tapped three into her hand. She closed the medicine cabinet door and met her reflection. Age touched the skin around her eyes, but there was something new in her reflection, a hint of the twenty-two-year-old woman she'd once been. In the years since her father's death, she'd lost so much, and now she was beginning to find herself again.

"Dixon?"

Robert was awake. "I'll bring you some coffee," she called out. She poured a cup and took it to him. He propped himself against the headboard.

She sat on the edge of the bed. "What a tragic night."

"This is going to be a dynamite story," he said.

"Are you going to interview Camille?"

"Not that. Willard Jones," he said. "We have a direct link between three state senators and a chemical company that's been run out of five other states. Those senators had given the chemical company the right to dump toxic waste, and your dad was going to blow them out of the water. This is going to be a Pulitzer for me."

"You're going to write the story of my father's murder?"

He looked at her as if he didn't know who she was. "Why do you think I've hung around here all this time? This is the story I came to do."

"What—"

"The missing-girl story is a good one, but it's really just about a crazy woman who killed her competition. Your story is about a great journalist who was silenced by political forces. Surely you can see the difference."

She stood up. "Did you ever intend to do a story on Chavez and the missing girls?"

"I had some interest in it. If Chavez had been the killer, it would be a better story. Now it's just a psycho wife who killed her husband's lover and some innocent people who got in the way."

Dixon retrieved her jeans from the floor. Still holding her coffee cup, she took her pants into the bathroom, closed the door, and leaned against it. Robert had betrayed her. Whether he realized it or not, he had.

She slid into her jeans, grabbed a T-shirt from a hook on the door and replaced it with her nightshirt. She brushed her teeth and got the taste of last night's cigarettes out of her mouth.

She could hear Robert dressing. She walked into the bedroom. He was tying his shoes.

"Do you think Olena Jones and Zander will talk to me today?" Robert asked.

"Robert, you sought me out because of my father's murder, didn't you?"

"I knew about you when I came to Jexville, if that's what you're asking."

"Would you have come here if Chavez hadn't?"

"Eventually. It was fortuitous that both threads drew us together."

"You slept with me, knowing your primary interest was a story?" She resisted a strong urge to throw her coffee cup at his head. "Do you have any idea how unethical that is?"

"One doesn't have anything to do with the other. I slept with you because I desire you."

"Somewhere in journalism school, didn't they teach you not to sleep with a source?"

He stood up abruptly. "You can turn this into something ugly if you want to, but that's not how it is."

"From my side of the bed, that's exactly how it is. I can't stop you from doing a story about my father's murder, but I won't help you. Get out of my house." She was trembling, and she didn't care.

"You need help," he said, stalking past her.

"And you need ethics."

He turned back to face her. "Mark Barrett used you. He knew those men were going to hurt your father, and he detained you. Is that what you're afraid to find out?"

"If Mark betrayed me, he certainly wasn't the last. Get out."

✝

The rolling farmland of Simpson and Hinds Counties had given way to congestion that marked the fringes of the Jackson growth district. Eighteen-wheelers and trailers full of pigs vied with a long line of SUVs for highway space as Dixon crept through the town of Richland. Not so long ago, this stretch of highway had been more rural, less congested, and there had been a stables where Dixon had taken horseback riding lessons as a child. Marilyn had complained that it was on the backside of nowhere. Now, it was part of the city. All of it had changed. And it was changing yet again, more asphalt, more growth. Traffic wasn't moving at all, so she pushed her air conditioner higher.

Mid-October had arrived with slightly cooler temperatures, but south Mississippi was still waiting for fall. Jexville had fallen back into small-town rhythms, with a few notable exceptions. Beatrice Smart was launching a recall campaign against Big Jim Welford. Camille and Eustace were back in the swamp, and Robert Medino had checked out of his room at the Magnolia. He was gone from Jexville, but one of her old friends at the *Clarion Ledger* had called and told her he was asking questions around Jackson.

The radio played a country tune, but Dixon beat a different rhythm on the steering wheel as she waited for a light to change. Traffic finally moved, and in fifteen minutes she was on the Interstate sweeping around the city. She exited at High Street and aimed toward the state capitol. A powerful state senator now, Mark Barrett had set his sights on the governor's office. He'd never pretended to be less than compulsively ambitious. She'd driven to Jackson to find out if his ambitions were stronger than his loyalty.

She parked on the square and hurried up the broad steps to the capitol building, where he had a second-floor office.

As her heels clicked across the marble floor, she realized how much she'd changed. She was no longer a young woman swept away by her feelings. Nor was she broken by her grief.

She pushed the elevator button and rode up. When she got off, she was calm and composed. The secretary asked her to take a seat, but she stood. In a moment, his office door opened, and Mark greeted her with a wide smile. He stepped across the carpet and drew her into his arms, hugging her tightly.

"Dixon Sinclair," he said. "I was afraid it was going to be an imposter." He hugged her tightly again.

It had been a long time since she'd loved Mark. She had loved him with the foolish abandon of youth.

When he released her, she stepped back. His face was more weathered, his hair sprinkled with gray, but his mouth was still firm and sensual. There seemed to be real warmth in his brown eyes.

"Come into my office," he said, ushering her past the curious secretary and closing the door. He stepped closer and took her hand. "What is it, Dixon?"

She'd thought she might ease into the subject, but she didn't have the reserve. "The day my father was killed . . ." She had to take a breath. "I was late meeting him. We were in bed, remember?"

"How could I forget? It was the last time you spoke to me."

Dixon saw the hurt in his eyes.

"Did you know what was going to happen to him? Did you detain me deliberately?"

He turned away and walked to the window. She couldn't tell if she'd wounded him or if he was preparing a lie.

"I loved you, Dixon. You were almost killed. If you'd been there on time, you'd be dead now."

"Either that, or my father would be alive, too."

He was silent for a long moment. "Willard Jones's execution date is coming up. Is that what's brought all of this up?"

She put her hand on his shoulder. "Willard Jones is innocent, and I need your help proving it. I've spent the last eleven years lying to myself. I never wanted to admit that I loved you. You were married, and I had no right to care about you. That lie cost me a lot, because I did love you."

He grasped her shoulders. "I wanted to marry you."

The future that could have been danced in front of her, then vanished.

"After the bombing, I was afraid you might have known that someone meant to hurt my father." She waited. "Did you?"

Mark's hands slid from her shoulder, and he walked to his impressive desk.

"Mark, if you ever cared for me, tell me the truth now. Willard Jones tried to hang himself. He's going to die for a crime he didn't commit. His family is suffering. If you know the truth, I'm asking you to tell me now."

He picked up a paperweight and examined it. "I didn't know for certain. I suspected. I got a phone call. Anonymous. The man told me to keep you away from the paper."

"Why didn't you warn me?"

"If I'd mentioned anything to you, you would have driven straight to the newspaper. You would have died, too."

Dixon had expected to feel anger. Instead, she was completely numb. For eleven years she'd suspected the worst, and now that she knew it, she could feel nothing. "Who did it?"

"I'm not certain. If I'd known who was behind it, I would have told you, and I would have called the authorities. I would have. I didn't really believe anything would happen. Keeping you with me was a precaution."

"They killed my father, and they let an innocent man rot in jail for eleven years." The words scalded her mouth. "Tell me who made that phone call."

He shook his head. "I don't know."

"I'm going to find out. And I'm going to make them pay." She opened the door and saw the secretary staring at her.

"What are you going to do, Dixon?" he asked.

"Exactly what my father would have wanted. I'm going to burn some people. In print."

"Wait. We may be able to get the phone records from that date. I'll make a few calls." He took a step toward her. "Dixon—"

She closed the door behind her and walked out of the building and into the sunshine.

She'd just gotten into her truck when her cell phone rang.

"I heard you went to Jackson," J.D. said. "Find anything?"

She hesitated. Confirmation of Mark's betrayal felt harsher after Robert's.

"Yeah. I found a lot more than I wanted to know."

J.D.'s question was cautious. "Good or bad?"

Dixon started her truck. She looked up at the capitol building. She'd come of age in this town, walking thoughtlessly through buildings where powerful men made decisions that affected every citizen of the state.

"Both. There was definitely a conspiracy to kill my father. It's going to take some digging, but I'll get the evidence."

"And the bad?"

"Betrayal is a bitter feast, J.D."

"You don't have to eat all the courses, you know."

His gentle tone made her smile, and she was glad he hadn't said "I told you so" about Robert.

"So you're a philosopher with a badge. You never cease to surprise me."

"I don't want to get your hopes up, but I think you already have enough evidence to get a stay of execution for Willard Jones. That'll buy you some time to find the rest of it, and I'll do what I can to help."

"Thank you." She gripped the phone tighter. "Just so you know, when I get the evidence, I'm going to burn them."

"I don't doubt that for an instant. Telling the truth can be a thankless task, but you know that. In a lot of ways, Dixon, we're both in the business of giving people what they deserve."

She pulled out of the parking lot and threaded her way toward the Interstate, toward Jexville and the new life she'd carved out for herself. "I'll be home in about three hours."

"Drive carefully."

"You bet." She punched off the cell phone and gripped the wheel with both hands. She had a lot of work ahead of her, but for the first time in a long while, she knew she could handle it.

Her father was dead, and the men who'd had him killed were living free while an innocent man remained in prison. Nothing could change what had already happened, but the truth would be told. That was what Ray Sinclair had taught her. That was her legacy.

ACKNOWLEDGMENTS

Sometimes a book takes many years and much effort on the part of both the writer and editor. Special thanks go to Ashley Gordon, my editor, and to Gail Waller and Carolyn Newman at River City Publishing. I owe them all a great deal.

As always, the road was less lonely with Marian Young to guide me.

Thanks and credit are due to my friends and fellow writers of the Deep South Writers Salon: Susan Tanner, Renee Paul, Stephanie Chisholm, Aleta Boudreaux, and Thomas Lakeman—who gave so generously of their time, energy, and talent.

Thank you all.